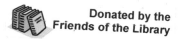

LOCKDOWN

ESCAPE FROM FURNACE

ALEXANDER GORDON SMITH

LOCKDOWN

ESCAPE FROM FURNACE

Farrar Straus Giroux
New York

www.furnacebooks.com

Library of Congress Cataloging-in-Publication Data
Smith, Alexander Gordon, date.
    Lockdown : Escape from Furnace / Alexander Gordon Smith.—
1st American ed.
        p.   cm.
    Summary: When fourteen-year-old Alex is framed for murder, he
becomes an inmate in the Furnace Penitentiary, where brutal inmates and
sadistic guards reign, boys who disappear in the middle of the night
sometimes return weirdly altered, and escape might just be possible.
    ISBN: 978-0-374-32491-9
    [1. Prisons—Fiction.   2. False imprisonment—Fiction.   3. Escapes—
Fiction.   4. Science fiction.]   I. Title.

PZ7.S6423Loc 2009
[Fic]—dc22

                                                    2008043439

For our little one,
and all the other lost children.
Always remembered.
Always loved.
Always free.

LOCKDOWN

ESCAPE FROM FURNACE

Beneath heaven is hell.
Beneath hell is Furnace.

NO WAY OUT

IF I STOPPED RUNNING I was dead.

My lungs were on fire, my heart pumping acid, every muscle in my body threatening to cramp. I couldn't even see where I was going anymore, my vision fading as my body prepared to give in. If the siren hadn't been hammering at my eardrums, then I'd have been able to hear my breaths, ragged and desperate, unable to pull in enough air to keep me going.

Just one more flight of stairs, one more and I might make it.

I forced myself to run faster, the metal staircase rattling beneath my clumsy steps. Everywhere around me other kids were panicking, all bolting the same way, to safety. I didn't look back to see what was behind us. I didn't need to. I could picture it in my head, its demonic muzzle, silver eyes, and those teeth — like razor wire.

Someone grabbed my arm, pulling me back. I lost my balance, spilling over the railing. For a second the yard appeared five stories beneath me and I almost let myself go. Better this way than to be devoured, right? Then the beast shrieked through its wet throat and I started running again before I even knew I was doing it.

I heard the rattle of the cell doors, knew they were closing. If I was caught out here, then I was history. I leaped up the last few steps, hurtling down the narrow landing. The inmates jeered from their cells, shouting for me to die. They stuck out their arms and legs to trip me, and it almost worked. I staggered, lurched forward, falling.

Somehow I made it, swinging through the door an instant before it slammed shut, the mechanism locking tight. The creature howled, a banshee's wail that made my skin crawl. I risked looking back through the bars, saw its huge bulk bounding past my cell, no skin to hide its grotesque muscles. There was a scream as it found another victim, but it didn't matter. I was safe.

For now.

"That was close," said a voice behind me. "You're getting good at this."

I didn't answer, just stared out across the prison. Six stories of cells beneath me and God only knew how many more above my head, all buried deep underground. I felt like the weight of the world was pressing down on me, like I'd been buried alive, and the panic began to set in. I closed my eyes, sucking in as much of the hot, stale air as I could, trying to picture the outside world, the sun, the ocean, my family.

All things I would never see again.

"Yup," came the voice, my cellmate. "Bet it's starting to feel like home already."

I opened my eyes and the prison was still there. Furnace Penitentiary. The place they send you to forget about you, to punish you for your crimes, even when you didn't commit them. Only one way in and no way out. Yeah, this was my home now, it would be until I died.

That wouldn't be long. Not with the gangs that eyeballed me from behind their bars. Not with the blacksuits, the guards who ran their shotguns along the railings as they checked the cells. Not with those creatures, raw fury in their eyes and blood on their breath.

And there were worse things in Furnace, much worse. Maybe tonight the blood watch would come, drag me from my cell. Maybe tonight they'd turn me into a monster.

I dropped to my knees, cradling my head in my hands. There had to be a way out of here, a way to escape. I tried to find one in the hurricane of my thoughts, tried to come up with a plan. But all I could think about was how I came to be here, how I went from being a normal kid to an inmate in the worst hellhole on Earth.

How I ended up in Furnace.

TO HELL

I CAN TELL YOU the exact moment that my life went to hell.

I was twelve, two years ago now, and there was trouble at school. No surprise there, I came from a rough part of town and everybody wanted to be a gangster. Each lunchtime the playing field became a battleground for the various groups of friends. Most of the war was fought with words—we'd call each other names, we'd tell one gang to move out of our area (we had control of the jungle gym, and we weren't going to give it up). I didn't realize until much later just how like a prison school can be.

Every now and again something would kick off and fists would start flying. I never threw a punch in all my time at school; even the thought of it makes me feel queasy. But that doesn't make me any better than the boys and girls who got their hands dirty. It makes me worse—at least fighting with your own two fists is kind of noble.

That Tuesday started off like a normal day. I had no idea that it was the beginning of the end, my first step on the road to hell. Me and Johnny and Scud had been sitting on the jungle gym, talking about soccer, and about who'd been the best English keeper of all time. It was one of those days where everything just seemed like it was perfect. You know, a blue sky that goes on forever, and so warm that it feels like the sun's wrapped you up in a blanket. When I think back to my life before it turned, I think about this day. I think about how things could have been different, if I'd just walked away.

But I didn't walk away when Toby and Brandon dragged this little kid across the playground. I didn't walk away when they started pushing and shoving him and asking him questions about why his daddy drove him to school in a Range Rover. I didn't walk away when Toby threw the first punch and the kid crumpled. I didn't walk away when Brandon dug the kid's wallet from his pocket and threw it to me.

Instead, I opened that wallet, took out two ten-pound notes, and crammed them into my pocket. Then I turned my back on the sound of muffled punches, and thought about what I'd buy.

That was the exact moment my life went to hell.

"ALWAYS TRUST YOUR instincts, Alex," was something my dad used to say. He was no stranger to trouble: nothing serious, but a couple of dodgy business deals that hadn't gone the way he'd wanted. A good man, if a little lost, and not the sort of person qualified to give you advice like that.

But he was right. Your instincts are there for a reason, and on the day that I walked out of school with Daniel Richards's twenty quid they were screaming for me to find the little kid and give it back. You can probably guess by now that I didn't. No, I learned to ignore my instincts, to switch off the little voice that tells you not to do things, to deny the fact that I hated myself for what I was doing.

And that's how I became a criminal.

The thing is, it was so easy. It started off with me, Toby, and Brandon walking around the playground demanding money from the other kids. The kind of thing you always see in films, just before the big, ugly bully gets his comeuppance. Only I was thin and scrawny, not bad-looking, and I didn't get my comeuppance for another two years.

Loose change, a fiver every now and again, and occasionally some candy—it wasn't enough. When Toby suggested we break into a house or two, Brandon backed out. I didn't. Greed wouldn't let me. So we did; we hit a small bungalow three roads over from my house, one we knew was empty for the night. Around three hundred quid stuffed in a fake can and a bundle of jewelry that we chickened out of selling and ended up throwing in the trash.

I still haven't forgotten the old lady who lived there— glimpsed with a long-dead husband in the faded photographs on the mantelpiece—and the knowledge that those rings meant more to her than any amount of money. But I buried my doubts just like I buried all my other uncomfortable thoughts. Committing any crime can be easy if you don't think about it.

And I never thought about the future, not once. Even though everybody was talking about the tougher police forces. Even though there was zero tolerance on youth crime after the so-called Summer of Slaughter, when the gangs went on killing sprees. Even though they'd built the Furnace Penitentiary—the toughest maximum-security prison in the world for young offenders, the place that would swallow you whole if you were ever unlucky enough to walk through its doors. I remember the shivers that went up my spine when I first saw pictures of Furnace on TV, but I never once thought I'd end up there. Not me.

Of course, I knew I couldn't go on like this forever, but so long as the money kept coming in I managed to convince myself that I was invincible, that nothing would ever happen to me. On my thirteenth birthday I bought myself a new bike, on my fourteenth a top-of-the-line computer. I was king of the world and nobody could stop me.

But all those dark, horrible feelings I'd buried were still there, I could feel them churning and growing somewhere inside of me. Deep down I knew I was heading for a fall, one that I'd never be able to pick myself up from.

And, as in all good crime movies, that fall came with one last job.

ONE LAST JOB

THE HOUSE WAS EMPTY, we knew it. Toby had been tipped off by a friend of a friend that the owners were away for the week, leaving behind enough electronic equipment to entertain a small country and a massive bundle of cash from their coffee-shop business.

But we were waiting outside just in case, cowering under a small bush in the back garden with only a solid wall of rain between us and a set of big windows.

"Come on, Alex," muttered Toby, wiping water from his face. "It's emptier than Elvis's coffin in there!"

Toby had a thing for Elvis. He loved his music so much that he refused to believe the King was dead. I ignored the comment and scanned the back of the house. The lights were all off and we hadn't seen a single movement from inside for the half hour we'd been here.

Toby was right, it was probably empty, but the last thing I wanted was to run into some furious guy who'd decided to stay home. It had happened once before when we'd hit a large house out in the countryside and I'd come face-to-face with a man on the way to the toilet. We'd both stared at each other in shock for

what seemed like hours, then screamed in perfect harmony. I'd
turned and legged it with him on my tail. It was even scarier than
it sounds — he'd been stark naked.

Fortunately nothing like that had happened since, but I was
eager to avoid any more encounters with homeowners, clothed
or not.

Toby nudged me and I nodded, feeling a trickle of cold water
slide down my back. We were sheltered from the worst of the
downpour by the bush, but every now and again drips would
snake down our faces and necks with an infuriating tickling sensation. Back then I thought it was like Chinese water torture. I
know different now.

"Okay," I whispered, getting to my feet and rubbing the life
back into my numb legs. It was a bitterly cold winter night, but
through a break in the clouds the light from the moon made the
world glow like it was covered in silver polish. If I hadn't been so
focused on breaking the law, I might have stopped to admire the
sight.

Taking a deep breath, I jogged across the garden to the sitting
room windows, trampling over the flower beds to avoid making a
noise on the gravel. I stopped when I heard an angry mutter
behind me and turned to see Toby hopping across the mud on
one leg and holding his other foot in his hands.

"Cat crap!" he hissed at me, his expression one of disgust
mixed with disbelief. "Why do I always manage to put my foot in
crap?"

I wanted to smile but I couldn't. I was too pumped up —
adrenaline flooded my whole body like it did before every job,
making my heart beat faster than a hummingbird's wings and

sharpening my senses. I felt like an animal, aware of every sound and sight and smell and ready to turn and flee at the first sign of trouble.

Reaching into the long pockets of my coat I pulled out the only two pieces of equipment, aside from a flashlight, that a burglar ever needs—a glass cutter and the sticky dart from a toy gun. Licking the suction cup on the tip of the dart I pressed it against the bottom right pane. After a couple of tugs to make sure it was secure I pressed the blade to the glass and cut a smooth circle. Pocketing the cutter I pulled the dart gently and the glass popped free, leaving a handy hole in the window.

"Voilà!" I whispered, grinning despite the unbearable tension of the situation. "Do the honors, Tobster."

I stood to one side and looked at Toby, who was trying to clean his shoe on the soil of the flower bed. Each time he wiped it giant clumps of mud stuck to the mess until his shoe was lost in a massive brown ball—like he'd just put his foot through a coconut.

"Toby!" I shouted. He snapped to attention, pouting.

"These cost a hundred quid," he said.

"Well, buy yourself some new ones with the money you make tonight," I replied, running my hands through my soaking hair. "Buy yourself twenty pairs."

Toby grinned back and walked to the window, sliding his small hand inside and fiddling with the clasp. After a few seconds there was a loud click and the window creaked open.

"Wow," he said, in shock. "That was almost too easy."

I thought so too. It *was* too easy. I should have guessed then that something funny was going on, but greed is a powerful thing, and all I wanted was to get inside and get out again with as much loot as I could carry. If all went to plan, the proceeds from tonight would mean neither of us had to hit another house for months.

"Right, let's do this," I said, gritting my teeth and pulling the window right open. The room inside was dark, but I could make out rows of shelves and a couple of sofas inside. Several unblinking red lights stared at us out of the shadows, and I imagined the eyes of some hellish guard dog that would bound from the darkness, fangs bared—ready to chew any intruders to pieces.

But they weren't eyes, they were the standby lights from a fortune in electronics that would soon be safely in our bags.

"I'll go first," said Toby. "Give me a leg up." He raised his foot but I didn't move.

"I'm not touching that," I said, looking at the giant clumps of mud and crap that looked like they'd been welded to his sneaker. "Why don't you give *me* a foot up."

He sighed and linked his two hands together to form a cradle. Bracing my foot in his grip, I pushed upward, getting one knee on the window frame and pulling myself inside. Scanning the dark interior to make sure it was empty, I skipped down onto the floor, not making a sound on the soft carpet.

Toby was at the window holding two duffel bags and I took them from him before grabbing his arm and hoisting him up. He was almost in when his soiled shoe slipped on the wood of the window frame. With a yelp that was deafening after the tense silence, he fell on me, sending us and a nearby plant stand crashing to the floor.

For a second, neither of us could move a muscle. I lay there with Toby's weight on top of me, barely able to hear anything over my thrashing heart. But there was no sound of slamming doors or terrified screams or feet trampling down the stairs. At least we knew for sure now that the house was empty—Toby's clumsiness would have woken the dead.

Pushing him off me, I got to my feet and picked up my bag, offering Toby a hand.

"Sorry about that," he said sheepishly, pulling himself up.

"Never mind, you lump," I replied. "You start putting away some of this electronic stuff, I'm gonna go find the cash."

"Ten-four," said Toby, pulling a flashlight from his bag and aiming the beam at the row of high-tech gadgets lined up underneath the enormous television. I left him to it, pulling out my own flashlight and making my way out of the door.

You never really get over the sensation of being in someone else's house without their permission. Everything is different—the smell, the atmosphere, even the air tastes strange. I guess that's something to do with the reason I'm always in another person's home. It's as if the building itself doesn't want you there, like it's just waiting for you to slip up before it sucks you into some dark room forever.

Trying to ignore my thoughts, I made my way down a small hallway toward the stairs. According to Toby's friend of a friend, the owners had stashed the week's takings in a tin inside their office, along with a bundle of cash from a charity gig they'd held at the weekend. It should be a piece of cake.

It was a fairly old house, but well taken care of and the stairs didn't creak once as I made my way up. I swung my light to and fro to see where I was going, the shadows seeming to dance in front of me like there was an army of goblins hiding in the corners and behind the furniture. I swallowed hard as I neared the top, cursing my imagination.

There were six doors on the long landing, all closed. Carefully twisting the handle of the first, I found myself staring into a pristine white bathroom. The second door opened outward, revealing an empty closet. Well, almost empty—as I was closing the door something rushed at me out of the darkness, slapping me on the forehead. I just about screamed, fighting off my attacker before realizing it was a mop. Shoving it back inside, I kicked the closet shut, no longer caring about noise, and walked past a small chest of drawers to the next door.

Third time lucky, as they say. This one opened into a large room with a desk against one wall. I made my way straight to it and couldn't believe my eyes. On its walnut surface lay a stack of ten- and twenty-pound notes plus several bags full of coins— what must have been a couple of grand in all.

It was as I was reaching for the cash, a massive grin on my face, that I heard the sound of screaming from downstairs.

I froze, my skin turning to ice, my scalp seeming to shrivel up so tightly that it hurt. The house wasn't empty. Toby had been rumbled by what sounded like a very shocked woman, which meant he'd make for the nearest exit. I, on the other hand, was stuck up here. I snatched the notes and stuffed them into my pocket.

When the shrieks started again, I realized I'd got it wrong. It wasn't the owner screaming—it was Toby.

But the shock of that was nothing compared to the fright I

got when I turned around. In the shadows behind the office door, right in front of me, was an enormous figure. A man whose black suit blended perfectly with the walls, but whose two glinting eyes and vast, sinister grin shone out of the darkness like those of a shark in the cold, dead water of the ocean.

FRAMED

I DON'T NEED TO tell you what I did next. I ran, straight for the open door. But the figure was too quick, slamming it shut and reaching out toward me with an arm the size of a tree trunk. I ducked but he moved like lightning, grabbing the flashlight from my fist and throwing it at the wall. It smashed as it hit a shelf, plunging the room into darkness.

Well, almost darkness. All I could see as I backed away from the man were his eyes, which still stood out from the shadows like two silver coins. They followed me each time I made a move, never blinking and so bright that they seemed to burn right into my soul.

I had to get out of the room. I had no idea who this guy was but I was in his house and, judging by the size of him, he could turn me inside out without breaking a sweat. I was wondering whether I could leap through the window without killing myself when he spoke.

"Where you gonna run to?" he said, his voice so deep that it sent a vibration through the floorboards. "I can see you, Alex."

My heart seemed to stop for an instant as I heard my name. He couldn't know who I was. There was no way. We lived more than a mile away and we never came to this part of town unless we were hitting a house. Then it struck me. He was a cop. He'd been following Toby and me after a previous job and had framed us by setting up this house as bait.

The thought filled me with panic. At last, the thing I never thought would happen was finally happening—I was about to be busted. Another ear-piercing scream penetrated the room from downstairs. What the hell were the police doing to Toby? I suddenly wished I was back at home, tucked away in bed and dreaming, wished I had never stolen that money from Daniel Richards. And I knew that if I didn't make it out of this room, I wouldn't be back in my own bed for months, maybe years.

I fingered the money in my pocket, realizing how pathetic I was to risk everything for a few hundred quid—money that would be useless behind bars. But maybe it could prove useful here. Grabbing as many of the notes as I could, I wrenched them from my pocket and threw them at the man. I didn't wait to see what effect they'd have, but dived to the floor, rolling under his reach and scrambling to my feet on the other side of the room.

I couldn't see the door: it was too dark. I slapped my hands furiously against the wall, knowing that I had only seconds before I felt the cop's huge hand on my shoulder. But there was nothing there except shelves and books. Risking a look behind me, I saw the man's two disembodied eyes race across the room, and it was all I could manage not to collapse to the floor screaming.

Just as he was above me, however, my hand hit the doorframe. Reaching across, I felt the handle and twisted it, ripping the door open so hard that it almost came off its hinges. It struck the man square in the face, but his only response was to laugh—a deep, grating rumble that followed me out onto the landing.

"Run, Alex, run, Alex, run, run, run," came his voice as I felt my way toward the stairs. What the hell was going on? What kind of cop would say that?

I was running too fast and tripped on the top stair, almost plunging into darkness before I managed to get a hold on the banister. I tried to plan my escape route as I descended. Obviously the room we came in through was now a no-go area—I had no intention of meeting whoever was in there with Toby. There was the front door, which lay directly ahead of the stairs, or I could try to find my way to the back of the house. Either way, I wouldn't get far in the dark.

As it turned out, though, it wasn't the dark that got me. Almost as soon as I propelled myself from the bottom step every light in the house was switched on simultaneously. I gasped and pressed my hands to my eyes, momentum flinging me into a wall. The illumination had completely thrown me, filling my head with stars and causing me to lose my bearings.

I squinted against the glare to see that the hall was empty. A quick glance at the front door told me there were too many locks to force it open, so I started running toward the back, hoping for a quick exit.

I couldn't tell you what happened next. I'm not sure if it was the fact that my eyes hadn't adjusted to the light, or if fear and adrenaline did something to my brain, but it was as if a figure simply stepped from the wall. One minute my path was clear, the next it was blocked by another mountainous man—so wide and so tall that he seemed to take up every centimeter of space.

I skidded to a halt, mouth agape. This man too was dressed in a slick black pinstriped suit, with a white shirt and black tie. He looked more like an undertaker than a cop. What scared me most about him, though, was his face. It seemed to be expressionless and grinning at the same time—his silver eyes staring down at me with unmistakable glee, like a boy about to squash a bug.

"Boo," he said, his thick voice just as deep and dangerous as that of the man upstairs.

I staggered backward, shaking my head. The man had left only one escape route—the way we'd come in. I bolted through the sitting room door, ready to fling myself screaming from the window. But what I saw in that room drained the strength from my body, turning my legs to jelly. It took everything I had to remain upright.

The room, which had been deserted less than five minutes ago, was now full of men. Each was almost identical in size, dwarfing the furniture and making the large space feel like a doll's house—each almost identical in looks too, like brothers. And they were all wearing the same immaculate black suits. I counted four in all, and the sound of footsteps behind me made it clear that the other two were in the hall.

But the figure I couldn't take my eyes off was standing in between the giants, twitching and shaking like he was having a fit. He looked tiny in comparison, barely reaching the elbows of his comrades, and wore a long, black leather coat that made his bald head look like pale parchment.

I knew now why Toby had been screaming. The man was wearing what looked like a gas mask—an antique, rusted device that covered the lower part of his face and stretched over his shoulder to a tank on his back, like the ones worn by divers. He wheezed noisily through the ancient contraption as if he was having an asthma attack. Peering over the top of the mask, like two raisins set into rancid porridge, were his eyes, and the way they stared at me made me want to curl up and die.

It took me a few moments to notice the frail, shaking body of Toby on the floor beneath one of the men in black. He stared at me with a look of pure terror, his eyes wide, pleading for me to help him. I didn't know what to do, I didn't even know who the men were. Taking another look at the shriveled figure by the window, I found myself praying for the familiar uniforms of the police, not this freak show of gas masks and goliaths.

"Nice of you to join us, Alex," said the huge, black-suited man who was standing above Toby. His face was a mirror image of the others', only with what looked like a small mole on his chin. His voice too was indistinguishable from those I had already heard, like distant thunder.

"It looks like everybody here knows my name," I said, the words coming out of my mouth before I even knew I was speaking. Despite the terror that rooted me to the spot, I was determined not to give these men the satisfaction of seeing my fear. "If I'd known there was a party here tonight I would have brought some cake."

To my surprise, the men all chuckled at my joke—a noise so deep that it made the remaining glass in the window vibrate. It was the most terrifying sound I'd ever heard.

"We wanted to surprise you," the man continued.

"Well then, arrest me—arrest us," I said, just waiting to get out of that room. "You've caught us red-handed; take us down to the station and we'll confess."

The same grating laughter that set my teeth on edge. When it had finished, the giant man turned to his smaller friend as if awaiting a command. Seconds rolled past while the freak in the gas mask studied me and Toby, then he turned his dark eyes to me and nodded.

"What?" I asked, desperate to know what was going on. "What the hell does that guy want?"

"He wants you to say goodbye to your friend," the man continued. I shook my head, the fear and confusion churning in my stomach. Were they just going to take me and not Toby?

"What?" I repeated. Toby was no longer looking at me, but was staring at the carpet, sobbing uncontrollably.

"They've got guns with silencers," he said, his voice little more than a whisper. "They're not police, Alex."

I didn't understand what Toby had said until the giant man opened his suit jacket to reveal a holstered pistol tucked beneath his armpit. For a second, I felt the world spin as if I was about to pass out, and by the time I'd regained my composure the man had pulled out the silenced handgun and was pointing it at me.

"Last chance to say goodbye," he said.

I looked at Toby, wanting this nightmare to end, thinking about the things I'd never be able to do if the man pulled the trigger, thinking about how much I'd miss my friends, how much I loved my family. All lost because of greed. It was so stupid! I couldn't control my emotions anymore and tears filled my eyes, blurring my vision. All I could see was the outline of the man, and the black shadow that was his gun.

"Goodbye, Toby," I said through sobs. "I'm sorry."

"Alex," was all I heard of his reply. Then the black shadow

moved, sweeping downward and emitting a low pop that was barely audible against the laughter that once again filled the room. I tried to blink the tears from my eyes, not quite believing what I'd seen. But when my vision had cleared I realized there was no escaping what had just happened.

Toby lay motionless, his eyes blank, the carpet beneath his body the same horrible color as the wound in his head.

It seemed like hours before anyone moved again. It felt as if the connection between my brain and my body had been severed, turning every limb numb. I wanted to feel anger, hatred, sorrow, anything, but all I could do was stare at my friend, at the body that would never move again—a corpse with one dirty shoe. My legs finally gave way and I sank to my knees.

"Catch," came the booming voice. The giant man tossed the gun to me and I reached out instinctively, grabbing it by the handle and staring at it in shock. For a second, I pointed it at the black-suited brute, but I'd barely held a toy gun before, let alone a real one, and quickly tossed it to the floor.

"Now, if I were you, Alex, I'd make a run for it," he continued. "I mean, you've just broken into a house, stolen a load of cash, and shot your best friend in the head in cold blood. The police aren't gonna like you one little bit, so why don't you put those sneakers to good use and run."

I couldn't respond, I didn't know what he was talking about. But suddenly I felt an enormous pair of hands grip me under my arms and hoist me effortlessly to my feet. The same hands turned me around and pushed me roughly toward the front door, which had been unlocked and opened.

"Good luck, Alex," came the voice from behind me. "Run as

hard as you can, or sit and cower outside. Either way we'll see you real soon."

I turned and saw the face of the man in black break into a monstrous smile—all teeth and slitted eyes. Then I took one last look at Toby, at rest on his crimson bed, and bolted out into the rain.

ON THE RUN

WHAT'S THE MOST SCARED you've ever been? Maybe at night, after a horror film, lying under your blankets convinced there's a monster in the room. Or one day in the city when you were younger, realizing you've lost sight of your mom and dad. Perhaps face-to-face on the playground with someone who wants to beat the living crap out of you.

Multiply those feelings by a million and you get me on a dark, wet night, running as fast as I could on the slippery streets to escape the people who'd shot my best friend. I didn't know which direction I was heading in, I just needed to get as far away from that house as possible, and I ran until my legs felt like they were made of lead, until my lungs were on fire and my heart stuttered and stammered like it was about to give out.

Then I collapsed by the side of the road, my wheezing sobs so loud that people in the nearby houses actually pulled back their curtains to see what was going on. But nobody came out to help me, and I didn't blame them. When you've committed a few crimes, something about you changes. It's like you've been marked with a tattoo that only other people can see, and it makes them wary so that they cross the street to avoid you. Even now, as helpless as a newborn baby, my tears conspiring with the rain to soak my jeans, I knew I was alone.

And I also knew that I couldn't stay out in the open. If what that man had said was true, then they were trying to frame me for murder. And that wasn't just a slapped wrist or a month or two in juvie, that was life in prison—in Furnace, with its pits and its punishments and its pain.

Pushing to my feet, I looked at the road sign to get my bearings, realizing that my school wasn't too far from here. I took a deep, shuddering breath and started jogging again, making my way down Brian Avenue and across an abandoned Trafford Road into the row houses that ran along the back of Eastmark High. Toby, Brandon, and I had snuck into school this way countless times to play soccer on the field.

I realized that Toby would never play soccer again, and the thought was like a punch to the gut. But I fought back the tears, tried to push the image of my dead friend from my mind as I cut through an overgrown garden and climbed over the worn fence into the dark, deserted field beyond.

I didn't learn the word *irony* until much later, but I guess it was ironic that I ended up walking across the slick grass to the jungle gym, which rose from the wispy layer of predawn mist like the rusted hull of some ghost ship. It was here that everything had started to go wrong.

It had only been two years since I stole my first cash, but it seemed like forever. I could barely even picture me before that day—a young boy who had never had a bad thought in his life, who wanted to grow up to be a magician, who couldn't care less about money.

I pictured that young boy now, saw him turning his back on

his friends and walking off into the sunshine to follow a different path. And I hoped that somewhere, in a different dimension, there was a version of me who wasn't sitting alone on an uncomfortable metal bar in the cold waiting for the police to lock him away forever.

The rain had almost stopped. I climbed a little higher to the platform at the top of the jungle gym and leaned against the rail, looking out across the misty field, eerie in the bright moonlight. Every now and again the glow would be shrouded by a passing rain cloud, throwing the whole world into darkness. Each time it happened I was gripped by terror—the fear that a monstrous dark figure would rise from the fog and snatch me up, carry me away forever. But the moon always fought back, bathing the field and its sole inhabitant in its liquid silver.

My options were few and far between. I could sit here and wait for morning, when the school would be full of people all looking for me. I could head home—surely the news about Toby's death wouldn't have broken yet, and I could talk to my mom and dad about what happened. I could head to Brandon's house, hide out there until I thought of a better plan. I could run, head for the hills and never look back. Or I could just go to the police, tell them what had really gone on in that house. I mean, there were six giant men and a freak in a gas mask, somebody else must have seen them.

None of those options seemed particularly appealing, so I put them in order of how bad they were. Running seemed like the worst thing I could do, closely followed by waiting here and going to the police. That left Brandon and my own home. I thought about seeing my mom again and it filled me with a strange mix of sadness and joy. Maybe she could just give me a hug and all this would go away. Surely moms had the power to make *anything* go away.

But the thought of confessing to her was almost as unbearable as the thought of a lifetime inside Furnace. It would have to be Brandon's.

I was so lost in thought that I didn't notice the change in light until it was almost too late. Looking at my jeans I saw they were shimmering with a red and blue haze, not unlike a disco light. But this was no disco. I snatched my head up to see two police cars sitting a hundred meters away outside the school's main gate, casting a web of color across the dark grass.

Several armored men were climbing out of the vehicles, most equipped with rifles and flashlights and one holding what looked like a bolt cutter. They walked to the gates, the cop with the cutters using them to snap through the heavy chain before kicking them open. He pointed at the school building, and two of the police with flashlights started running toward it. Then he scanned the playing field, his eyes coming to rest on my jungle gym. He gestured my way.

I ducked behind the rail as two beams of light struck the metal frame, seeking me out. There wasn't much cover, but the police were too far away to see me. Not for long, though. As I watched, the two men started jogging across the grass in my direction. I shuffled backward across the platform until I reached the rear edge, ready to drop down to the ground.

But before I could, my eye caught a piece of graffiti that I swear had never been there before. Carved into the soft wood of the platform, in large, even letters, were three words that made my blood freeze.

Keep running, Alex.

I traced my fingers across the markings to make sure they were real, but the sensation of splinters in my skin let me know that this was no dream. The men, whoever they were, had known what I'd do before I did.

The sound of footsteps pounding the wet grass reminded me that the police were getting closer. I shoved myself off the rear of the frame, landing awkwardly on the soft ground and backing into the darkness. Turning, I sprinted toward the fence, forcing my tired legs to work. Scrambling out into the overgrown garden, I scanned the street to make sure it was empty, then turned left and started walking toward Brandon's house.

I hadn't spoken to Brandon much since Toby and I had started robbing houses instead of students. It was as if he could see that invisible tattoo too, and it was pretty clear from the way he acted now that he was scared of us, of what we'd become. But we'd been close friends once, and even when you've been to hell and back your friends stick by you.

I cut up Edwards Avenue, taking another left at the top of the hill and making my way toward Bessemer Road. The houses in this part of town were all huge, their four stories staring out across the tract housing below like they were laughing at them. I guess that's one of the reasons Brandon had backed out—even though his parents only owned an apartment up here, they weren't exactly poor. Not that I was stealing bread so that I could stay alive. I'm no Oliver Twist.

I spotted the building that Brandon's apartment was in and crossed the road, trying to stick to the blanket of shadows that kept most of the street in darkness. All the lights were off, which wasn't surprising given that it was long after midnight, but I knew which room was his. Sneaking in through the front gate, I picked up a couple of small stones from the graveled path and pulled back my arm to launch them at the second-floor window.

Before I could, something grabbed my wrist—a vise-like grip that felt like it could have torn the whole limb off. I yelped, as much from the shock as the pain, and spun around to see a horribly familiar face standing right behind me, his silver eyes glinting, the same tiny mole on his chin and his soulless smile beaming at me like the Cheshire Cat's. It was impossible—he hadn't been there seconds before, and nobody could move that quickly, that quietly.

"Didn't your mother tell you never to throw stones?" the man in the suit asked, his voice so powerful that it felt as if it was being transmitted right into the center of my brain. I couldn't respond, my whole body felt numb. The man tightened his grip on my arm, bending down until his face was almost touching mine. "Not long till sunrise, Alex," he said, the scent of his breath like sour milk. "And now you've got these guys to deal with."

He twisted my wrist, spinning me around and giving me a shove that propelled me back out of the gate. I tripped on my own feet, staggering backward off the curb and landing in a heap in the road. I glanced up just in time to see a police car slam on its brakes, squealing to a stop seconds before its front bumper made friends with my forehead. I looked back to Brandon's garden, but it was empty—the man in black had vanished just as quickly as he had appeared.

I heard the sound of the car doors opening and I leaped to my feet, backing away from the vehicle. A policeman in beetle-black body armor was making his way toward me, his expression one of concern. A policewoman held back, one hand on her radio, the other on the nasty-looking nightstick that hung from her belt.

"You okay?" the man asked, stepping closer. "You just came out of nowhere. Did we hit you?"

I kept on retreating, my eyes flitting back and forth from the man to the woman. Her radio bleeped, the sound filling the whole street, before a voice spoke from the static. I couldn't make out what it said, but I knew from the way she looked at me that it wasn't good.

"It's him!" she shouted, wrenching the stick from her belt and advancing. Her partner's expression instantly morphed into one of anger, and he pounced, leaping toward me.

Up until tonight, I'd have thought he was a big guy, and quick too. But compared with the men in black the cop looked tiny, and his move was sluggish. I darted to my left, angling my body so that his hands missed me, then swiveled, pushing him square in the back and sending him sprawling onto the wet road. His partner shrieked at me to stop, vaulting over the car's hood with her nightstick held high, ready to knock me into next week.

I don't know how I did it, but somehow I managed to start running again. You must remember how your legs feel after running laps in gym class, when they're so exhausted that it seems like you're running underwater. That was how it felt—leaping back onto the pavement and hurtling down that road, trying to hold off the sobs so I could breathe. When I look back, remembering that policewoman, who only chased me to the end of the street before returning to her car, it doesn't seem too bad. I mean, I've run screaming from far worse things since that night, creatures that never stop chasing you.

There was only one place left to go, and I headed there at full pelt. I don't remember the journey, it was as if my brain had shut down so that all my energy could be directed to my feet. And I couldn't stop running, even when I reached my house. If I kept moving, then nobody could catch me—not the police who were gathered outside, not the men in black suits who were waiting in the shadows, watching everything through silver eyes. If I could just make it inside, then all the bad things would go away.

So I didn't stop. Not when the police started shouting, not when officers in black masks and bulletproof vests ran into the street with rifles, not when my mom came racing out of the front door dressed in her pink nightie and slippers, screaming at me to give myself up. I just put my head down and cried to her with all my strength.

I don't know how I even managed to stay upright, the world was spinning so fast, but I made it past the first policeman, my sheer momentum sending him flying. The second backed out of my way, his expression of shock almost comical. I could see my mom, tears streaming down her face, being held back by two policewomen. I could see the open door behind her, the warm glow of the kitchen. If I could just make it, ten more steps, then maybe all this could end. Maybe I could find Daniel Richards, give him his money back. It was only twenty quid!

I hit the third policeman square on. He was built like a fireplug—all chest and shoulders—and I bounced off, the wind knocked out of me. I charged forward again but it was too much. My legs cramped and I dropped to my knees for the second time that night. I reached out to my mom, and she reached out to me, but the air between us was instantly flooded with black uniforms, blotting her out like flies. Then I was on the ground, strangers' knees in my back, their nightsticks against my skull, and sharp metal around my wrists.

"I didn't do it!" I sobbed. "I didn't do it!"

But I couldn't even lift my head from the sidewalk, and with the weight of the world on my shoulders only the cold, wet concrete beneath me heard my denial.

DENIAL AND DAMNATION

"I DIDN'T DO IT."

It seemed like the only thing I said for the next few days, a kind of mantra that I kept pumping out as a defense against all the questions and accusations. The first ones at my throat were the cops who threw me into a van, whose taunts and threats cut into me with far more force than the cuffs that bound me to the seat.

"How could you do it?"

"I didn't do it."

"He was your friend."

"I didn't do it."

"Well, you're gonna pay, kid."

"I didn't do it."

Next it was the detectives. They started nice, like they always do in the movies, offering deals and leniency if I just confessed. But the more I denied it the harder they got, their questions so relentless that by the third day when they were kicking over my chair and blowing cigarette smoke in my face I barely knew whether I was guilty or not.

Then came Toby's parents, who sat on the other side of a table clutching each other and screaming at me, their eyes burning with more hatred than I had ever seen in anyone, their anger only held in check by the cops who rested hands on their quivering shoulders and told them I'd get what was coming to me. By this time my mantra was a whisper, little more than a breath, but I kept saying it because, like a breath, it was the only thing keeping me alive.

The worst questions came from the people I loved, my mom and dad. I was separated from them by a dirty plastic window, but there was a far greater barrier between us. I could tell by the way my mom couldn't meet my eye that she thought I was guilty, and she refused to listen to my pleas just like everybody else. There may as well have been a gorge between us, or a mountain, and by the time she was guided out of the room by my dad's unsteady hands I couldn't even find the energy to whisper my denials.

For three weeks I endured an interrogation every day and was thrown into a cell each night. Of course, I told them everything that had happened—the men in the black suits, the sinister figure in the gas mask, the way they had shot Toby in cold blood—but even as I was talking the words seemed ludicrous, hollow. I didn't blame them for laughing at me, I'd never have believed my story either if I hadn't lived the nightmare myself.

My TRIAL WAS an extension of the same empty process. I was marched into court with an armed escort, and chained inside a cage—the kind better suited to serial killers and military generals accused of war crimes, not terrified kids. The heavy bars didn't stop the hatred directed at me when the hearing began. It

poured through like ice water from a judge who was already convinced I was a killer, from a jury that had made up its mind about
this case as soon as it started, and from the crowd in the public
gallery who bayed for my punishment like hyenas. I felt like I
was drowning in their contempt, and just prayed for it to be over,
even if it meant sinking without a trace.

My spirits were lifted only once, when midway through the
second day the doors of the courtroom opened and two men
strode through. Dressed in black and larger than life, they were
instantly recognizable—the men who had sent me here. The
room fell silent as soon as they entered, even the judge lowering
his voice from respect, or maybe fear.

"That's them!" I shouted as they took their seats. "They're the
men who framed me. They killed Toby!"

But the judge simply banged his gavel and fixed me with a
contemptuous stare.

"Of course they are," he said, his voice oily with sarcasm.
"These men are representatives from Furnace Penitentiary. Is
this what your defense has come to? Accusing anybody of your
crimes. Was I there? Did I have a disagreement with your ac-
complice and pull the trigger too?"

The jury laughed, and the men in black suits unveiled their
shark grins and flashed their silver eyes at me. I was like a fish on
the end of a line, waiting to be reeled in.

It took the jury less than forty minutes to decide my fate.
Twelve men and women in a room with my life in their hands,
and they condemned me in less time than the first half of a soccer match. Not that I'm trying to pass the buck. I hadn't killed
Toby, but his blood was on my hands just like my blood was on

his. If we hadn't been so stupid, then none of this would have happened. We'd both have been at school just like any other day, tormenting teachers, chasing girls, and being kids.

I'll never forget the judge's closing speech when the jury announced the guilty verdict. He stood, his walnut desk like a pulpit and his booming voice and thrashing limbs like those of a preacher damning the devil.

"Your crimes are heinous and unforgivable," he shouted, the flecks of foam around his mouth visible even from where I was standing. "Like so many of today's youth you have taken your life and squandered it, turning to crime instead of honor, sickness instead of decency. You have killed in cold blood, you are a coward and a thief and a murderer, and like all the other festering waste of society who come through this court I am happy to sentence you without remorse and without pity."

He leaned forward, never taking his eyes off me.

"You knew very well when you pulled that trigger what your punishment would be," he hissed. "There is no longer any leniency for child offenders, not since the Summer of Slaughter. And like those murderous teenagers you will never again see the light of day. If it was up to me, I would see you hanged by the neck until you were dead. But alas I must settle for this." He paused again, smiling wickedly to himself. "Or perhaps *settle* is the wrong word. Perhaps this is a fate even worse."

I knew what was coming. I clenched my fingers around the bars, praying one last time that something would happen to end this sick and twisted dream. But it was too late. It was over.

"Alex Sawyer, I hereby sentence you to life imprisonment at the Furnace Penitentiary with no possibility of parole. You will be taken from here this afternoon and incarcerated for the remainder of your days."

The resulting wave of cheers and shouts, the banging of the gavel and the roaring in my ears as the truth sank in drowned out the only thing I could think of to say.

"I didn't do it."

I DON'T REMEMBER much else about that day. I have a vague recollection of being dragged from the courtroom by the armed guards, the men in black holding open the door and telling me once again that they'd see me very soon. I couldn't quite remember how to use my legs, so they literally pulled me along the marble-clad corridors, past the crowds with their expressions of hatred and disgust, past my own parents, whose faces I could not make out because they turned away.

I recall only one thing with any clarity. As I was passing a second courtroom the doors flew open to reveal another boy, a similar age to me, being hauled kicking and screaming from inside. He was giving the bailiffs a hard time, his flailing body sending one crashing to the floor and causing the other to reach for his taser. With a flash fifty thousand volts sent the boy hurtling across the corridor, leaving him in a groaning, smoking pile. But even then I could make out his protests and they sent a chill down my spine.

"It wasn't me," he whispered as the men picked him up. "It wasn't me."

For the briefest of seconds our eyes met. It was like looking into a mirror—the fear, the panic, the defiance. I knew instantly that what had happened to me had also happened to him. Our dark fates entwined by the same men, our lives broken by an identical deception.

And then he was gone. I was carried down the corridor, my memories of the moment lessening with each step and fading away completely as I climbed into the truck that would take me to my new home. To the place I would spend the rest of my life. To my own personal hell.

To Furnace.

BURIED ALIVE

I'M BETTING YOU'VE ALL seen some prison films, or watched
cop shows where the bad guys get sent to jail. You know what
they look like: miles of fences topped with razor wire so sharp it
hurts just to look at it; sprawling grounds watched over at all
times by million-watt spotlights and towers with guns; lifeless
buildings that rise up from the ground like great gray tomb-
stones; tiny windows from which ghostly faces stare at an outside
world they can no longer know.

Not Furnace.

Our prison bus took us straight there. Me, the kid who'd been
stunned, and two other teenage guys, all as pale as church can-
dles and cowering back into our seats as if somehow we could
avoid arriving at our inevitable destination. All the while the
police guards shook their shotguns at us and jeered, asking us if
we'd seen Furnace on the newscasts, if we knew what it looked
like, if we had any idea of the horrors that lay ahead.

I knew. I'd seen Furnace on TV like everybody else. After
that summer when so many kids had turned to murder, they
made sure that everyone in the country got a good look at the
prison. They thought it would make us too scared to break

the law, too scared to carry knives and to cut people up for just looking at them the wrong way, too scared to take a human life. Looking around, I guessed they hadn't been too successful.

There had been protesters, of course, the human rights supporters who claimed that locking a child away for life was wrong. But you can only argue with the truth for so long, and that summer when the gangs ran wild and the streets ran red everything changed. Even in the eyes of the liberals we weren't kids anymore, we were killers. All of us.

I used to always think that the waiting was the worst part, but when we rounded a corner and Furnace finally came into sight, I knew I'd rather have stayed on that bus for an eternity than get any closer to the monstrosity ahead.

It was just like on the news: a towering sculpture of dark stone, bent and scarred like it had been burned into existence. The Black Fort, the way in. The windowless building stretched upward, its body merging with a crooked spire that resembled a finger beckoning us forward. Smoke rose from a chimney hidden behind the building, a cloud of poisoned breath waiting to engulf us. All in all it looked more like something from Mordor than a modern prison.

As we neared I could make out some of the details that the news crews had left out. Carved into the cold stone were vast sculptures designed to inspire fear into anybody who saw them— tortured statues, each five meters tall, showing prisoners on the gibbets, hanging from ropes, on guillotines, pleading to executioners, being dragged from loved ones, and, worst of all, a giant head on each corner impaled on a spike. The dead faces watched us, and if I didn't know better I could have sworn their expressions were of pity, their sorrowful eyes wet from the gentle rain that fell.

"Doesn't look so bad," said one of the other boys, his quivering voice betraying his true feelings.

"Well, that ain't the half of it, boyo," replied one of the guards, tapping his shotgun on the window. "That there is Furnace's better side. You know where you're going." He lowered his weapon so it was pointing at the floor. "Down."

He was right, of course. The building ahead was only the entrance, the gateway to the fiery pits below, the mouth that led to the sprawling guts of Furnace, which lay hundreds of meters beneath the ground. I remember when they started building it— I must have been six or seven, a different person—how they'd found a crevice in the rock that seemed to go on forever. They had built the prison inside the hole and plugged the only way out with a fortress. Anyone wanting to dig himself out of this mess only had a couple of miles of solid rock to get through before he was free.

I guess that's when it finally sank in. The thought of being down there, underground, for the rest of my life suddenly hit me like a hammer in the face. I couldn't breathe, my head started to swim, the bile rose in my throat. I sat forward in my seat and stared at the floor, desperately trying to think about something else, something good. But all I could see now were the stains of a hundred other prisoners who had thrown their guts up on confronting the reality of their fate.

I couldn't hold it back. I puked, the mess hitting the seat in front and causing the guard to leap away. I retched a couple more times, then looked up through blurry eyes, expecting a furious reaction. But they were laughing.

"Looks like you win again," said one, reaching into his pocket and pulling out a ten-quid note. "How do you always guess which one is gonna hurl first?"

"When you've been on the job as long as I have," came the reply, "you just know."

There was more, but I couldn't hear it over the sound of the retching and sobbing that echoed back at me from the stained upholstery.

WHEN THE BUS eventually stopped we were herded out like sheep. I felt like I'd thrown up a couple of vital organs as well as the contents of my stomach, and my legs were so wobbly that I thought I was going to collapse when I stood. But as soon as we were outside, the sensation of rain on my face perked me up a little. Well, it did until I remembered that this might be the last time I would ever stand in the rain.

We were right outside the main gate, in a giant cage that gave off a sinister hum and made my head throb whenever I got too close to the bars. I didn't have to know much about physics to guess that it took a hell of an electrical charge to have that effect. The entrance to Furnace was suitably terrifying—two enormous black gates topped with a plinth marked with the word GUILTY. As soon as we were lined up, the gates swung open with a sound not unlike fingernails running down a blackboard, revealing a gray room with nothing in it except two men dressed in black leaning casually against the walls and a nasty-looking gun mounted on the ceiling.

The men grinned at us and stepped forward. I felt my legs going weak again just at the sight of them, and I wasn't alone.

The three other boys shuffled away in fear, and even the armed guards moved back toward the bus.

"They're all yours," said one of the guards, his voice little more than a whisper. He pulled a palmtop from his jacket and held it out with a shaking hand. "If you could just print here."

One of the giants in suits strode forward and snatched the device, pressing his thumb against the screen until it bleeped loudly. He watched the armed guards scramble into the bus, then turned his attention to us. I studied his face. With their glinting eyes and their menacing smiles the men in black all looked the same, but I recognized this one—the mole on his chin letting me know it was the man who had shot Toby.

"We told you," he said, placing his hand on the shoulder of the boy beside me but talking to us all. "You could run but you couldn't hide. And now here you are, guests of honor at Furnace Penitentiary."

The other man walked to the front of the line and grabbed the kid by the scruff of his shirt, pulling him forward.

"This way," he said, his voice like the sound of continents shifting.

We shuffled forward, our steps tiny in the hope that maybe we'd never reach the threshold. It was as the first boy passed through the doors that the second—the guy who'd been stunned at the court—suddenly made a break for it. He pounced to the side and stepped backward, all the while looking at the men guarding us.

"You framed me," he shouted, his face twisted into a mask of anger and fear. "I didn't kill anybody and now I'm spending the rest of my life in this nightmare. I won't let you do it."

The two men started laughing, their thunderous peals echoing off the stone walls. Then in the blink of an eye the one to the right of me burst across the dusty ground and with a mighty crack sent the boy flying toward the fence. If I hadn't seen it with my own eyes, I wouldn't have believed the speed of the man. He had moved so fast he'd left traces in the air, like sparklers on a summer night. The boy hit the floor and rolled, ending in a crumpled heap perilously close to the electrified bars.

"You wouldn't be the first one to fry on that cage," said the man, walking until he stood over the boy. "But it's a shame to waste you on something as quick and painless as the Barbecue."

He reached down and picked the boy up by his collar, like a bear scooping up a rag doll, then carried him back to the line. The kid had a bloody lip and a dazed expression like he'd just been hit by a freight train, yet somehow he was managing to stand. He lowered his eyes to the floor, but I saw him flash the man a murderous look as soon as his back was turned.

"Now that little rebellion is out of the way I hope you realize just how serious this is," said the first man, walking to the front of the line and ushering us forward. "This is a private institution sanctioned by the government, which means that we now own you. You have been sentenced to life in prison with no possibility of parole. So, short of a revolution in the country or an act of God, you will die here. Not that God would ever mess with Furnace."

I faltered as I reached the threshold, staring at the line that separated the ground outside from the polished stone of the room ahead. It was just one more step, but it was the last one I would take as a free person. With a shuddering sigh I lifted my leg and planted my foot down on the other side of the wall. It might have just been my imagination, but the sound of that footstep seemed to reverberate around the room, a death knell mourning a lost life.

"As you can see, the manner of your death isn't important to us," the man continued, guiding our group through the feature-less room toward a metal door in one wall. "Of course the state has no death penalty, but any attempt at escape will be dealt with using lethal force."

The door opened to reveal a long corridor ahead, as feature-less as the room we'd just left. I cast one final look behind me, catching a glimpse of dark cloud through the main gates before they slammed shut. It was a fleeting image, but one I will never forget.

"There's no one you can cry to, no one you can beg to. The public have judged you and found you guilty. As far as they are concerned, you are already dead."

The corridor ended with another door, this one guarded by a third man, also in black. He nodded to his colleagues as he unlocked the gate, and winked a silver eye at us as he waited for it to slide open. We passed through, finding ourselves in a small room with a hole in one wall.

"Line up and take your prison uniforms," the man continued. "One each. Then go through that door for purging."

We obeyed. What choice did we have? One by one we walked by the hole in the wall, and from the shadows we were passed a pair of paper shoes, underwear that felt like sandpaper, and a hunk of stiff, striped cloth that was better suited to holding potatoes than wearing. The white uniform was branded with the Furnace symbol—three circles arranged in a triangle, a dot in the middle of each and thin lines joining them. I followed the boys in front through the door to find another room, this one full of tiny cubicles.

"Get in, strip, and wash," came the booming voice behind us. I picked a door, left my new uniform on a shelf outside, and entered. There were directions on the wall and I followed them, taking off my clothes and placing them into a chute where they vanished from sight. Shivering in the cold, I pressed a large red button in front of me and was instantly hit by a fist of freezing water. I doubled over, pressing myself against the wall to avoid the stream. But the cubicle was too small, and I had to endure it for what seemed like an eternity.

When the spray stopped, I followed the instructions again and held my breath while a cloud of gas was pumped in. It stung my eyes and my skin, and even after the directed thirty seconds when I took a gasping breath, the gas still flooded my lungs, making my chest feel like it was on fire.

Staggering out of the door, I put on my uncomfortable uniform and watched as the other three boys emerged from their cubicles—each one red-eyed, pale-skinned, and coughing. We looked like phantoms haunting the room where we'd died, which wasn't too far from the truth, I guess.

His malicious grin as wide as ever, the man steered us across the room to a set of elevator doors. He whispered something into his collar and seconds later the doors opened, revealing a machine gun on the ceiling of the elevator car which swung around to face us.

"This is where we part company, for now," he said. "This elevator will take you all to your cells. Don't try anything funny or you'll end up decorating the walls."

He pushed us forward with his massive hands and we entered the cabin, the remote turret following our every move.

"It's quite a ride down to the bowels of the earth," he said as the doors began to close. "So I hope none of you are claustrophobic."

Then he was gone, and with a deafening whir of gears the armored elevator began its descent to the darkness at the bottom of the world.

THE DESCENT

FOR THE FIRST MINUTE or so none of us spoke. We didn't even look each other in the eye. It was a strange mix of emotions. There was fear, of course, so thick you could almost smell it beyond the stink of dust and oil, but there was also something else. I guess it was pride—if we acknowledged each other, then we were also acknowledging our own helplessness, our own panic, and after what we'd just been through, nobody wanted to do that.

In the end, it was me who broke the ice.

"I just want to get this out in the open," I said above the sound of the elevator's descent. "I didn't kill anyone. They framed me, they shot my friend and set me up for the fall. I'm not a killer."

Gradually, the other three boys raised their heads, and for the first time we all got a good look at each other.

"Join the club," said the kid who I'd seen in court. He was shorter than me, but wider, his body tensed like a cat that's puffed up its fur. He brushed a strand of untidy dark hair away from his face and cast a nervous gaze up at the machine gun in the ceiling before continuing. "Those guys in black drove a car into some old woman. Killed her. They knew everything about me, they got my prints onto the wheel, they knew I wouldn't have an alibi that night or any way of proving I didn't do it. Name's Zee, by the way."

"Zee?" I asked, raising an eyebrow. The question brought a brief smile to his face.

"Got four older brothers and sisters. Mom was adamant that I was the last one, so she called me Zee. What about you?"

"Alex," I replied. I looked at the other two kids. They were the complete opposite of each other—one resembled a beanpole, his uniform hanging off him like rags on a scarecrow, the other had probably eaten way too many chocolate bars in his time, but his green eyes were sharp and his gaze fierce.

"Jimmy," said the beanpole, hoisting up his trousers. "Yeah, I didn't kill nobody either. Same story as you, Alex, they murdered a friend of mine. Stabbed him, though."

We all turned to look at the fat kid. For a minute it seemed like he was going to cry, then his expression hardened and with his fists clenched he spat out two words that sent chills down all of us.

"My sister."

There was still no sign of the elevator stopping. It might just have been a psychological trick to make us feel like we were going deeper than we were, but I doubted it. It takes a long time to travel a mile underground.

"You saying they framed us all?" asked Zee, shaking his head. "Doesn't make any sense. Why would they do it?"

"Maybe they've got cells to fill, targets to reach," suggested Jimmy, but his tone of voice made it clear he didn't know. None of us did. Not then.

"Listen," I said, certain that the elevator car was bugged and motioning for the other boys to come closer. "Whatever happens in there, whatever they've got in store for us, we've got to stick together. Right?"

"I've got your back," said Zee. "I'm getting out of here no matter what."

"The only way you're getting out is in a coffin," hissed the kid who had lost his sister. "Haven't you heard about this place? There is no way out."

"Well, I'm with you guys," said Jimmy, ignoring the remark. "Ain't no way I'm spending the rest of my life in this hole."

The noise of the elevator shifted pitch and with a bone-breaking shudder it came to a halt. Before the doors could open, however, there was one last hate-filled remark from the corner of the cabin.

"We're all going to die in here."

THE MOMENT THE elevator doors opened my senses came under attack. I can describe what I saw when I stepped out into Furnace but I can't tell you how I felt. I was so overloaded by what lay before me that I'm sure part of my brain shut down just so that it wouldn't overheat. It was like a survival mechanism to stop me going insane. I took in the details but they didn't register on any emotional scale.

The elevator had taken us to the very depths of the prison—a stretch of bare stone that was easily the size of a soccer field—and above us for as far as we could see lay its tortured, twisted interior. Furnace certainly deserved its name. The walls were made from the very rock of the earth, their surfaces rough and red, and the half-light of the room made them flicker as if they were on fire. The sunless yard was vast and circular, and arranged in rings around the outside were countless cells, the gray metal platforms and jagged staircases resembling a rib cage against the fleshy walls.

I stared at the elevator shaft, which rose in a relentless line above our heads, the top barely visible where it entered the red rock of the ceiling—broken only by a giant video screen hanging over the doors. The elevator was the only way in or out, and there was absolutely no other means of getting back up.

The hiss of pneumatics snapped my attention back to the walls beside us and I saw two more machine guns protruding from the rock like black limbs. They trained their sights on us as we staggered from the elevator into the vast chamber, each with an unblinking red eye that seemed to assess our every move. I wondered whether there was a human at the other end of the controls, or whether some dark robotic intelligence had its finger on the trigger, ready to fire at the smallest sign of trouble. I couldn't decide which would be worse.

I was so overawed by the prison itself that it took me a while to notice it was full of people. They swarmed across the courtyard in front of us, mostly kids about my age, some a little older and even a couple who looked like they should still be in middle school. Some hung out in groups, their stares and swaggers a clear message that they were in charge. Others hung back in the shadows or peered over the bars of the platforms, all sickly faces and baggy eyes. Most were staring at us, some laughing and shouting "new fish," others shaking their heads in compassion. Their gaze made my cheeks burn, and I lowered my head so nobody would see.

It didn't take long for a few of the kids to step forward, but it was pretty clear that they weren't a welcoming party. Each of the six boys wore a black bandanna with a crude picture of a skull painted on the front. It would have been laughable if they didn't all look as though they were about to make us walk the plank.

"Let me guess," I said, starting to speak before I even knew I was doing it. "You're in here for piracy."

I heard Zee snigger to my side, but there wasn't even a hint of a smile in the pockmarked faces before me. One of the boys, not the biggest but by far the ugliest, stepped right up to me, so close that I could see the dirt clogging his pores.

"Get this straight from the start, new fish," he said, jabbing me in the chest with a filthy fingernail. "You on our turf now, so you take orders from me."

My heart was pounding so hard it felt like something inside me was about to burst. I tried meeting his glare with one of my own, and was holding up pretty well until I suddenly started thinking that this was how the kids at school must have felt when Toby and I had pressed them for money—powerless, furious, ashamed. The thought washed through me like acid, and my head dropped. Looking back, that little moment of self-realization probably saved my life. I've seen the Skulls kill people for nothing more than standing up to them.

"You all belong to me," the kid continued, speaking slowly and emphasizing each word by prodding us one by one in the chest. "No getting away from that. You all Skull Fodder now."

Zee started to say something—it sounded like it was going to be a witty comeback—but fortunately for him he was interrupted by the sound of a siren. It was deafening, cutting through my head and reverberating up the steep walls of the prison until the echoes died out near enough twenty seconds later. By that time the boys had backed away, joining the rest of the inmates who were flooding toward the center of the giant courtyard. I noticed a yellow ring painted onto the floor and wondered whether we should be heading toward it too.

But it was too late to move. The siren rang out again, and a metal door the size of a bus to the left of the elevator began to hiss and rumble, mechanisms inside grinding and turning as they released a series of locks. With a blast of steam the vault door swung open lazily on its enormous hinges, revealing a sight that I knew there and then I would take with me to my grave.

THE GUARDS CAME OUT FIRST, three of them all in black suits and all holding shotguns in their massive fists. They strolled from the steam-filled corridor beyond like they were going for a walk in the park, their silver eyes full of cold humor. They made me nervous, no doubt about it, but that wasn't what filled me with terror.

Behind them came two more figures that looked horribly familiar—their stunted bodies covered by leather overcoats, their shriveled, pasty faces concealed by ancient gas masks that wheezed noisily. They were almost lost in the shadows of their guards as they twitched and shook their way out, but their black eyes—which looked as lifeless as the lumps of coal in a snowman's face—never left us. I recalled the first time I'd met one of these monstrosities, the way it had picked Toby to die without the slightest trace of emotion. I felt anger well up inside me, but I was powerless to do anything about it.

Besides, it wasn't even these freaks who made the scene ahead so horrific. It was the man who walked out after them. At first glance he seemed like an ordinary guy in his forties—pretty tall, very lean, dark hair, and a clean gray suit. But the more I studied him the more I realized there was something very wrong with the way he looked. His face was too angular, the skin pulled tight against the bone beneath like he was a skeleton dressed in someone else's flesh—flesh that looked more like leather when it caught the light.

The weird thing was that I tried looking him in the eye but I simply couldn't do it. My gaze just bounced off, like there was some kind of force field around his face. I know that sounds stupid, but I can't think of any other way to describe it; whenever I looked him right in the eye, I found myself staring at something else instead—his chin, his suit, the wall. I mean, what the hell was that all about?

The cherries on the sick cake that lay before me—the sight that really struck fear into my heart—were the two creatures who trotted out after their master. If the devil had dogs, it would be these. They were huge, bigger than Irish wolfhounds, their heads easily level with my shoulders. The creatures glistened in the red light of the prison, and it took me a while to work out why. When I realized, I almost threw up my guts again.

They didn't have any skin. Their slick bodies were made up of muscles and tendons that bulged in plain view, throbbing gently with the beating of their hearts. As they moved you could see their insides working, the muscles stretching then contracting, finally tensing when the group came to a halt. Their faces too were entirely devoid of fur, two silver eyes embedded into their flesh and glaring at our group like we were dinner.

I took an involuntary step back but stopped dead when the dogs started growling.

"It doesn't take long to learn obedience in this place," came a voice so gravelly and deep that for a second I thought it was being broadcast directly into my skull. But the man with the dogs was moving his mouth, so I assumed the words came from him.

"And obedience is the difference between life, death, and the other varieties of existence on offer here in Furnace." The man stepped forward, his dogs trotting by his heels. "Obey my rules and you'll do just fine. Disobey them and you'll soon learn that here your nightmares exist on the same plane as you, they stalk the same corridors and haunt your cells. It's only me that stands between you and insanity.

"Anyway, where are my manners? My name is Warden Cross, and I run this institution. I know who you are, and I know your crimes. But here everybody is guilty, so we do not judge you by the paths you took, only by the way you choose to live in this prison."

He stopped a short distance before us and I could swear the temperature dropped several degrees. I don't know why but I started to think of him as a black hole, like he sucked all the life and warmth and goodness from whatever was nearby. The closer he got the more it felt as though something was being wrenched out of my body. I squirmed in discomfort, beads of sweat forming on my forehead.

"You've already broken the first and most important rule of Furnace," the warden went on. "But since you didn't know it, I guess we'll excuse you this once. When the siren sounds, you must be either in your cell or in the yellow circle in the yard. Anyone breaks that rule then I can't guarantee their safety." He gestured at the guns on the wall. "It's a precautionary measure, you understand." I didn't, but I kept mum.

"If you hear one long blast on the siren, then you must get to your cells. That means lockdown, and that's when things really turn nasty if you're left outside." This time he nodded at his dogs, which began to drool messily on the stone floor.

"There are, of course, other codes of conduct, and you will all have plenty of time to become acquainted with them. But let's get you settled in. I mean, we're not monsters." His face erupted into a crooked smile. "Well, not all of us."

One of the men in black handed the warden a sheet of paper, and he studied it for a moment.

"Zee Hatcher," he read. "Prisoner number 2013832. Your cell is D24, fourth level. Cellmate Carlton Jones." There was a shuffling from the crowd of inmates, and a small, redheaded boy stepped to the edge of the yellow circle. He nodded nervously in the direction of the warden, then motioned for Zee to approach him. I watched him go, feeling like I'd been robbed of my best friend even though we'd only just met.

"Montgomery Earl," the warden continued, looking at the doughy kid. "Prisoner number 2013833. Cell number E15, fifth level. Cellmate Kevin Arnold."

"Hell no," came a voice from the crowd. It was the ugly kid dressed like a pirate. I felt my heart sink for poor Montgomery. I knew exactly what life would be like for him paired with that thug. The warden glared at Kevin and the boy stopped his protests, muttering something to the other Skulls who stood nearby.

"Better get moving," the warden said. Montgomery trotted off toward the yellow circle but I couldn't watch to see what happened.

"Alex Sawyer. Prisoner number 2013834. Cell number F11, sixth level. Cellmate Carl Donovan."

I looked over at the crowd but nobody came forward.

"I said Carl Donovan," the warden hissed, his leathery face creasing in displeasure. Gradually a tall, well-built kid a little older than me stepped forward, pushing past the people in front of him and staring at me like I was something his cat had coughed up. I ran a hand through my hair, then walked slowly across the uneven stone. The warden was dishing out a cell to Jimmy, but I wasn't really listening.

"Hey," I said meekly when I reached the boy who I'd be living with for God only knew how long. He looked down his nose at me and just snorted, then turned and started walking back through the crowd. Behind me I heard the warden shout out across the courtyard.

"Beneath heaven is hell, boys, and beneath hell is Furnace. I hope you enjoy your stay."

SETTLING IN

THE KID CALLED CARL led me across to the back of the courtyard, never once turning to see if I was following. He bounded up a set of stairs and I ran to keep up with him—tripping on more than one step in my desperation not to be left behind. At one point I heard the siren again and completely missed my footing, scraping my shin on the sharp metal and crying out in pain. I looked back out over the yard to see the massive vault door swing open and the macabre group vanish into the wall—all except for the men in black suits who stalked the floor with their shotguns.

Carl leaped up five more flights of stairs without so much as panting. By the time I'd caught up with him I was breathing like a broken vacuum cleaner and sweating like a sumo wrestler in a sauna. He was standing outside our cell looking impatient, and I apologized as I walked past him through the door.

I don't really know what I'd been expecting. I knew it wouldn't be the Hilton, or even a Travelodge, but when I'd thought about my cell I'd pictured something the same size as my old room, with a bed and a wardrobe and maybe even a plant or something. As it was, I had to stop short as soon as I entered the tiny room or else I'd have banged my nose on the far wall.

The cell was little bigger than our garden shed, and most of that was taken up by a set of metal bunk beds that looked better suited to eight-year-olds having a sleepover. Aside from a toilet wedged into one corner, the only other thing in there was a bad smell.

"You've got to be kidding me," I muttered under my breath. I felt another wave of panic wash over me as I pictured the rest of my life crammed into this tiny space, and I bit my lip hard to get it under control.

"It ain't much, but it's home," said Carl, pushing me out of the way and leaping onto the top bunk. "And this one's mine."

I sat down on the lower bed and stared out of the bars, which made up one whole wall of the cell. All I could see, on the other side of the giant pit, were more cells and more prisoners, their gray faces a reflection of my own. I thought about just running out of the cell and jumping over the balcony ahead. Six floors up and hard rock below—three or four seconds and it would all be over. But there was no way, I couldn't bring myself to do it. Not yet, anyway.

"Six floors isn't enough," came a voice above me, deep but surprisingly tuneful. I raised an eyebrow, wondering if he'd been reading my mind. "S'okay. It's the first thing any of us think about. And I've seen people do it, too. Jump from pretty much every level. Well, the ones that are open, anyway. First couple of floors, you get sprained ankles and a few bruises. Levels three through six you get broken up pretty bad but you don't die. Not unless you hit headfirst, which isn't easy. You really wanna bite the dust, then you got to go up, level seven or eight. That ought to do it."

I heard the bed creak and shake as he changed position.

"Funny thing is," he went on, "you go any higher, then you don't die either. I saw one kid go from the tenth floor, but he just bounced and screamed. Died a bit later, yeah, but I don't wanna know what he went through first."

I shuddered at the thought and promised myself I'd never jump, no matter how bad things got. The bed creaked again and a head appeared from over the top bunk. I was surprised to see it smiling.

"Name's Donovan," he said. "Always thought it sounded better than Carl. You're Sawyer, right?"

"Alex," I replied, not quite ready to abandon my first name.

"Alex, right." He sprang from the bunk and landed gracefully on the cell floor before sitting next to me and looking me up and down. "You seem like a good kid, anyway. You have to be careful around here, you get some real nasty freaks. Killers, you know?" He laughed. "Well, we're all killers, but there are two kinds—the ones who did it for fun and the ones who did it 'cause they had no choice."

"And the ones who didn't do it," I added with a sad smile.

"Yeah, we been getting a few of them around here lately."

I poked my flat pillow mournfully and lifted the sheet. It was so thin I could see right through it, like greaseproof paper. Not that I thought I'd get cold. The air in here was hot and heavy, like we were sitting in an oven.

"Have you been here long?" I asked. He gave a kind of spluttered laugh that had absolutely no humor in it.

"Five years, Alex. I'm first generation. I'd already been in prison for a couple of months, miles away from here. Jeez that place was nice—spacious cells, leisure facilities, rec room. It was like a country club compared to this. They transferred everyone under eighteen to Furnace as soon as it opened so that all you other kids could see what happened when you did bad things."

"But you were framed, right? By the men in black?"

"Me, no." He paused for a minute, looking out through the bars but obviously miles away. "The blacksuits have framed a lot of the people in here, but I'm as guilty as they come. I killed my mom's boyfriend 'cause he was beating her up every night. Just couldn't take it anymore. I snapped, hit him with a candlestick. Was a lucky hit, I guess, for an eleven-year-old. Or unlucky, depending on how you look at it."

"And they put you away?" I asked incredulously.

"New laws had just come in, the ones clamping down on youth crime. That was the year of all the murders, the Summer of Slaughter as everyone calls it. Even though I had nothing to do with the gangs, the government was using all cases of juvie murder as warnings, so they gave me life. The irony is my mom . . . Well, she couldn't handle it. She . . ."

He stopped and looked away, and I swear I could feel his rage like some kind of force emanating from him.

"How do you tell the time in here anyway?" I asked, trying to change the subject. "No sun, no clocks."

"You can't," he replied, obviously glad for the new topic of conversation. "You just go by the sirens and by lockdown at the end of the day. Rhythms here are completely different, but you get used to them." He got up and walked to the cell door. "On that note, let me show you around. I could do with some grub and it's trough time soon."

I pushed myself up off the bed but not before noticing a series of gashes that ran along the wall—five lines etched into the rock from the bed to the door. He saw me looking at them and frowned.

"You'll get to know all about that soon enough," he whispered.

"What are they? They look like they were made by finger-nails." I was joking, but from the way his expression hardened I realized it was true.

"This place isn't right," he went on, leaning in toward me so close I could feel his spit on my face. "You're never safe here because one day it will be your turn to be taken—maybe a week, maybe years, maybe tonight. Some go quietly, some don't. Adam didn't, he went screaming and clawing at the wall and fighting for his life."

He ran his finger along one of the grooves, then he turned his attention back to me.

"In the dead of night they come for you, Alex," he said. "Sooner or later they come for everyone."

THE GOOSE BUMPS stayed on my arms all the way down the stairs as I fired question after question at Donovan's back, but now that we were out of the cell his air of hard indifference had returned and he ignored me. He only started talking again as we were walking across the courtyard, but the smile was nowhere to be seen.

"Sorry about the Jekyll and Hyde act, kid," he said through a mouth of stone, his eyes glaring hard at everyone we passed. "In this place you gotta act tough all the time or else they pick you off." When I asked who "they" were, he nodded at the group of boys in the corner wearing the black bandannas. Kevin was there, but Montgomery, the fat kid, was nowhere to be seen.

"The pirates?" I asked. Donovan made a noise from his nose that I thought might have been a laugh.

"Yeah, the pirates. Otherwise known as the Skulls. They were one of the groups responsible for the Slaughter. They're not the only gang here but they're easily the worst. They all carry shanks." He noticed my confusion. "Homemade knives. They make them out of anything and everything they can find. Rock, cutlery, even bone. Not afraid to use them either."

We had crossed the courtyard and arrived at a large crack in the rock that led into a tunnel. Like everything else it blended into the red walls perfectly, which was why I hadn't spotted it before. There were two more wall-mounted machine guns here, one pointing right at us and one directed through the opening. Ignoring them, Donovan strode forward.

"Give the gangs a wide berth if you want to stay in one piece," he went on as we made our way through the tunnel. "Around here the guards don't give a crap if we kill each other, and those kids don't have anything to lose. It's not like their sentence can get any longer if they kill anyone else, if you follow me."

I did, although I couldn't quite believe what I was hearing.

"So is that who comes at night? The gangs?"

This time Donovan laughed out loud, the sound echoing off the walls and making me jump. He simply shook his head and walked on, leading me out into another chamber of bare rock. This one was full of tables and benches, most of which were currently empty. At the far end of the room was a deserted canteen, not unlike the one at school. The ceiling here was much lower, bearing down on me as we walked toward the nearest table. The fleshy walls made me feel like I was in the stomach of some giant monster—a place to get digested, not to eat.

"Welcome to the trough room," he said. "This is where you get your three tasty, nutritious meals of the day. Steak, salmon, venison, champagne truffles. The works!"

"Seriously?" I asked, a flicker of hope igniting inside me like a drug.

"Sure, I guess. Trouble is you can never be too sure what you're getting because it's blended up with about a ton of sawdust and served as a paste. I like to think that what we're eating used to be real food."

The flicker died, along with my appetite. We took seats opposite one another as the prisoners slowly made their way into the canteen, where the food was served. A few minutes later two short bursts of the siren sounded and the crowd inside the canteen started to swell.

"How did you know what time it was?" I asked as a door behind the canteen opened and a sweaty inmate emerged struggling to hold a vast container.

"Like I said, you just get a knack for it," Donovan replied. He got to his feet and started walking toward the canteen. I made to follow, but he waved for me to sit back down again, shouting over his shoulder, "Allow me."

I watched him go. The inmates were all hovering around the canteen but there was no queue—not that I really expected one in a place like this. It was more like vultures picking at a corpse. The strong ones got priority, barging past everyone else to be served first. I don't know whether it was a relief or a shock to see Donovan plow his way to the front, the smaller kids backing away from him and hovering on the outside of the throng. But even he stood to one side to let the Skulls through, never taking his eyes off them as they snatched their food and walked away.

I was distracted from the spectacle by a gentle hand on my shoulder and swung my head around to see Zee. He sat down on the bench beside me and leaned in close, his face twisted in panic.

"This place is like a death camp," he whispered. "What with the gangs and the guns and those scary guards—"

"The blacksuits," I said.

Zee shuddered. "I've even got bloodstains on the floor of my cell, for Christ's sake." I thought about the marks on my wall but didn't say anything. "What's your guy like? Carl?"

"Donovan," I answered, watching him cross the floor with two trays of food. "Nice. I was lucky, I think. What about you?"

"Yeah okay. Quiet kid. Wouldn't say boo to a goose, as my gran used to say."

"I don't blame him," I answered. "I once got chased around a park by a goose. I could swear it was trying to break my arm. They're evil."

We were both giggling when Donovan arrived back, and he looked at us as if we were crazy.

"It usually takes a few weeks for people to crack up in here," he said as he sat down, sliding my tray across the table. "Don't tell me you two have lost it already."

"Donovan, this is Zee." They nodded at each other, although both remained wary.

"Another new fish," said Donovan, shoveling his food into his mouth. "I'd get it while it's hot if I were you. Not that this crap is hot."

I looked at the mound of gray mush in front of me and instantly thought about the mess I'd made on the prison bus. They looked alike, and the smell wasn't too dissimilar either. It felt like my stomach was tying itself in knots, and I pushed the tray toward Zee.

"Help yourself," I said. But he had turned green at the sight of the food and looked like he was on the verge of chundering as well. Donovan's eyes were twinkling with affectionate humor.

"A few more days and this will seem like heavenly macaroni and cheese," he said, pulling the tray toward him. "It's surprising what you can get used to when you're starving."

SKIRMISH

DESPITE THE FOOD, I began to feel a bit more relaxed during trough time. With a little imagination I could almost pretend that I was back at school, chatting with friends over hot lunches (which admittedly hadn't been much prettier than this anyway) and just enjoying time away from lessons. Instead of talking about teachers, soccer, and girls, though, we discussed life inside Furnace. But even that seemed distant, like we were chatting about a film we'd seen on television or some new computer game.

"So there really is no way out?" Zee asked when Donovan had finished eating. The older boy had scoffed two helpings of muck and was eyeing the canteen hopefully on the chance there was any left. "I mean, no tunnels, no secret exits?"

"First off, you better watch what you say and who you say it to," he answered, giving up on thirds and returning his attention to the table. "To the warden, talking about escaping is the same as escaping. And I can't even bring myself to tell you what happened to the last guy who actually made a break for it.

"Second, yeah, this place is full of tunnels but they all only go in one direction: down. This prison is wedged in a massive gorge, and as far as I know there are tunnels in the rock that go much deeper than this. They use some of them for storage, and some for the warden's offices, and I know from personal experience that the hole is down there."

"The hole?" Zee and I both asked together.

"Solitary. I was down there for three days after I got into a fight with some gang wranglers—not the Skulls, the Leopards. They're not really around anymore. Anyway, it's just a hole in the ground right at the bottom of the prison, and they lock you in it with no light or food and only a pipe for a toilet. The only water you get is the condensation on the walls." His face had paled from the memory.

"After a day you think you're going crazy. After two days you think you're in hell. After three days you lose a little piece of yourself that you don't get back. I never heard of anyone being in there more than four days and surviving. That place drives your soul right out of your body. It's the screams you hear when you're down there, like demons. They don't ever shut up."

He shook his head, seeming to come out of a trance.

"I'll die before I go back in there."

I didn't know what to say, so I kept my mouth closed. But Zee didn't seem as fazed by the threat of solitary confinement.

"But some of those tunnels must go somewhere. I mean, underground passageways, that sort of thing."

"Well, you're welcome to try," replied Donovan with more than a hint of sarcasm. "I don't think you'd be the first and I doubt you'll be the last. But believe me when I say that the hole isn't the worst thing you'll find behind these walls. Hey, maybe you'll get lucky. Maybe they'll take you tonight and you'll see for yourself."

"Take me?" asked Zee. "Take me where?"

But Donovan wasn't listening. Zee turned to me but I just shrugged. He slumped back on the bench, obviously annoyed.

"So, your old cellmate, Adam. Was he your friend?" I asked, changing the subject.

"Friend?" Donovan replied, as if trying to remember the word. "You don't have friends in here, you'll soon come to understand that. You get attached to someone, then you'll just lose them. They'll get shanked or they'll jump or they'll be taken one night. When they reach eighteen they get sent up to level fifteen and you'll lose them then, too. Not that many survive to eighteen."

He paused when a shout echoed across the room, starting again when it died away. "Don't make friends, don't make connections. They'll see it, and it will get you both killed. Don't make the mistake of bringing your heart down here with you, there is no place for it in Furnace."

The shout rang out again, angrier this time. Donovan seemed to freeze, his hackles raised, and I felt my heartbeat quicken. There was a growing tension in the room. You could almost see it—like a black shadow seeping over the tables and compressing the air. It was emanating from a bench on the opposite side of the trough room where two inmates were on their feet and nose to nose.

"Let's go," Donovan hissed, getting up. Other people were doing the same, eyeing the confrontation warily as they made for the exit.

"What's going on?" Zee asked.

"Trouble," was his reply. "And we don't want to be anywhere near it."

As if on cue there was another sound and a metallic crash. I looked back to see one of the boys reeling backward, a red gash in his head where something had struck him. His attacker was preparing for another blow, the tray raised above his head, the sharp edge directed forward like an ax.

"Can't we do something?" I asked. But we'd reached the tunnel and Donovan was already walking inside.

"Feel free," he shouted over his shoulder. I stood and watched for a moment longer, but as the makeshift blade descended I was pushed forward by the crowd, and the moment was lost behind the bloodred wall.

FOR THE NEXT few minutes chaos reigned in Furnace. We emerged into the yard just as one long blast rang out from the siren. The sound seemed to activate the machine guns lined up along the walls. They spun out toward the crowd of panicking inmates, their slick, smooth movements reminding me of some crazy, homicidal robot on the rampage.

The deafening wail of the siren had the effect of a fuel injection on everybody in the giant room. It was like somebody had hit the fast-forward button, making the inmates move at a ridiculous speed. Most were running for the stairs, their fear palpable as they pushed each other out of the way. Even Donovan was jogging across the yard, his usual calm expression twisted into a mask of apprehension. He shouted something, but it was lost in the noise of the stampede and the unending scream of the siren.

The terror was contagious, flooding my mind and making my head swim. I felt something crash into me from behind and I sprawled out over the hard ground, a sharp pain running up my arm from a twisted wrist. Ahead of me lay an engine of legs, each a piston that trampled anything in its path. I struggled to get up, but something struck my arm out from under me. I wrapped my hands around my head and curled into a ball as the kicks rained in from every side—just wishing for it to be over, to wake up from this sick nightmare.

After what seemed like an eternity I felt somebody grab my wrist, hard, and haul me up. I resisted for a second but the force was insistent, and I relented. Opening my eyes, I saw Donovan above me, his expression furious. Digging his fingers into my flesh, he pulled me along with the tide, shoving other kids out of the way until we reached the stairs. I followed without thinking, my brain too exhausted to do anything other than put one foot in front of the other—and it wasn't very successful at that either.

Like the aftermath of a tsunami, the flood had died to a trickle by the time we reached the sixth level, buoying us into our cell only seconds before the siren cut out. The absence of sound was almost as disturbing as the noise itself. The prison had been plunged into a gulf of silence broken only by the occasional sob. But it didn't last. With a noise a little like the one a roller coaster makes as it's being pulled up a slope the cell doors began to slide shut, a thousand gates sealing with a boom that made the very stone tremble.

Donovan had slumped onto my bed and was wiping beads of sweat off his brow. I didn't even have the energy to make it to the bunks, and just slid down the cold metal bars until my knees hit the floor. For a moment neither of us did anything but pant. My whole body was aching, my stomach felt like it was unpeeling itself, like I was coming apart. I offered silent prayers of thanks that I hadn't eaten dinner.

Below, on the ground floor, I could see the vault door opening and a dark shadow sweep across the yard toward the trough room. There must have been twelve or thirteen blacksuits down there, armed with guns.

"Dogs?" asked Donovan in a whisper. Then, when I didn't answer: "The dogs, are they out there?"

I watched the vault door swing shut, but nothing else had come out. I shook my head, not quite able to speak. Donovan muttered a thank-you to someone, or something, and I heard him collapse back onto the bed.

"Is anyone out of their cell?" he went on.

I scanned the circumference of the prison and saw dozens of faces peering out through the bars at the events unfolding below. But everybody seemed to be locked up pretty tight. I shook my head again, then twisted around on my knees and found a more comfortable position leaning against the wall.

"Jesus," Donovan said eventually, directing his words at the bunk above him. "Talk about an induction. You've been here a couple of hours and you've seen a skirmish and a lockdown. You should consider yourself lucky."

"Lockdown?" I asked, not feeling in the least bit lucky.

"That siren, that long one, it translates as 'get the hell back in your cell in the next minute or your ass is grass,' " he explained, finally turning to look at me. "Lockdown is one of the worst things that can happen here. This one isn't too bad, it's just the guards. That skirmish in the trough room must have triggered it. Sometimes fights do, sometimes they don't.

"The worst lockdowns come for no reason. One minute you're playing cards in the yard and the next you're all running for your lives, trampling each other so you don't get torn to pieces when . . ." He paused, his voice catching in his throat. I didn't want to press him, something about his expression made me hold my tongue. Besides, I wasn't sure I wanted to know any more.

I clambered up off the floor and walked to the bunk, sitting down at the foot of the bed and putting my head in my hands. He swung himself around so we were sitting side by side.

"Look," I said sheepishly. "I just wanted to say thanks. Thanks for coming back for me. I would have been pummeled out there."

He looked at me and nodded, but his eyes were cold.

"Don't mention it. But don't expect it again. I told you, there are no friendships here, no loyalties. I helped you because you're new, and because when there's two people in a cell then there's only a fifty percent chance they'll take you. You'd better wise up, Alex, I'm not your guardian angel."

I knew already that Carl Donovan was many things, but he was a terrible liar. I found myself smiling inside, although a sliver of that smile must have escaped through my eyes because Donovan caught it.

"I don't know what you're so happy about," he muttered, but that tiny smile was contagious, and took strength from the adrenaline that still pounded through our arteries. He flashed a wide grin at me, all white teeth against his dark skin, and gave me a gentle cuff around the back of the head. "You crazy, you know that? You belong in here, no doubt about that."

I just nodded. We sat in silence for a few minutes, our heart-beats gradually slowing and the rasps disappearing from our breaths. It wasn't long before I saw movement below, and walked over to the bars to see the crowd of blacksuits head back across the yard carrying the wounded kid between them. He wasn't moving, and there was a thin red line on the stone floor that trailed behind the group as they disappeared through the massive door.

"Are they taking him to the infirmary?" I asked, quite pleased with myself despite everything for remembering the posh word for a prison hospital.

"Something like that." Donovan clambered up into his own bunk and lay facing the ceiling. "Anyway, lockdowns this late don't tend to finish until morning, so I'd make myself comfortable if I were you. Be lights-out in an hour or two."

I looked around the cell and tried to imagine what I'd do for an hour or two. The thought felt like a weight pressing on my chest, and once again I found myself panicking at the idea of spending the rest of my life in this tiny cell. The sensation ran up through my body, and when it reached my brain it was so powerful that for a moment I saw lights popping on and off before my eyes. I wanted to tear through the bars and fight my way back to the surface so I could be free again. Instead, I just stamped my foot against the floor, so pathetically that not even Donovan heard it. The feeling ebbed from my body, unsatisfied, and I collapsed on my bunk.

"So is that what you do all evening, then?" I asked eventually. "Sit and stare at the ceiling and rot away quietly?"

"Pretty much," he replied, laughing. The bed squeaked as he turned over. "To be honest, with jobs and all you're usually dead to the world by lights-out, so you don't mind the peace and quiet."

"Jobs?"

"You'll find out all about it tomorrow," he replied. I could hear his voice starting to slur, like he was drifting off already. "You think we just sit about all day?"

Sitting around, dueling with canteen trays, and running from guards. Yeah.

"Oh, and listen," he said, his voice alive again. He popped his head over the bunk and fixed me with a glare that made my pulse race. "If you hear a siren during lights-out, and the blood lights are on, then you don't get out of bed for any reason, okay? Doesn't matter what you hear outside those bars. Keep your eyes closed and pretend to be asleep, don't draw attention to yourself and especially not to this cell." I tried to say something but he cut me off. "No exceptions. They catch you looking, then you're as good as dead already."

He vanished, leaving me wide awake and terrified.

"Sweet dreams, Alex."

DARKNESS FALLS

I DON'T BELIEVE THAT anyone truly loses their fear of the dark. Yeah, grownups act like they feel at home when the lights are out, they say there's nothing to be afraid of, that nothing's changed just because you can't see anything.

But they're bluffing. I defy even the bravest adult to spend the night in a place like Furnace in the pitch black without thinking that every noise is something right behind you with dagger teeth and eyes of silver and blood on its breath; that every whisper of air that runs over your skin is the rush of a descending blade; that every flicker of movement is a tendril of darkness wrapping itself around your throat and coiling in the pit of your belly, where it feasts on your soul.

The darkness came without warning. One minute I was lying in my bed thinking pretty rationally about my life behind bars, the next I was plunged into a void so profound that I thought I'd gone blind. It was such a sudden change that I sat bolt upright, clawing at my eyes and desperately looking for even the slightest hint of light to prove that I still had the ability to see.

I stumbled out of my bunk, crawling across the rough floor with my stomach in my mouth. I was in such a panic that I crashed right into the bars, but through them, far below, I caught a glimpse of the giant screen mounted above the elevator, a white Furnace logo rotating lazily on a black background. The darkness was doing its best to smother the image, but its weak illumination reached out like a beacon. I clung to the bars and watched it, the sensation of relief so powerful that it brought tears to my eyes.

It was here, holding the bars of my cell like they were my only friends, that I first heard the symphony of Furnace. It started with the sobs, which rose up out of the darkness all around me like the gentle strings in an orchestra. They began as hushed moans choked back by the countless musicians that crafted them, merging together from every level to create a fountain of sound that ran down to the deserted yard below.

Next came the jeers, the tuneful taunts of "new fish" and "you better cry, they're coming for you," which punctuated the sobbing like sharp blasts from trumpets. As the callous taunts grew in volume so did the cries, swelling into desperate wails hurled out into the artificial night mixed with calls for help and pleas that were heartbreaking to hear. Somewhere, somebody was singing a song, his deep voice a bizarre bass line to the symphony, a mournful cello that kept the two halves of the orchestra in harmony.

I don't know how long it went on, rising gradually to a crescendo of screams and whistles and sobs and songs that took hold of me, forcing a cry from my own traitorous throat. For what I knew would be the first time of many, I reluctantly added my voice to that symphony, crying and screaming until, exhausted, the music died and the prison once again found silence.

I KNOW I don't have to tell you that I didn't get much sleep that night. I lay in my bed with my eyes open, projecting pictures onto the blank black canvas before me. Images of my home, of my family, of my friends, of television, of school, of birthday cakes and bike rides and trips to the country, of the sea, skimming stones, ice cream on the sand, soccer matches and kickarounds in the playground, building models with my dad, weeding the garden with my mom, of sunshine, of rain, of snowmen and Christmas and playing with new toys in the flickering light of the fire.

But each happy image was smothered by the darkness, vanishing without a trace into the dead night. Furnace was claiming my memories as well as my body, its hold on my life now absolute, unforgiving.

All the time I lay there I expected to hear the siren. I wasn't sure what Donovan had been talking about when he said they came at night, but my imagination provided plenty of scenarios: the blacksuits appearing at the bars, ready to drag me into the abyss; the gas masks and their pockmark eyes, pointing at me like I was the next delicacy they were going to drop down their sick throats; the skinless dogs, wet to the touch as they pulled me to the warden and his leather face.

Whenever I did manage to drop off to sleep, these terrifying images followed me, making themselves at home in dreams they had no right to be in. In some I was being buried in a grave cut into the rock, the blacksuits covering me with rubble that pressed my body flat and choked my lungs. In others I actually sank into the floor, the stone like red quicksand that sucked me in until I was lost in shadow.

In the worst dreams, though, I was inside a glass prison, on the surface. Through the walls I could see my house, my family going about their life without me. I shouted to them and banged on the glass, but there was a gas mask right in front of me, preventing them from hearing. And I saw the blacksuits approaching my front door, the gas mask freaks closing in on the back of the house, the dogs leaping through the windows, spraying my mom and dad with glass. I tried to smash the walls of my prison but they wouldn't even crack, the wheezer in front of me blocking my every move, and I could do nothing but watch as they met the same fate as Toby, their blood pooling over the kitchen floor as their killers retreated.

It was only at the end of the dream that I realized the figure before me, on the other side of the glass, wasn't a gas mask at all. It was my reflection.

AFTER EACH DREAM I'd wake up screaming, sweat pouring from me and my heart in overdrive. Each time it took me ages to drift off again and each time the same thing happened—nightmares that tried to eat me alive.

By the time the lights came on, serenaded in by a short blast from the siren, I felt like I'd been lying on that bed for a thousand years, tormented by every demon possible. My sheet was drenched and my head was pounding, and when I swung my legs over the bunk, every limb was shaking like a leaf. It took only one glance through the bars at the prison beyond to send me stumble-running across the cell to the toilet, throwing up my guts into the dull metal pan. Nothing came out apart from a thin trail of bile, but it made me feel better—like I'd purged myself of some of the thoughts from the previous night.

The sound of my retching had woken Donovan, and by the time I'd pulled my head from the toilet he was sitting up in bed watching me with a sympathetic smile.

"Takes a while for the nightmares to leave," he said. "But they do. Trust me—that toilet and me were best friends for the first few days I was here."

I laughed, despite myself. Wiping my mouth with my sleeve, I realized that puking wasn't the only thing I needed the toilet for. I glanced at Donovan sheepishly.

"Um, do you mind . . . ?"

He raised an eyebrow, then cottoned on to what I meant, his head disappearing as he lay back down.

"Sorry, Alex," he said as I went about my business. "That's the other thing you never really get used to. Pooping in public."

"Well, it would be a lot easier to relax if you'd keep quiet for a second," I scolded. The bed creaked as he laughed, but fortunately he didn't say another word until he heard the flush.

"My turn," he said, jumping from the bunk.

"All yours."

Doing my best to ignore the noises behind me, I stared through the bars at the cells directly opposite. Inmates were climbing from their bunks, all pasty faces and crumpled uniforms. Judging by some of their expressions, I wasn't the only one who'd had nightmares.

My eyes fell on one cell, on the next level below. It was pretty far away, and sat at a strange angle, but I thought I could make out Montgomery curled up on the stone next to the bars. I saw a pair of legs on the upper bunk, which no doubt belonged to chief Skull Kevin. From the looks of things, the bottom bunk was stripped bare. I wondered if poor Montgomery had spent the whole night on the floor.

"So, you ready for some hard labor?" asked Donovan, flushing the toilet. He had an apologetic look on his face and was wafting the air with both hands. "That mush plays havoc downstairs, you know?"

"You're not kidding," I replied, holding my nose and wishing—not for the last time during my stay in Furnace—that we had separate bathrooms. "Anyway, what do you mean, 'hard labor'?"

He grinned as he pulled on his shoes, then offered the same infuriating reply I'd already heard so many times.

"You'll find out soon enough."

HARD LABOR

TEN MINUTES OR SO after the lights had come back on the siren cut through my head a second time and the cell doors rattled open. With a series of whoops and cheers the inmates on every level crashed along the platforms and down the stairs, filling the prison with the sound of thunder.

"When you're locked up in here for life, you learn to welcome the little freedoms," explained Donovan as we made our way from our cell. His face was once again a mask of defiance, challenging anyone to mess with him, but his tone was light enough. "Getting out of our cells every morning feels a little bit like we're breaking free, if you know what I mean."

I didn't. Not then. But I soon came to understand. Part of you soon forgets about the outside world. There is just lockdown and out there, and out there—in the yard, in the trough room, at hard labor—feels a hell of a lot freer than a two-meter-square cell.

As we made our way down to the yard Donovan explained about the jobs. Mornings were spent working. Slopwork was in the kitchen. Greaseup meant cleaning duties, which sometimes included the Stink, or mopping the toilets. Bleaching was in the laundry. According to the duty roster—displayed in crisp white letters on the giant screen above the elevator—Donovan and I were chippers for the day.

"It's the hardest of hard labors," he said as we followed the crowd through to the trough room. We picked up a couple of bowls of mush from the canteen and found an empty bench— close enough to the scene of yesterday's incident that I could make out a weird rust-colored stain on the floor. I focused on my breakfast to try to take my mind off the fight. It was a pile of sawdust-colored paste that looked identical to yesterday's dinner.

"The same thing?" I asked, feeling my stomach grumble. I wasn't sure if it was because I was hungry, or because my gut was warning me not to go near the dish.

"Yeah," Donovan replied, lifting a heap of paste up with his spoon and eyeing it suspiciously. "Exactly the same. They make it in batches, each lasts a few days. You have it for breakfast, lunch, and dinner."

"Great," I muttered. I knew I was going to have to eat something sooner or later, so I scraped a thin layer off the top of my breakfast and touched my tongue to it. I was expecting the flavor of vomit, or crap, or something equally nasty, but to my surprise I couldn't taste anything. Taking a deep breath, I closed my mouth around the spoon and felt the runny mixture drop onto my tongue. For a second I gagged, but then I managed to control the reflex and noticed that the goo was completely flavorless, except for the pleasant tang of salt.

"The texture is the worst part," Donovan explained, scooping the last dollop from his bowl. "Just think of it as salty porridge and it isn't too bad."

I remembered how my dad always put about a kilo of salt in his porridge—as opposed to honey or sugar or jam like sane people—and the thought made me feel better. My appetite took over and I wolfed down the paste with a passion, almost sucking the plastic from the spoon in my eagerness. The gunk was lukewarm, but it settled in my stomach and radiated a pleasant, comforting heat.

The morning's third short siren blast saw everybody making their way out of the trough room back into the yard, where the crowd gradually split into a number of groups. I followed Donovan to the other side of the huge space toward a cavernous fissure in the rock guarded by a blacksuit and his shotgun. I felt my legs go weak at the sight of him, but the sheer density of the people around me held me up as we stomped past.

The short tunnel ahead led us to a room filled to bursting with mining equipment—picks, shovels, wheelbarrows, and dozens of hard hats that clung to the walls like yellow fungus. Around the outside of the room were three more cracks: gaping black mouths in the rock. Two were open but a third, in the center, was sealed off with enormous wooden planks bolted into the rock.

Donovan slammed a hard hat onto his head, switching on the lamp fixed to the front, and held another one out for me. I took it as the blacksuit walked to the center of the cluttered space and began to speak.

"You know the drill: dig and clear." His voice was like the rumbling of some subterranean river muted by the rock. "Shaft props every three meters, hats on at all times—we want you fit to work again tomorrow. Anyone caught smuggling equipment out gets two days in the hole. Any skirmishing gets you three."

By now most of the hundred or so inmates in the room were kitted up. Some held picks or shovels and others were hoisting the ancient metal wheelbarrows off the ground. Not knowing what to do, I grabbed a pick from the wall. It was so heavy I nearly dropped it, the spike coming worryingly close to the foot of the guy standing next to me. I tensed my muscles and managed to stop its descent, but Donovan was already flashing me a concerned look.

"Levels one through three, you're through the first door," the blacksuit went on. "Levels four through six, get in the third door. Room Two is out of bounds. Move it."

Our huddle of prisoners shuffled forward with about as much enthusiasm as if there had been an electric chair waiting beyond that hole in the wall. I could almost imagine them as old-time miners, singing "Hi ho, hi ho" as they marched into darkness. Only these workers were calling out insults to one another and making threatening gestures with their picks. I kept my head down and trailed Donovan.

"Don't worry, kid," he said as we stomped through the tunnel. "Only another twenty thousand or so days of this to go."

My pick suddenly got a lot heavier, as did my heart.

We emerged into a wide cavern, the ceiling so low that I had to stoop in places to avoid the drooping rock. Everywhere I looked there were long, thin beams propping up the ceiling, a forest of twigs that didn't look anywhere near strong enough to hold up the million or so tons of stone above our heads. I pictured what would happen if gravity took over, bringing down the roof of the cave and squashing us like a boot crushing a bug. At least it would be quick.

Swallowing hard, I managed to force the claustrophobic panic from my mind.

"Better pray there isn't a cave-in today," said Donovan, his words practically turning my stomach inside out.

The rock walls of the cave had been battered and broken into weird shapes. Most looked like curtains in a theater, full of shadowy folds that stood out against the rich red surface. They might be good hiding places, and I stored the information away in the back of my mind in case I ever needed it. Then I remembered the flayed dogs and instantly dismissed the thought. Donovan led the way to a distant section of the cave and rested his pick against the rock.

"Don't need a degree in rocket science to do this job," he said. "Just keep whacking until downtime. When you can't see your feet for rubble, give a shout to one of the wheelies and they'll come clear up. 'Kay?"

"And to think my mom and dad never thought I'd hold down a job," I answered. We both fought to hide our grins, then, motioning for me to stand out of the way, Donovan swung his pick to one side and brought it forward with a cry of rage. The metal blade struck the rock with a flash of light and a pistol crack, showering us both with shrapnel.

"Ow!" I yelled, hurriedly pulling down the hard hat's visor to avoid being blinded.

"Some fun, huh?" Donovan shouted as he swung again.

Making sure there was nobody around me that I could inadvertently injure, I hoisted the pick above my head ready to swing. I'd completely forgotten about the low ceiling, however, and the move generated a shower of rock that drummed off my hat. Donovan frowned through his visor and I felt my cheeks redden. I tensed my arms again and this time swung the pick in a sideways arc. It struck the rock with a deafening clang and a vibration that traveled up my arms and practically dislodged the vertebrae in my spine. Wincing, I waited until the pain had subsided before trying again. This time I gave the rock a delicate tap that barely shaved off a whisker of dust.

"Takes a bit of time to get used to the impact," said Donovan between strikes. "But that's okay. In here time is the only thing you've got plenty of."

I tried twice more, ignoring the sensation that my spine was being ripped out with each strike. After a few minutes tiredness set in, but with it came a pleasant numbness that spread through my body.

The lamp on my helmet threw the rock face into a mosaic of light and shadow. I started looking for features in the stone that resembled faces—ridges for foreheads, scratches that might have been noses, pick marks as lips, and loose pebbles like sightless eyes—and pretended they were blacksuits. Each time I swung right for the center of the face, releasing a scream of anger and hatred that lent power to the attack. And when the faces crumpled into fragments, I felt a little shiver of pleasure.

The strength of my feelings was a little unnerving—the knowledge that, at that moment, I could have driven a pick right through the real guard who would appear in the cave every now and again to check that everybody was working. Hatred— real, murderous hatred—was an emotion I'd never really experienced before, and I wasn't sure whether it excited me or terrified me.

IT'S INCREDIBLE HOW much stamina you can find when you're fighting an enemy in battle, even if that enemy is just in your imagination. For what must have been three or four hours everyone in that cave swung their picks at the rock relentlessly, like barbarians bringing down the walls of a castle. The sound of picks striking rock, the flash of the sparks, and the screams that powered each swing made my ears ring and my blood pound. It really was like an ancient battle, and I started to wonder just how long the blacksuits would last if all of Furnace's inmates picked up their tools and turned on their captors.

Donovan and I must have cleared away a good meter of rock by ourselves. It doesn't sound like much, but we're not talking about chalk here—these walls were tough. The rubble built up around our feet and was cleared away by the guys with wheelbarrows to be deposited in some unknown place. Probably mixed with our food, I thought, eyeing the piles of dust slumped like fallen soldiers on the ground between us.

I was still pummeling the wall with a passion when the blacksuit appeared again and called for us to put down the tools. It was only as we all wove our way back through the ceiling props, dragging our picks behind us, that the pain slowly started to ebb back into my body. It began as a dull throb, but by the time we'd hung up our equipment it felt as though every muscle I had was on fire.

We were told to wait until the other group marched back into the equipment room, then the blacksuit herded us out of the tunnel back into the yard. I wondered why nobody had bothered to search us—the picks may have been impossible to smuggle out, but some of the rock fragments we had chipped away were sharper than scalpels. It soon became clear when we were led through another rough-cut door to a long room full of showers.

"Five minutes," shouted the blacksuit. I watched as everybody began to strip, heaping their uniforms and underwear into a pile in the corner then drifting out to stand beneath the overhanging showerheads. I did the same, feeling extremely self-conscious as I pulled off my clothes. But we were all in the same big naked boat and nobody seemed the least bit bothered by it. I picked a spot at the far side of the room and to my surprise found that Donovan had followed me.

"Brace yourself," he said. Seconds later there was an alarming squeal followed by a hiss, then the showerheads all erupted. I flinched as a jet of freezing water hit me square in the back, forcing the air from my lungs, but thankfully the temperature soon adjusted—still cold, just not arctic. I frantically scrubbed myself down, noticing the water turn red from the dust that clung to me, pooling around the drains as if we were all being bled dry. I shook the image from my head as Donovan started talking.

"Bet your arms feel like they're made of putty," he said, his voice raised above the spray.

"Yeah. What were we doing in there anyway? I never heard of guards encouraging their prisoners to tunnel through the walls before."

"Well, most prison walls aren't several miles thick," he replied, wiping water from his eyes and spitting red. "We're carving out new rooms. We chipped out this very room here, stone by stone. Took three years. Before then we washed in our cells. Buckets and sponges. Like some shantytown."

I tried whistling to demonstrate how impressed I was at the sheer size of the room, but all that came out of my wet lips was a bubbly farting sound.

"To be honest, though," he went on, "I think they just make us hammer away for a few hours every day so we're exhausted. It gets something out of our systems. Knackered inmates are a lot easier to control than pumped-up ones." He paused for thought. "And sometimes there are cave-ins, like in Room Two the other week. And dead inmates are even easier to control, if you follow me."

I wasn't sure if he was joking or not, but given what I already knew about Furnace, I was guessing that he was deadly serious. I gave my hair a quick rinse just as the showers shut off, and we all marched back across the room. While we'd been washing, someone had taken away our dirty clothes and there was a pile of new uniforms, underwear, and paper shoes by the door. Donovan slapped his way past several pink, shivering bodies and scrambled into his duds, but I was happy to wait. It's not like there was a variety of sizes and colors—the jumpsuit I eventually put on hung off me with the same disregard for my body shape as the last one.

We traipsed back out into the yard, which was a flurry of activity as the various groups of workers returned from their jobs. It was weird, but as we crossed over to the trough room I actually started to feel like I was getting into the swing of Furnace. This place was dangerous, yes, but there was a routine here that was almost comforting. Sleep, work, and relax; sleep, work, and relax. The system was like a heartbeat that kept us all functioning, a rhythm that made me feel like maybe things wouldn't be so bad here.

Of course, it was right at that very moment that all hell broke loose.

SKULL FODDER

DONOVAN AND I ENTERED the trough room to the sound of jeering. At first I couldn't pinpoint precisely where it was coming from above the general chatter—the hall was half full of inmates who had obviously beaten us to the showers, their cheeks glowing above starched collars. As we strolled across the floor, however, it became clear that the noise was emanating from behind the canteen.

Four Skulls were standing on the other side of the counter, each wearing the trademark black bandanna. Two of the kids were dishing out bowls of slop to the huddle of waiting inmates, but the others were looking at something at their feet, something hidden behind the stainless steel canteen counters. From the way they moved, it looked like they were kicking out at whatever it was, and the evil glint in their eyes stripped my appetite away in seconds.

I couldn't face getting any closer to the Skulls, so I let Donovan go ahead while I scanned the hall for a familiar face. Zee was sitting on his own in the middle of the room, poking his slop forlornly with a spoon. I walked over to the other side of his bench, doing my best to ignore the pain in my legs as I sat down. He barely even raised his head to acknowledge me, and his expression told me something terrible had happened.

"Something terrible *has* happened!" he said when I uttered my thoughts out loud. "Y'know, I thought I could take it here, put up with anything they threw at me until I found a way out. But I just don't know anymore."

"Did someone attack you?" I asked, alarmed. "The blacksuits? The Skulls?"

He shook his head, then looked up at me as if about to reveal the most shameful secret of all time.

"They made me clean the toilets, Alex," he whispered. "Every single bowl on the first level. That's nearly one hundred crappers, for your information, most of which still had evidence of . . ." He looked like he was about to gag. "I've had a shower but I can still smell it on me."

I did my best to hold it in but I couldn't help myself. The laugh bubbled up from deep inside me like a fountain, and I howled so loudly that practically the entire hall turned and scowled in my direction. It was a good few seconds before I managed to plug it, but by that time Zee was struggling to maintain his mask of distaste. The lines around his eyes eventually relaxed and his face opened up like a flower.

"I thought you'd been in a fight or something," I said, his grin letting me know it was safe to go on. "You looked like you were about to jump."

"Well, let's see how you feel when you're cleaning someone else's crap out of your fingernails," came his response.

The jeering was still ongoing from the far side of the room, but I couldn't face turning around to see what was happening. Instead, I asked Zee.

"Some poor kid," he answered. "They've had him pinned to
the floor for the last quarter of an hour. As far as I can tell,
they're making him lick up anything they drop. It's horrible, but
what can you do?" He looked sheepishly at his lunch. "I mean,
better him than us, right?"

Luckily I was saved from having to answer as Donovan
crashed down onto the bench beside me and tucked into a massive bowl of slop.

"How was your first morning?" he asked Zee as he chewed.
"What job you get?"

"The Stink," he hissed.

Donovan pulled a face that was half grimace, half grin. "Tough
break for a new fish. Still, we all gotta do it."

"Well next time you *do it*, can you try to miss the seat?"

This time we all laughed, but it was short-lived. I heard a
crunch behind me and a peal of ugly laughter. Beneath it all was a
quiet sob that seemed to claw its way into my chest and burrow
right inside my heart.

"Did you see who it was?" I asked Donovan. He was lifting a
spoonful of food to his mouth and paused to consider the question.

"No one you know, kiddo," he said eventually. But his hesita-
tion had already given away too much.

"It's Montgomery, isn't it?" I said. Donovan let the spoon fall
to his dish and nodded. "Christ, I saw him in his cell this morning. Kevin made him sleep on the floor, as far as I could see.
They're going to kill him at this rate."

Both Donovan and Zee were staring at the table like there
was an escape plan written on it.

"This place is full of unwritten rules," whispered Donovan without looking up. "There always has to be someone to take the punches. That's how it works. It isn't fair, it isn't right, but that kid licking slop off the floor over there means that we get to eat in peace. If there was no scapegoat then we'd all be in danger, if you fol—"

"I follow you," I barked. My anger surprised me; it didn't make any sense. Back in school Toby and I had always picked on the weaker kids, guys just like Montgomery. They didn't fight back, they didn't argue, they gave you what you wanted, then went and cried in the corner. I wasn't sure why I felt such a burning anger inside me at the thought of Montgomery getting picked on now, such rage at the idea that nobody was going to help him. "So we just leave him until he can't go on anymore then hope the next scapegoat isn't one of us, right?"

"Listen," spat Donovan, his fraying temper obvious from the way he glared at his bowl. "You've been here one day and you think you can change things. I've been here five years and I know how the system works. You try to be a hero then you'll get a shank in the back, you try to help that kid then tomorrow it's gonna be you both licking crap off the floor. Let me know if you're going to do something stupid, kid, 'cause I'll ditch you like that." He snapped his fingers.

The thin, wet cry from the canteen had coated Donovan's every word, leaving me with a gut-wrenching mixture of frustration and fury and fear. I couldn't work out which emotion was which, they all sat like unwanted guests in the pit of my stomach. I looked at Zee but he still wouldn't meet my eyes. I called his name, gently, and he raised his head like it was made of stone.

"I want to help him, but . . ." He trailed off. "If this was at school, y'know, I'd do what I could. But we're a long way from the playground."

The moan behind me changed pitch into a shriek and this time I couldn't help myself. I glanced over my shoulder and saw one of the Skulls grinding his foot down while the other flicked slop from a ladle onto the unseen figure below.

"What about the guards?" I asked. "Surely they don't allow this."

"They don't care," said Donovan. "Nobody cares. You shouldn't either."

But I did. Every fiber of my body wanted to step in and help, and every fiber of my body wanted to stay on that bench and forget it was happening. I thought that any minute I'd literally be torn in two, reduced to a quivering, bloody mess on the canteen floor.

It was the smallest of things that made up my mind. One of the Skulls looked up at his friend and flashed him a wicked smile. It was an expression I knew well, I'd worn it a thousand times at school after getting a good haul. Looking at it now was like staring into a mirror, seeing a side of myself full of greed and treachery and violence and without a shred of compassion. I hated myself right then, and the overpowering feeling brought a red shadow down over my thoughts, blotting out any rational argument.

Before I even knew what I was doing I was out of my seat, ignoring the protests from Donovan and Zee. My blind rage drove me across that room like a bulldozer. I pushed straight past the inmates still waiting to be served and jumped onto the counter. Everything was in slow motion and strangely distorted, like I was watching it through water. I saw two faces right before me, looking up in shock. The other Skulls hadn't even noticed, they were too busy tormenting the round, sobbing figure beneath their feet.

Then, as if the whole world had been holding its breath and finally decided to gulp down some air, time snapped back to normal. With a scream I kicked out hard with my right foot. Years of playing soccer paid off as my paper shoe connected with the face of the first Skull and, with a crack that might have been his nose or my toe breaking, his head jerked backward and he crumpled to the floor.

I tried to direct a second kick but the Skull was quicker, grabbing my foot and pulling me off balance. I half jumped, half fell, and by some miracle of chance tumbled off the canteen serving counter right on top of him. He hit the ground hard and I landed knee-first in the center of his chest, crushing his lungs. Momentum carried me forward and I crashed into the wall behind the canteen, stars exploding in my vision.

Panicking that somebody would stab me in the back, I whipped my body around, scrabbling for purchase on the smooth stone. The other two Skulls were charging at me, and I had to duck as the ladle flew past my ear, showering me with gunk. I had never been in a full-on fight like this and I had no idea what to do next. Fortunately adrenaline was making me act without thinking, and I threw myself at the kid who'd just swung the ladle. The move was half punch, half jump, and missed entirely. Denied contact, my flailing arms shot out. I lost my balance again and I staggered straight into an oncoming fist.

I'd always thought that getting punched would be painful, but it isn't. Not at the moment of impact, anyway. It's like your body switches off its senses during a fight to stop you getting over-loaded. You hear a wet thump, and for a moment your world spins, but there is no pain. The absence of sensation caught me by surprise, and suddenly I felt like a superman—unbeatable, impervious to everything.

I angled my head to the side to avoid the next punch that came in, then planted my palms in the middle of the Skull's chest and shoved with all my might. He tripped on the still prone body of Montgomery and almost did a backflip before tumbling earthward. I detected movement in the corner of my eye and ducked instinctively, the ladle skimming over my head. I swung an elbow in the direction of the attack and felt it connect. The Skull whose cheekbone I'd just fractured yelped before slumping back against the canteen.

I grabbed his collar with my left hand and with my right started to pound him. They weren't hammer blows by any stretch of the imagination, but they came hard and fast, and after three or four he was bruised, bloody, and bleating through his split lips. He looked at me with real fear in his eyes, and I tried to picture what my expression must look like. The word *demonic* sprang to mind.

But then his bloody mouth twisted into a smile and I suddenly realized things had taken a turn for the worse.

I felt a pair of strong arms wrap themselves around my chest, pinning my arms. I thrashed from side to side but it was no good, the Skull had me locked tight and I was powerless to defend myself as the kid in front started throwing punches of his own. He was much better at it than I was, and each strike made my world fade closer to black. There was still no pain, but there was something worse—a creeping numbness that was spreading through my body, and the unmistakable, terrifying sensation that I was being seriously damaged.

I put my final reserves of energy into a last bid for escape, and managed to push back with my legs. I and the kid holding me collapsed to the ground as one, but he still didn't let go. I looked up to see the guy who'd been thumping me and the Skull I'd winded. Both were advancing like lions on a wounded gazelle, with nothing but murder in their eyes.

All this had taken place in less than a minute, but the trough room was almost deserted. From the angle I was lying in I could see past the canteen, and watched as the last few people hurried from the hall. Only one figure remained, and for a second, hope flared as I pictured Donovan coming to help. But he simply shook his head at me, turned, and walked toward the yard. Even Montgomery had struggled to his feet and was trotting off without so much as a backward glance.

The bloodlust inside me suddenly subsided, leaving me utterly alone. The adrenaline had escaped my veins, and it felt like it had left lead weights in its place. Even without the guy beneath me and his bear hug I still don't think I would have had the energy to move a muscle. My fearless expression had deserted me too, and I could do nothing but stare at the predators before me with wide eyes and a trembling jaw.

The two Skulls knelt down beside me and, to my horror, one of them slid something from his belt. It was a wooden spoon, but the handle had been filed down to a deadly point. He waved it in front of my face.

"Gonna pay for that, new fish," he said, his breathing still labored from where I'd landed on his chest. "Gonna be the shortest stay in Furnace of all time."

"Quick," said his friend, wiping the blood from his lip. "Siren gonna go off any time. Lockdown."

"This creep doesn't deserve a quick death," the first Skull hissed, raising his weapon above my stomach. "Gonna bleed you."

I closed my eyes and prayed that this wouldn't hurt too much. At that moment I didn't even care about dying, I just didn't want to feel any pain. I tried to relax my muscles and picture myself somewhere else—on the beach with my family, basking on the hot sand and cocooned by the sound and smell of the ocean.

But the illusion was shattered by a roar. I thought at first that it was the Skull screaming as he plunged the shank into my guts, but when my stomach remained intact I opened my eyes to see a blurred shape flying past and my attacker reeling backward. The shape stopped and swiveled, bringing something hard down onto the head of the other Skull. The tray made a satisfying crack as it hit, and behind it I saw Zee's face.

"I'm not doing this," he said as he kicked the kid beneath me in the ribs. The figure writhed and his arms loosened, letting me wriggle my way free. "I'm not doing this. I'm not doing this."

Past the roar of blood in my ears I heard the sound of a siren, and knew that lockdown was imminent.

"Run," Zee shouted, throwing the tray to the floor with a crash and grabbing my sleeve. We careened across the trough room, leaping onto the tables to avoid the scattered benches and remains of lunch. I tried to remember what Donovan had said about lockdown, about how long the siren sounded before the cells were sealed. Was it a minute? Thirty seconds?

We emerged into the yard to find it free of people but full of noise. From the hundreds of cells that lined the hall came shouts and cheers and whoops and whistles, all directed at us as we ran for the stairs.

But we weren't going to make it. Halfway across the yard I heard the rattle of the cells shutting tight, followed by the hiss of pneumatics that signaled the vault door opening. I should never have stopped running, but I did. Fear and morbid curiosity forced me to a halt, made me watch in horror as the massive portal swung open and the dogs bounded out.

HELL HOUNDS

REMEMBER I TOLD YOU I'd run from worse things in my life than the cops? Well, this was one of those occasions. They burst from the shadows like hounds from hell, sent by the devil to tear sinners to pieces and drag their screaming souls back to the underworld. The sheer power of their twisted bodies was betrayed by their lack of skin, their exposed muscles and tendons flexing and glistening in the unforgiving light of Furnace as they came to a halt in the middle of the yard.

Worst of all were their eyes—two emotionless silver pennies that shone from their wet faces, scanning the ground and eventually fixing on me. I stared back, lost in the twin moons of each creature, the glare an invisible fishing line that hooked itself into my eyes and stopped me from running. For a moment, nobody moved. But then one of the hounds raised its head and unleashed a howl—a sickening noise that sounded like the screams of a dying man—and they charged.

"Come on," I heard Zee shout, grabbing my shoulder. I turned and bolted after him as he made for the nearest staircase, hearing the dogs scream again as they closed in for the kill, hearing the noise in the surrounding cells reach a crescendo as the inmates settled in for the show.

We scaled the steps three at a time, fear and adrenaline turning us into Olympic champions. I was shouting curse after curse, a torrent of swear words that I hoped would block the staircase behind me. It didn't work. By the time we had reached the top of the stairs the dogs were advancing on the bottom. They had slowed their run to a leisurely prowl, knowing we had nowhere to go. The creatures seemed to relish the thought, their massive jaws twisting into a grimace and dripping great gobs of saliva onto the steps.

And they were right, there *was* nowhere to go. All the cells were locked tight.

"Next floor," hissed Zee, and we started climbing again, my legs burning and my head spinning from the effort. We reached the second level and turned to see both dogs following us up the stairs, sparks flying from their feet every time their claws connected with the metal. Zee bounded up one more flight of steps and started running along the platform, ignoring the whoops and hollers from the other side of the bars.

"Think," he screamed at me. "Where are we going?"

"Just head for the other stairwell," I replied, trying to make it sound like I had a plan.

We bolted down the platform, the inmates inside watching half in horror and half in fascination as the dogs followed us. One of the beasts was distracted by something inside a cell and threw itself at the bars, buckling them like they were made of plastic. My legs almost gave way there and then, as well as other parts of my body that I don't really want to mention, but I managed to keep going.

Halfway along the platform the dogs got bored of prowling and broke into a trot, their huge feet making the platform shake in its casings every time they made contact, their eyes narrowing as they fixed on their prey. We reached the stairs and clambered up them, trying to look at where we were going and what was behind us at the same time. As long as we kept a stairwell in between us and the creatures I felt okay.

Talk about tempting fate. Tiring of the chase, the first dog hurled itself from the platform, leaping through the air above the courtyard and landing with a crash on the other side of the banister from me. Up close its face was even more horrific, I could see past a set of stained and crooked teeth right down its raw red throat, a glistening abyss where I was about to meet my fate. Of all the ways I could have thought of to die, this was the worst—chewed to pieces by a mutant dog. I staggered backward, tripping on a step and landing on my ass.

The monster dug its claws into the metal and pulled itself over the stairwell, never taking its silver eyes off me. I could smell its fetid breath as it panted—the stench of death and de-cay that would accompany me to my end. It lowered itself ungracefully to the platform, making the whole thing tremble, and raised its head for the kill. I took one look at Zee, frozen at the top of the stairs, then resigned myself to the inevitable, pray-ing for the second time that day that my death wouldn't be too painful.

But from the yard below came the sound of sobbing. The dog whipped its head around and stared through the metal railings, and I did the same. One of the Skulls from the trough room—

the one who had tried to kill me—was limping across the floor, begging at the top of his voice to be allowed back in his cell.

The dog unleashed a deafening howl and leaped off the staircase. Despite being three floors up it landed perfectly, speeding across the stone. I felt Zee's hand on my shoulder and let him help me to my feet. He started running up the stairs again but I couldn't pull myself away from the events below.

The second dog had also leaped from the platform and both were now closing in on their new victim. The Skull was backing off, his face a mask of fear. He still held the sharpened wooden spoon in one hand and he waved it in front of him. It looked like someone trying to stop a train with a toothpick.

"Come on, Alex," Zee whispered. "They're gonna be back up here any minute."

The dogs crouched down on their haunches, looking for a second as if they were about to curl up and go to sleep. But then they both sprang forward, jaws open impossibly wide. The place where the Skull had been standing was suddenly a blur of color, different shades of red battling it out with flashes of silver and shards of dirty white for supremacy in the sickening tableau.

It was over in seconds. I didn't watch the dogs finish their meal, I just followed Zee as he leaped up the stairs again. Beneath us I heard a pair of blood-curdling howls gargled through wet throats, then the sound of claws on metal as the dogs once again scaled the stairwell.

"What's the point?" I hissed breathlessly as we reached the fourth level and kept on running. "They're going to catch us."

But Zee didn't answer. I stopped for an instant to catch my breath and stole a glance through the stairs. One dog was below, bounding up the steps with frightening speed. The other was scaling the steps at the far end of the platforms. They were boxing us in.

Fear lending us strength, we pushed ourselves up past the fifth level to the sixth, and were about to keep climbing when I saw a sight that I didn't quite believe. Midway down the row my cell door was half open, wedged in place by a toilet seat, of all things. Standing on the platform waving frantically at us was Donovan. I felt my entire body flood with relief and we both charged toward him, but before we'd made it past more than a couple of cells the dog appeared at the far end and began hurtling our way.

Zee kept running but I slammed to a halt and grabbed his sleeve.

"We'll never make it, that thing's going too fast," I said, pulling him back to the staircase we'd just left. "We need to go up."

Zee started to argue but I held up my hand.

"Trust me."

We reached the staircase seconds before the first dog. It thrust its giant muzzle through the stairs from the platform below, twisting the metal and almost shearing off my foot. I leaped over it as it struggled to pull its wedged jaw free, and looked back to see that the second dog was retreating to the far staircase.

Leaping up the last couple of steps we raced down the seventh-level platform. A howl from behind us signaled that the creature was hot on our heels, and up ahead I saw the second dog emerge from the stairwell and crash down the walkway in our direction. In a matter of seconds we were both going to be Pedigree dog food.

"What now?" Zee screamed. I stopped running and placed my hands on the railing that separated the platform from the yard seven floors below. The view made my stomach twist unpleasantly, and for a second I didn't think I could do it. But the dogs were closing in, fast. We had no choice.

I started clambering over the railing. Zee just stared at me.

"You can't be serious," he said.

The dogs were ten steps away at most, bounding along the metal so fast it looked like they were flying. Zee stopped arguing, swung a leg up and threw his body over the railing so we were both standing on the other side, hovering above the drop.

"It's only one floor," I said. "Just drop and grab."

"I can't," he said.

But he could. At that instant the dogs reached us, launching themselves toward the railing in a frenzy of teeth and claws. I couldn't have held on to that bar even if I wanted to, my strength giving out milliseconds before the dog's jaws snapped shut where my head had been. The second creature threw itself at Zee but he managed to let go. It soared over his head, snapping at us relentlessly as we all plummeted earthward.

There was barely any time to react. The railing of the platform below shot toward me like a bullet. I reached out a hand and more from blind luck than anything else managed to grip the metal bar. It felt like my arm had been wrenched out of its socket but I held on tight. Zee had missed the bar but held on to the floor, his legs dangling helplessly above the void.

The dog wasn't so lucky, hitting the ground below with a dull thud. It whimpered as it struggled to its feet, the sound of broken bones grinding against one another setting my teeth on edge. It wouldn't be long before its friend worked out where we were, so I pulled myself over the banister and reached down for Zee. Donovan appeared at my side, grabbing the boy's other hand, and together we pulled him to safety.

"Quick," Donovan shouted, sprinting back down the platform to our cell. The door was still open, the automatic mechanism whining as it strained to slide shut. There was a howl behind us and I snapped around to see the remaining dog charge along the platform. I could swear that its face was twisted into an expression of fury at what we had done to its brother.

We jumped into the cell, Donovan coming in last and wrestling with the toilet seat. I helped him, gripping the stained metal and pulling with all my might. The dog was gaining. We were going to be trapped inside the cell with the creature at this rate.

But when all seemed lost the toilet seat popped free, sending Donovan and me flying backward onto the bed. The cell door slid home, bolts securing it in place, and the dog crashed into the bars. They bent alarmingly, but they held. The creature thrashed against the metal for a few seconds before the siren cut through the prison again. It stood outside the cell, fixing us all with a silver glare like it was remembering our faces. Then it howled and fled back to the staircase.

I'M NOT ASHAMED to say that I spent the next few minutes crying my eyes out. Zee did too. We sat huddled on the bottom bunk sobbing helplessly, our exhausted bodies and fear-stricken minds unable to do anything else.

As soon as the dogs had vanished back inside the vault door— the injured one barely able to drag itself over the threshold—

Donovan started shouting at me, telling me how utterly stupid I had been to start a fight I couldn't win. But after a couple of insults he stopped, staring at us both like we were a couple of upset toddlers, his expression half frustration and half pity. Eventually he just shook his head and climbed onto his bunk.

I wept solidly until I felt like I'd cried out my very soul, until it seemed as if there was nothing left inside me. Then I lay back on the bed, staring into space and trying to forget that I even existed. I don't know whether it was minutes or hours later that I finally remembered my manners.

"Thanks," I breathed, little more than a whisper. "Thanks for saving our lives."

The bed creaked as Donovan shifted his weight above me, and I heard a grunt that might have been an acknowledgment. There was a gentle cough from my side and I turned to see Zee looking at me expectantly.

"Oh, yeah, thanks to you too," I said, recalling the events in the trough room, events that seemed like they belonged in another lifetime. "You saved my ass, Zee."

"You owe me one, big-time," was his reply. But his mouth was bent up in what I thought was probably a smile. "Big-time."

"At least we made it," I said. "We survived."

I was surprised to hear Donovan laughing, a chuckle that was entirely devoid of humor.

"You made it, yeah, but for how long?" he asked. "Those dogs don't forget a face, especially when you leave one of them with broken legs. And as for the Skulls . . ."

He didn't need to finish. I knew that as soon as I got out of my cell they would be coming after me. I mean, we'd just got one of their number killed. I was truly Skull Fodder now. Part of me started wishing that the dogs had eaten all of the gang members from the canteen, but the thought made me feel sick.

"Do you see now?" Donovan continued. "This place isn't a joke. It's not some film or book or computer game where you get infinite lives. You foul up out there, then you die. It's as simple as that. And you two fouled up today, *big-time.*" He echoed Zee's accent. "Big-time."

"What happened to the other Skulls?" I asked, trying to change the subject. "The ones from the trough room."

"Holed up someplace, probably trembling in their little bandannas. Guards'll flush 'em out in a minute."

"What about us, will we get punished?" asked Zee. I suddenly pictured what Donovan had said about solitary confinement, tried not to think about going mad in a lightless pit at the bottom of the world.

"Maybe, maybe not," he replied. "You never know what's gonna happen in this place. Could end up in the hole, could just be left alone. Could be taken tonight. All a mystery till it happens."

The siren pierced my skull as once again the vault door opened. This time two blacksuits strode out, armed with shotguns, and made their way toward the canteen. They passed the pool of dark liquid that was all that remained of the Skull, then vanished through the wall. Less than a minute later the three remaining Skulls emerged from the trough room, hands clasped above their heads, one of the shotguns pointed at their backs as they marched toward the stairs. They disappeared from view, but I heard one of the blacksuits shout out a cell number followed by the muffled sound of a door opening.

It happened twice more, then the thunderous sound of the blacksuits' boots began to get louder as they made their way along our platform. I pressed myself back against the far wall, but there was nowhere to go and I was helpless as the two grinning faces appeared at the bars.

"Always the fresh meat," said one. "New kids, think they can cause trouble."

I tried to apologize, but my mouth was so dry I couldn't make my tongue work. One of the blacksuits ran his hands along the bars, curved inward from the weight of the dog.

"Open F11," he boomed. The cell door moved a few centimeters before the buckled bars jammed against their casings. The man grabbed hold of the door and pulled, the muscles beneath his suit straining so hard that I thought the fabric would rip. With the sound of screeching metal the solid bars relented, snapping back into place and allowing the door to slide open. The men didn't enter, they just pointed at Zee.

"You, come with us."

"Me?" he asked, his voice barely audible. Zee looked at me as if I could help. I swallowed hard then stood up, hands held out in submission.

"It's me you want," I said slowly. "I started it."

"Well, look at Mr. Noble," said the blacksuit who had bent the door. "Don't kiss ass, kid. You're in the right cell, he's not. It's a breach of lockdown rules. Now get over here, Hatcher."

Zee reluctantly stood and walked toward the cell door. The men raised their evil-looking weapons and ushered him outside.

"I'm so sorry, Zee," I said, but he was already walking off. I had a sudden flashback to Toby, lying dead on the floor of a stranger's house, his life taken because of my stupidity, my greed. I couldn't believe it was happening again.

"Close F11."

The cell door rumbled shut and I gripped the bars, trying to see what was happening. Zee was marched to the stairs, vanishing as he was led down to his fate.

"Where are they taking him?" I asked Donovan. "What are they going to do to him? It's my fault all this happened, not his."

The answer came a second later when I heard a shot sound out across the prison, echoing off the stone walls and piercing my heart. I sank down to my knees, trying to force time to reverse, trying to undo what I'd made happen.

But then the noise came again, not a shot but the crack of metal on metal.

"Open D24," came a voice, and the sound continued, the noise of a cell door opening. I rested my forehead against the cold bars, offering a prayer of thanks to anything that was listening. I heard the door close, followed a short while later by the siren as the men in black retreated.

"He's okay," I muttered. "We're okay."

But Donovan simply laughed that chilling laugh.

"No, Alex. You're dead, you just don't know it yet."

THE WARDEN'S WARNING

WHEN I WOKE UP the next morning I actually thought I was on fire. Every single fiber in my body was in agony. I had pains in every muscle, pains in muscles I didn't know existed, pains in muscles in *places* I didn't even know I had. My head was drumming some sort of ancient tribal dance, my throat felt like I'd swallowed a cheese grater, and my eyes were watering as if I was wearing contact lenses soaked in vinegar. I uttered what must have been a pretty pathetic groan, then tried to swing my useless legs out of bed.

"Kill me now," I whispered. My spine sounded like a bowl of Rice Krispies as I stood, all snaps, crackles, and pops, but after hobbling round the cell a couple of times like an old man I felt the pain start to subside. On my second round I saw Donovan leaning up in bed looking at me sympathetically.

"First time anybody does chipping they ache the morning after," he mumbled through a yawn. "But I can't imagine how you feel after chipping, fighting, and trying to escape the dogs."

"I feel like every nerve in my body is being pricked with a red-hot needle," I replied, making Donovan wince. "I feel like someone has skinned me alive and is now toasting my internal organs with a blowtorch." He actually turned a little pale at that one. "I feel like I've been bathed in acid—"

"Okay, enough," he interrupted, holding up a hand. "I'm about to eat breakfast."

We chatted while we waited for the morning siren to sound, which it did as I was using the toilet, leading to a number of "pardon you" jokes from Donovan. I didn't know why we were both in such good spirits, considering the events of the previous day. Being locked up does strange things to your state of mind, I guess. You're so relieved to have made it through each day and night that the simple act of waking up makes you euphoric— even when you do feel like you've just wrestled an elephant.

Our moods soon changed when the cells opened. We traipsed down to the yard with sour faces, each marked with a hint of fear, scanning the crowds for any sign of attack. I spotted a number of painted bandannas—lifeless black eyes daubed above lifeless gray faces—but aside from a handful of scowls aimed in my direction they seemed to ignore me. I kept my arms tensed by my sides, ready to lash out, just in case.

For some reason, things this morning were a little different from the day before. Two blacksuits stood by the elevator, beneath the massive screen, and were herding us in front of it like cattle. I almost made a mooing sound, but it was more from fear than from an attempt at humor. I managed to keep my mouth shut as we reached the courtyard and moved to the back of the group. It took a few minutes for everybody to make it down the stairs, but eventually every inmate in the prison was shuffling nervously beneath the flickering screen. It felt like we were waiting for our execution.

One of the blacksuits raised his shotgun in the air and fired a single shot. Behind the deafening report I heard the ammunition pinging off bars above my head, and hoped that everybody was on the ground floor. Anyone left upstairs could have some ugly holes in them. The yard instantly fell quiet, the prisoners clamping their mouths shut to avoid drawing attention to themselves.

"Looks like you've made quite an impression," Donovan risked whispering in my ear. I hoped this didn't have anything to do with the previous day's events, but judging by the way people were staring at me I knew it was a pretty pointless wish.

Eventually the screen exploded into static, a fizzing snowstorm that settled into a fuzzy image of a dark figure. The man was sitting in the shadows, but a single slice of light illuminated a flash of teeth and a crooked nose that I knew belonged to the warden. He sat forward and suddenly his whole face came into view. Unlike when he was standing in front of me, I was able to look into his eyes. But I wished I hadn't. They were like black pools inside his head, vortices that seemed to suck me in. It was like staring into an abyss. I thought I could see planets in those eyes, galaxies of stars. I saw madness and chaos, I saw eternity. I saw my own death.

Then I blinked, and they were just eyes. Dark, yes, but normal. I realized I was drenched with sweat. It sat on my skin like a damp towel and I shivered in its grip. The entire room was cowering before the image of the warden, who resembled a giant staring down at his prey from the vast monitor.

"Obedience is the difference between life, death, and the other varieties of existence on offer here in Furnace," the image spoke, the voice amplified through hidden speakers to a volume that made the ground vibrate. It was the same thing he had said on the day I arrived, and I don't know why but I felt like he was speaking to me personally. After everything that had happened, I guess he probably was.

"Yesterday was a disgrace. Fighting in the canteen, a flagrant breach of lockdown rules, and one of my dogs had to be relieved of its pitiful existence because of two broken legs."

I felt a sudden and surprising pang of guilt that the dog had been put down. They were monsters, but the whimper it made as it tried to stand up after the fall was still fresh in my mind.

"I know who was responsible, and so do you. But you are a colony of pests, you no longer have individual personalities. A crime committed by a few is a crime committed by you all, and therefore you are all subject to reprisal." There was an audible groan in the yard. "So today, the trough room is out of bounds. No meals, no water. If you animals want to fight over your food, then you don't deserve to eat."

He smiled, and for a moment I felt myself sucked back into the pits of his eyes. It was like the world around me was unpeeling, dropping away, leaving blackness and madness in its place. I wrenched my head down, my stomach churning the same way it does on a roller coaster.

"For the moment I'll forget about yesterday's other incident," the warden went on, sitting back so that his face was once again shrouded in shadow. "But pay heed. Any more infractions, any more fights, and the perpetrator will go to the hole for a week." This time there were actual shouts of distress from inside the crowd of inmates. "And a week down there is as good as the electric chair. I hope I make myself clear."

The screen fizzed again, then the static gave way to the rotating list of names for work duty. But nobody was paying attention.

Something was building up from the center of the crowd, a wave of tension that threatened to break at any minute. It was cut short by another warning shot from the same guard, who stepped menacingly toward the unhappy inmates and aimed his smoking weapon at the nearest prisoner.

"You heard the boss," he growled. "Shut up and get to work. If you ask me, you all got off lightly."

Somehow the prisoners managed to batten down their tempers, and one by one they drifted off toward their stations. I was dismayed to see that Donovan and I were chippers again. My body didn't feel up to lifting a pretzel, let alone a pickax, and the thought of being in a room full of people who hated me, all armed with mining equipment, didn't really make me feel any better. There wasn't even going to be any breakfast. I felt like my stomach had been surgically removed, leaving a gaping hole in my torso, and the thought of a day without food or water—even the gunk they served up here—was frightening.

We set off across the yard, but it was a good few seconds before either of us opened our mouths.

"Don't worry," said Donovan, speaking loudly over the shouts and insults that were being fired at me. "Not the first time the canteen's been shut down for a day and it won't be the last. We're used to it. Got sealed off for three days when the Skulls took on the Leopards. That was a full-blown riot though."

What little measure of relief I felt was quickly snatched away when a kid I had never seen before ran up to me and shouted, "Nice going, moron." I found myself pulling closer to Donovan as if his mere presence would somehow protect me, although I hadn't forgotten the way he had walked off yesterday when I had been getting pounded. I sensed someone else running toward me and I flinched, but I recognized Zee's accent and straightened myself, trying to pretend that I'd just tripped on the stone.

"Hostile crowd," he said. "Why do I feel like today's my last day on earth?"

"You'll be fine, for now," said Donovan as Zee fell into line with us. "Nobody will start a skirmish knowing it'll get them a week in the hole. Never been a survivor after that long. The record is four days, and he was a hollow man afterward."

There was a distinct rumbling of stomachs but I couldn't tell whether it came from Donovan, Zee, or my own gut, which was still churning. It probably emanated from all three of us, a chorus of protest at a day without sustenance.

We marched in silence through the hole in the wall, past a blacksuit whose silver eyes promised a world of pain if we stepped out of line. It was only my second day, but I felt like an old hand at chipping, donning my visor with a world-weary sigh, flicking on my helmet lamp, and hefting the pick onto my shoulder to avoid piercing anybody's foot. My muscles complained at the effort, but it was only a halfhearted gripe. They knew what had to be done.

Zee had been put with us today, and he stuck close by, following my lead and selecting his own tools. The blacksuit split us into teams, and once again we marched into the third room. Donovan and I staked out the same spot at the far end of the half-finished cavern, and I filled Zee in on the job description.

"Pound and clear, that's it. Oh, and watch your head!"

The steady percussion of metal and rock began again in earnest. At times the noise sounded exactly like what it was—a load of kids smashing a rock wall. But occasionally a rhythm would start up, some mysterious force of coincidence turning the relentless plinks into a staccato tune. It would only last for a few seconds before once again fading out of sync, but it always brought a smile to my face.

It was only after ten minutes or so of painful chipping that I felt like I was being watched. I put the sensation down to the fact that people were still scowling at me, but it was so powerful it felt like something boring into the back of my neck. I swung around and scanned the inmates before me. Most were hidden behind visors and a layer of red dust, but there was one familiar face that turned away as soon as I saw it. It was Montgomery.

I laid my pick down on the ground and walked over, weaving my way carefully around the wooden posts holding up the ceiling. He tried to back away, then stopped, then turned, then lifted his pick as though to start work, then let it drop. Finally, he slumped his shoulders and acknowledged me with a nod. Behind the shine on his visor I made out bruised cheeks and a swollen lip, but his expression was as hard as ever.

"How are you?" I asked softly. He fixed me with a glare that caught me by surprise, like I'd been the one beating him up.

"I guess you want me to thank you," he spat. I raised my eyebrows and opened my mouth, but I had absolutely no idea how to respond. "I didn't ask you to help me. I'm not some charity case. What? You want a big reward for rescuing helpless little Monty? Well, you're not getting one." Flecks of foam dotted the plastic screen in front of him. "Now we're not even allowed any food. A whole day. It's your fault."

He lifted his pick and waved it at me. It reminded me of an

old man shaking his cane at a group of kids. I held up my hands in surrender, my eyebrows refusing to return to their normal position.

"Jeez," was all I could manage. I felt the familiar burn of anger flare up inside my chest, but I swallowed hard and it faded. Monty's face was creased in hostile determination, but I could tell that it was fear making him react this way. I hoped it was, anyway, otherwise he was an ungrateful little wretch.

I opened my mouth to try to reason with him, then thought better of it, turning my back on him and returning to my pick.

"He didn't look like he was bursting with gratitude," said Zee, pulling up his visor and wiping a gloved hand across his brow. The move left a trail of wet dust on his forehead that looked like blood in the half-light of the room. "Did he even say thanks?"

I shook my head and Zee scowled over at Monty.

"That's so out of order. We could have died yesterday saving his fat ass. We should have just left him."

"Told you so," said Donovan between swings. I ignored him, but they were both right. It had been a stupid thing to do. I'm no hero, no action star. I'm a villain, not a saint. I should have abandoned Monty to lick up after the Skulls, then we'd never have got on the warden's bad side and we'd all have had breakfast. I took one last look at him—standing by himself, still holding his pick up like a weapon and staring at the floor—then started pummeling the wall again. I'm a little ashamed to say that this time, when I saw faces in the rock, I imagined they were his.

DOWNTIME

NOBODY IN FURNACE KNEW exactly how long work duty went on for. Donovan claimed that it was five or six hours—from breakfast to lunch—but that second day of hard labor felt more like a full twenty-four-hour stretch.

With no fuel to keep us going, we all quickly began to falter. The oppressive air of Furnace beat down on us like dragon's breath—hot, stale, and at times stripped of oxygen so we felt like we were choking. It was the lack of water that really took its toll, drying us out like prunes and forcing us to lay our picks down every couple of minutes to avoid blacking out. I even found myself eyeing the sweat on Donovan's forehead in the hope it would quench my thirst.

There were a couple of times I felt the world spin uncontrollably, the rush of vertigo like I'd just fallen off a cliff. I had to clamp my eyes shut and lean on my pick to avoid losing it completely. Other kids weren't so lucky. Two passed out that morning, the second midway through a swing. He fell forward like a dead weight, landing face-first on a jagged strip of rock. The sight of gushing blood usually would have turned my stomach, but I'd already seen far worse than that here in Furnace. His prone body was dragged from the room by a blacksuit, a slick crimson trail betraying his route.

By the time the siren sounded—half a lifetime later—the rhythm of picks against rock had dwindled to a sorry tapping from the couple of inmates who still had the strength to lift their tools. We were so desperate to leave that we all pushed our way through the door before the echoes of the siren had faded away, and in less than a minute we'd dumped our stuff and were waiting in the equipment room for the order to move through to the showers. Obviously another group had beaten us to them, as the blacksuit showed no sign of letting us pass.

To avoid the growing sense of frustration, which could explode into violence at any moment, Donovan, Zee, and I drifted to the back of the room. For some reason it seemed calmer here, cooler, but I couldn't work out why. The other guys felt it too; it seemed to relax them, loosen their tense limbs, and tease a smile from the corner of their lips. I found myself thinking of mountains, of all things, snow-tipped and windblown, as high above the world as we were below it, drenched in light and air.

All three of us took a deep, shuddering breath in unison, then laughed at the fact it had happened. Something about this spot was euphoric, and we all had to pinch our noses to avoid giggling helplessly. Fortunately at that point the blacksuit gave the order to move out, and the noise of our spluttered laughs was lost in the clomp of feet.

It was only as we made our way out of the room that I fathomed the source of our bizarre rapture. Looking back I saw the splintered black hole in the rock that led into Room Two. It was still sealed off with heavy wooden boards because of the cave-in, but there was no mistaking the nature of what was emanating from that portal.

It was fresh air.

AFTER THE HEAT and hardship of the chipping room the showers were like paradise. For once the cold water was a blessing, not a curse, and we all stood under the flow letting the icy blast cool and cleanse our bodies and gulping down as much liquid as we could. I swear more water went down our throats than down the drains that afternoon.

I thought the abundant supply of cool liquid might have kept things civil in the showers, but I've learned that in Furnace you can't have more than a few minutes without cruelty of some kind. Behind the roar of the flow I heard jeering again, wolf whistles and laughter that seemed to be both muffled and amplified by the vapor in the air.

I wiped the drips from my eyes and glanced across the shower room to see who was being persecuted this time, but I needn't have bothered. Monty was pressed up against the wall farther along the same row as me, while a pack of inmates sucked up water with their mouths and spat it at him. The poor kid was trying to cover something on his upper arm, and when he raised his hand to block a spout of spitwater I saw what it was—a brown birthmark the size of a grapefruit and the shape of a heart.

One of the kids stepped right up to Monty, cheeks full, and let loose a veritable torrent right into the kid's face.

"Nice tattoo, lover boy," he shouted through a twisted grin. I felt that familiar tug of anger, a beast inside me that wanted to be unleashed, but I fought it, reminding myself how Monty had reacted earlier. Besides, he spotted me staring at him and his green eyes narrowed in a way that once again made me feel like I was the one tormenting him. It was an expression of defiance, one that warned me not to help him. I didn't really understand it, but I respected it, and turned my back to let him know. I was glad I did, as the wet thump and cry that sounded from behind me would have been too much to witness.

Colder than glaciers, and dressed in clean new uniforms and paper shoes, we marched from the shower room into the court-yard. An armed blacksuit stood in front of the tunnel that led to the trough room, but I wasn't too upset about the thought of not going in there again after yesterday. Instead, Donovan led me and Zee across the yard toward the stairs.

"Things get heated down here when the trough room's out of bounds," he explained. "Hundreds of prisoners all starving and thirsty and bored is like dynamite waiting to go off. I don't think anything will happen, not with the warden's warning and all—no one's gonna blow if they've been promised a week in the hole—but best to stay clear just in case."

I wasn't going to argue with that. We reached the stairs and traipsed upward, but not before I noticed another door tucked beneath the stairwell, the gap in the rock so narrow that it was almost invisible. Two inmates stood outside, casually leaning on the wall. One was a Skull, the other had two black lines across each cheek—a mark I'd seen on another couple of prisoners.

"What's in there?" I asked, pointing. Donovan bent down to peer through the steps and nodded when he caught the eye of the inmate with the painted cheeks. The guy tilted his head in Donovan's direction in acknowledgment.

"That's the gym," he replied, continuing up the stairs. "But don't get your hopes up. That's private property, owned by the Skulls and the Fifty-niners—the guys with the lines on their faces."

"Why Fifty-niners?" Zee asked as we reached the second platform. Donovan snorted.

"Ask them, it's how many people they killed during the Summer of Slaughter, before they got sent down. There's fifteen of them so you do the math. They claim to have been one of the biggest gangs in the capital, east of the river. Don't believe it myself, though. They weren't big enough to take on the Skulls when they got here, just arranged some kiss-ass pact where they both control the gym. Ask me, fifty-nine is their combined IQ."

We reached the fourth platform with a series of huffs and puffs, each of us using the banister to pull ourselves up.

"They let a handful of people in to use the equipment, including yours truly," Donovan went on. "But nobody else gets in. They use it for cards and organized skirmishes. Floor in there is permanently red, if you follow me."

"Who wants to use the gym anyway," grumbled Zee as we hauled ourselves onto the fifth level. "Get worked hard enough in here without worrying about weights and rowing machines and all that crap."

"It's okay for you," Donovan replied, turning and flexing his arms at us. It looked for a minute like there were a couple of melons where his biceps should be. "You don't have a body like this to look after."

We laughed, but like all good moments in Furnace it was short-lived. As we neared our cell, two spotty faces emerged from behind the bars and blocked our way. It was Kevin Arnold and one of his lieutenants, a scar-faced kid called Bodie. Donovan seemed to expand when he saw them, his body swelling as he tensed his arms, and for a second the Skulls looked anxious.

"Don't have any beef with you, Donovan," Kevin said. I thought I could hear another sound from inside the cell, the noise of running water. "Just your jerkweed bunk buddy."

The Skulls turned their attention to me and I prepared to defend myself, nervously eyeing the six-story drop to my right and praying that I wouldn't end up flying over the railing. Donovan didn't say anything, but he didn't back down either.

"Got our man killed yesterday," Kevin went on. "Don't take that offense lightly. Gotta pay, blood for blood. You know the rules."

"Actually, I wasn't given a copy of the pirate handbook when I arrived, so I don't," I replied, cursing my voice, which trembled as I spoke.

Kevin smiled, and I noticed that he didn't have any of his front teeth.

"You funny now," he hissed. "But dead men don't laugh so loud."

I wasn't sure whether to laugh or cry. It sounded like some terrible Sunday afternoon horror film, but I knew that Kevin would skewer me with a shank without thinking twice.

"Soon as the warden lifts his warning, we'll shut you up for good, new fish. You and your little girlfriend there."

Zee spluttered in shock at the comment but didn't say anything. Kevin and Bodie barged past us and started walking up the platform. They were followed by a third inmate, who strolled from our cell still buttoning up his fly.

"Sleep well tonight," he said as he followed his friends, and I suddenly realized what the noise of running water had been. I dashed into the cell to see a dark stain spreading across my sheet.

"No way!" I blustered. "They can't. I mean, what did they do that for? Where am I going to sleep?" I went on like that for the best part of a minute before recovering my senses and pulling the wet mess off my bed. From the way it dropped to the floor with a splat I was pretty sure that all three boys had relieved themselves on my bunk. I dragged the sheet out of the cell onto the platform, then looked up at Donovan and Zee.

"What am I supposed to do now?"

"Laundry's in a couple of days," Donovan answered with a shrug. "Till then, I guess you'll just be sleeping al dente."

"Al dente?" I asked, frowning. Zee chuckled.

"I think he means al fresco," he said. "Out in the open."

"What am I, Italian?" Donovan replied, raising his arm as if to whack Zee but giving him a gentle clip on the ear. "Al dente, al fresco, Al Pacino, it's all the same to me."

The sharp tang of urine was making our eyes water, so we walked a few steps along the landing and sat down, our feet dangling over the drop and our faces pressed through the railings. The inmates looked like toy soldiers below, separated into different units that occupied various sections of the courtyard. Like oil and water, each group seemed repelled from every other, never straying into enemy territory. Some milled around like packs of dogs, looking for any sign of weakness. Others sat at the scattered tables arm wrestling and playing cards.

There was even a group of younger inmates playing tag, yelling in excitement as they chased one another around the yard, avoiding the bigger boys. I don't know why, but the sight of them running brought a lump to my throat—they were kids who should have been tearing across the school playground between lessons, or on their way home to a hot meal and a loving family. Some looked like they were ten years old, for Christ's sake—they never even had a chance to enjoy being young.

"The warden's not going to lift his warning, is he?" asked Zee, taking my mind off events below.

"He'll lift it in time," explained Donovan. "This place is like a pressure cooker and he knows it. He'll leave the threat of the hole hanging over us for a few days, but he can't keep it up forever or he'll have a riot on his hands." He idly picked some rust from the bar and flicked it out into the void. "He won't announce that he's lifted it, there will just be a skirmish one day and all that will happen will be a lockdown. Like I said, you never really know what's gonna happen in this place."

"So what's the deal with the warden anyway?" Zee went on after a chorus of sighs. "He's a pretty scary guy. Those eyes."

"You saw it too?" I asked, remembering the way that the world had dissolved when I met the warden's stare. "I felt like he was stripping away my soul or something."

"Yeah," Donovan replied, "eyes like fingers, they go right into your brain. Did you notice that you can't meet his gaze when he's standing in front of you?" We both nodded. "Nobody here can. None of us get it, but then there's plenty of things in Furnace that none of us get."

"But what about when he was on the screen?" I said. "I mean, I thought I saw, well, planets or space or something." I couldn't quite remember what I'd seen, and talking about it now, it seemed ridiculous. "I saw death, I guess. Stuff like that."

"I just saw nothing," Zee added. "It was like looking into a space that had once been full of stuff but that was now just full of emptiness. I thought I was being sucked in."

"Just take it from me," Donovan said. "Stay well clear of the warden. Some here think he's the devil. I don't, I don't believe in that religious talk, but I know evil when I see it. He's something rotten they dragged up from the bowels of the earth, something they patched together from darkness and filth. He'll be the death of us all, every single one of us here in Furnace. Only question is when."

"I know one thing," I added. "The warden certainly brings out people's dramatic sides." Zee and Donovan both laughed through their noses.

"So does he own this place then?" Zee asked. Both Donovan and I shook our heads, but I let the big guy explain.

"There's a reason it's called Furnace, dumb-ass," he said. "It was built by some guy called Alfred Furnace. Businessman or something, rich enough to pay for this place anyway. Nobody really knows anything about him, he never visits. Probably just sits on a throne somewhere counting the money the government pays him to take lowlifes like us off the streets."

We sat in silence for a little while, listening to the noise filter up from below. I gazed at the distant ceiling, lost in shadow at least twenty more floors above, and wondered what the weather was like, but the thought was just too depressing.

"Well," I said eventually, "we've witnessed fights, giant mutant dogs, and a warden who may or may not be Satan himself. Surely there can't be much worse to see at Furnace?"

"Kid," said Donovan matter-of-factly, "you ain't seen nothing yet. You can't truly understand what a nightmare this place is until the wheezers come for you in the dead of night. You want horror? The sight of them outside your cell could scare you to death by itself."

I didn't believe him, of course. I mean, after what I'd seen already I couldn't imagine anything more terrifying. But I was wrong; the dogs and the warden, they were just a warm-up act for the sickest show in Furnace—a show that I would only have to wait another four days to witness.

SLOP

FOUR DAYS. EACH ONE longer than the last, each dictated by the sirens that cut through the prison every other hour, each plagued by the same unending sense of terror. Every time I laid my head down at night and heard the symphony of Furnace I wondered how I had managed to get through the day, and as my heavy eyes closed and the waking world dissolved I would panic that this was the night they would come, that it would be my last night on earth.

But I was always surprised to find each new morning arriving on time and me still in it—exhausted and frightened, yes, but alive. The day after the warden's warning the trough room reopened to a cheer from the inmates gathered outside, myself included. The stampede for breakfast had been so ferocious that the kids serving up mush had run off, telling everybody to help themselves. We did, piling mountainous heaps of the anonymous dish on our trays. I can honestly say that, after a day without food, the salty gunk was the best thing I'd ever eaten.

That third full day of my incarceration Donovan and I had been chippers again, while Zee had been back on cleaning duty—although thankfully for him not the Stink. Day four was my first taste of a different job, working in the hot, steamy sweatshop that was the prison laundry. We had the same shift for the fifth day, where an accident with one of the machines left me with a painful scald all along my left arm. At least I had clean sheets again after that, though.

After hard labor Donovan, Zee, and I would hang out in the yard. Most of the time we just sat and chatted, but occasionally we'd nab a pack of cards and play pontoon or cheat or even snap. It was difficult to relax knowing you might feel a cold blade in your back at any moment, but we kept our eyes out for each other and just moved on if we saw the Skulls coming.

I learned that downtime in Furnace was like a strange dance where each group maneuvered around the others with surprising grace and timing. I also learned not to mention this insight to anybody in case they thought I was calling them a ballet dancer.

There wasn't too much violence in those few days. Every now and again tempers would fray and a skirmish would be on the verge of breaking out, but fear of the hole meant that it was always kept under control. There were a couple of punches thrown, a shank or two waved in somebody's face, and Monty and a few of the other kids suffered kicks and shoves and numerous humiliations, but I didn't see much blood. Occasionally somebody would stagger from the gym with various cuts and bruises, but they'd be grinning through their wounds. I guess organized fights didn't count as a breach of the warden's rules.

On day six Donovan and I traipsed down the stairs after the wake-up siren to see that we were on slopwork duty, along with Zee. I was actually a little excited to finally be able to see the inside of the kitchen, and when we pushed through the double doors at the back of the canteen I wasn't disappointed.

Unlike the rest of Furnace—which was all red rock and bruised shadows—the kitchen was a haven of brushed aluminum drenched in white light. The walls here had been plastered and painted, presumably for health and safety reasons. Not that Furnace was too concerned about the health and safety of its inmates, of course, but I guess even this hellhole must have had to pass a few inspections before being allowed to open. Walking through those doors into the illuminated interior was like walking from a garbage heap into a church, and I felt oddly uplifted.

It didn't last. As soon as I saw what we'd be doing, I realized that the kitchen was just a different sort of garbage heap. In one corner lay crates full of what I could only describe as leftovers— onion peels, chicken bones with scraps of meat clinging to them, bread with unmistakable green spores, cheese that was dripping from the bottom of the crates onto the floor, fruit that had already started to liquefy and rot, even a bag that looked like it was full of hair.

Worst of all were five or six boxes stuffed full of wet flesh. I swear I saw some things in those boxes that put me off meat for life—intestines, hooves, and even a bloody cow's eyeball staring up at the ceiling as if in deep thought. The glistening mess reminded me of the warden's dogs and I almost added my own guts to the mixture.

"Now you know why they call it slopwork," said Donovan, pulling on a paper apron and some sturdy rubber gloves from a box under the counter. "This is stuff from above that they wouldn't even give to pigs."

"Yeah but these are going out, aren't they?" Zee asked, picking an apron for himself and throwing one to me. "They're rubbish?"

"In a manner of speaking," was Donovan's reply. "If by 'out' you mean 'in' and by 'rubbish' you mean 'ingredients.' What do you think is in that gunk they feed us? Salmon soufflé?"

The best thing about slopwork was that you only needed a few people to work a shift. Ten inmates were posted to the kitchen at a time—four went to serve the sty outside, and the rest mopped up the mess and prepared the next batch of gunk. That morning Donovan, Zee, and I gave ourselves the job of cooking up slop, and we retreated to the massive industrial stove at the far end of the kitchen. I noticed that Monty had been posted on slopwork duty too. He picked up a mop and kept his distance, but repeatedly glanced up at the stove as if it contained some hidden secret.

"Don't suppose either of you know how to cook?" Donovan asked, lifting one of the crates from the floor and dumping it down onto the counter beside the stove. With a tug he broke the crisscrossed strings that kept the vile contents inside. We both shook our heads. I could just about manage toast and cheese at home, but even then I tended to burn the bread.

"Well, it isn't exactly cordon bleu," he went on, making Zee snigger. "Grab one of those pots and put it on the burner."

I looked beneath the counter to see rows of giant pots, each resembling a witch's cauldron. It took both me and Zee to heft it onto the burner. Donovan grabbed a massive bottle of oil and poured about half of it into the pot, then he opened up a panel on the side of the stove and reached inside. I heard something pop gently, followed by the hiss of gas.

"Grab one of those safety lighters," he said, nodding to one of three long, thin lighters chained to the other side of the oven. Zee lifted it and held it beneath the pot, pressing the button to produce a pathetic flame. I noticed the pungent smell of gas hanging in the air and took a step back. "Gotta get this right or the whole prison will go kaboom," Donovan went on, fiddling with the gas supply inside. "Hold it closer."

"What, and lose my fingers? I don't think so," Zee retorted. But he inched the flame closer to the burner until, with a roar and a splutter, the gas ignited.

"And we have liftoff," said Donovan, getting to his feet. I glanced through the panel and saw three or four vast canisters of gas inside, bolted securely to the wall. Donovan wasn't kidding— if one of them were to explode then we'd all resemble the meat in those crates, only barbecued.

Donovan began pulling handfuls of leftover food from the crate and dropping them into a sink embedded in the counter beside the stove. He motioned for us to do the same, and after pulling on the uncomfortable rubber gloves Zee and I lifted a couple of crates and began chucking slops into the sink, trying to ignore the smell of rot and decay. When Donovan's crate was empty he threw it to the floor, picked up a stick, and began prodding the disgusting mixture down the drain.

"Stand back," he said, reaching across the counter and punching a switch. A sound not unlike a chain saw in mud rose up from the sink and the slop slowly began to disappear.

"Is that a garbage disposal?" I asked, speaking over a series of gargles and wheezes from the spinning blades down the drain.

"Nope, this is Furnace's patented flavor mixer," he replied, ramming the stick down the drain to clear a blockage. "Guaranteed to blend ingredients in just the right order to produce a scrumptious meal."

We forced a couple more crates of food into the sink, watching as it was sucked into the hole. Donovan even risked a carton of meat, holding it upside down until the flesh inside gave in to gravity and plummeted earthward like so much pink porridge. I thought I glimpsed a number of pale forms wriggling their way free of the rotting guts, but I put it down to my imagination. Surely even this place wouldn't feed us maggots.

Donovan switched off the machine and opened a door in the counter. Beneath the sink was a huge bucket, practically overflowing with the brown goo that dripped from the pipe above. Grunting, he picked it up and tipped it into the cauldron. There was a brutal hiss as the gunge met the boiling oil.

"Another couple of bucket loads and you'll have made your first batch of trough slop," he said as he repositioned the bucket. "Leave it to boil for an hour or so until it loses all taste and color, add in some filler and salt, and bingo, perfection on a plate."

"Doesn't seem so bad," I heard Zee mutter.

"Well, let's see if you're still saying that when you've made your thirtieth pot of the day," Donovan answered. "Got a lot of bellies to fill in here."

Like everything in Furnace, slopwork was a dirty and draining duty, but being with Donovan and Zee made it feel a lot less like a chore. We chatted and joked as we processed the stinking crates, filling each other in on our histories, our likes and dislikes, our proudest moments and most embarrassing memories. I doubt any of us were really telling the whole truth—I know my boasts about captaining the school soccer team and getting a story published in *Sci-Fi Monthly* were a far cry from reality—but the simple act of bragging about ourselves and remembering a lost world took some of the crushing weight from our chests, let us breathe a little easier.

"That's one thing I really wish I'd done before I came here," Donovan said when the topic of conversation eventually came around to food. "I'd do anything to know how to cook a decent meal."

"With you there," I replied. "Never even thought twice about cooking. Mom and Dad did it all."

"I used to bake a few cakes and things with my gran," Zee added. "But I wouldn't have a clue how to start that now. Never really paid attention, just did what I was told."

"Yeah," Donovan went on as if he hadn't heard us. "What I wouldn't give to be able to rustle up some meatballs and pasta, a bacon cheeseburger, a little sausage casserole."

We all licked our lips and nodded, lost in the memory of good food.

"I used to cook," came a voice from behind us. I swung around to see Monty standing at our backs, holding his mop and staring at the remaining crates. His voice was soft and distant, and when he carried on speaking, his shining eyes never left the floor. "Me and my sister made up our own recipes. Garden-gnome spaghetti. We had a vegetable patch in our back garden and it was guarded by this gnome. We had to try to dig up what we needed without him spotting us, otherwise we had to do the dishes after dinner."

It was the most I'd ever heard him say, and after his outburst the other morning I was shocked to see this side of him. All three of us stood in silence, letting him speak.

"Susan always got to do the chopping because she was older

than me. But I stirred the pots. That was the important job, stirring. Too little and it burned, too much and it didn't cook properly."

Abruptly he let his mop fall to the ground and leaned over the crates. Rummaging through one he selected a few bruised peppers and held them out. Nobody moved, staring at the faded vegetables in his hands like they were a monster turd. We stood like that, a bizarre tableau, until Monty raised his head and studied us.

"I was never much good at anything, outside," he said. "But I could always cook." He shook the hand holding the peppers and I stepped forward to take them from him. He rooted through another couple of crates, selecting things that hadn't deteriorated too badly in the heat, and we took them, placing them on the counter. Finally, he poked tentatively through a crate of meat until he found what looked like a brown steak. Walking to the counter, he studied his ingredients. Then, before our astonished eyes, he began to cook.

There were no knives or cutlery of any kind in the kitchen, so he hacked at the meat with the edge of a tray until it lay in rough cubes on the surface. He gave me and Zee instructions to heat up another pot, which we did with enthusiastic giggles while Donovan crushed some overripe tomatoes in a bowl.

It was amazing watching Monty work. Where practically every action had been clumsy and graceless until now, his plump fingers moved like lightning over the food, blending, mixing, seasoning, and shaking with expert skill until he'd turned the disparate ingredients into something actually resembling food. With a little flourish, performed with nervous embarrassment, he tipped the bowl into the second pan and slapped his hands together. Almost immediately the smell of simmering vegetables and meat rose from the cauldron, so good I started dribbling.

"Susan used to say that being a good chef isn't about cooking a good meal," he said, using a spoon to carefully stir his creation. "It's about cooking for good people."

"Monty," I started, but he cut me off with a look that almost resembled the hate-filled expression I'd seen so many times before. It didn't last, and he returned his attention to the pot.

"Just eat," he said.

We let Monty serve up the dish without saying a word, but as soon as we wrapped our lips around his masterpiece we just couldn't shut up. Donovan especially. It had been so long since he had last tasted anything but prison food that he shouted out gleeful comments between every spoonful, even telling Monty how much he loved him.

Eventually he couldn't help himself and started crying, his shoulders rocking uncontrollably as he devoured each great mouthful. I almost joined him, the taste of salted beef and tomato sauce and gently cooked peppers making me feel like I was back at home. We were all transported out of Furnace for those few minutes. I'll never forget that. Until the last morsel of meat spilled down our throats and the final splash of sauce was licked from our plastic bowls we were free.

Afterward we cleared up our mess with howls of laughter, delirious with excitement. We even had a food fight with cores and peels, ducking behind counters and deflecting incoming missiles with pot lids, filling up the rubber gloves with water and lobbing them across the kitchen. Monty didn't join in, he didn't laugh. But he watched us with a glint in his eye and a twitch of a smile and I felt like I could see right through that expression to happier times—a large kitchen and two kids cooking garden-gnome spaghetti with the same love and laughter that we were clinging to so furiously now.

I wanted that moment to last forever, we all did. But of course it had to end. And there was never another day like it. How could there be? That night they came. They crawled from the darkness and came for Monty.

THE BLOOD WATCH

THEY CAME WITHOUT WARNING. They came without mercy.

One minute I was asleep, embraced by blissful dreams of Sunday afternoon picnics, the next I was shunted back into Furnace by a siren that wouldn't end—a continuous blast that wove itself around its own echo until the prison quaked and my ears stung. At first I thought it was the wake-up call, but it was still pitch-black and I knew from my internal clock that it was the dead of night.

As soon as I made that calculation I knew it was finally happening. They were coming. I shot up in bed, my heart beating so hard I was convinced it was trying to pound its way free from my chest. A wave of murmured wails and panicked cries circled the prison, ending with Donovan, who seemed to choke back a sob.

"Please, God, not tonight," I heard him whisper above the klaxon. "And not me. Not me. Please, God."

The darkness pressed against me like a coffin lining, and my light-starved eyes played tricks. Strange figures pulled themselves from the black cloth, always in the corner of my vision, stretching out for me with decaying fingers and hollow eyes. I expected to feel bony hands grab my arm any second, a cold embrace dragging me into the pit. I struck the air helplessly, and each time the phantoms dissolved only to form again, their pursuit relentless.

The wail of the siren cut out, and at the same time a thousand red lights embedded in the prison walls burst into life. I was plunged into a thick, choking silence, like someone had thrown me into a pool of blood. I saw the world in shades of red and black, and quickly found myself praying for night again. At least you can hide in the dark.

From the yard below came a hiss, then a bone-shattering boom as the vault door was unlocked. It swung open to reveal a procession of hunched forms who marched slowly from the gloom like they were heading a funeral procession. From my cell I couldn't make out who they were, the red light turning them into vague phantoms who drifted out into the yard. From the sound of wheezing, however, I could guess. I craned my neck to get a better view, but as soon as I moved I heard Donovan cry out.

"Just keep your head down, you idiot," he hissed. "Don't draw attention to the cell."

You could have heard a pin drop. Every single prisoner in Furnace had clamped his mouth shut, not even daring to take a breath for fear of alerting the twisted figures below. My own breaths sounded like hurricanes, my heartbeat like a drum punching out a rhythm that could probably be heard on the surface. Some perverse element of my brain started silently singing along to the twin beat—*take me, take me, take me*—and I had to bite my lip hard in order to make it shut up.

The five figures below stopped in the middle of the yard, wreathed in shadow. Then, as one, they screamed. The sound made my blood curdle. It was like a death cry from some wounded animal, like the noise a rabbit makes when it's snared in a trap. But it was an angry noise too—the howl of somebody who has just seen a loved one die. The shriek grated up the prison walls, turning each of us to stone. Then the figures lifted their heads and I saw who they were.

It was the gas masks, the wheezers, piggy-eyed and pasty-fleshed.

The wet screech came again, this time from only one of the grotesque figures, and the group separated. Two turned and made for the staircases on the far side of the prison, taking long, distorted steps, while the other three came our way, eventually disappearing under the platform outside my cell. Seeing the freaks below was one thing, but not seeing them was far worse. It meant they were coming up the stairs.

"What are they doing?" I whispered. When there was no reply I started to repeat myself, only to be cut off by a hiss from above.

"If you don't shut up I swear to God I'm gonna come down and kill you myself," Donovan said, his harsh words barely audible. "This isn't a joke. If they mark this cell, then you're going somewhere that makes death look like a holiday."

I opened my mouth to ask again but from the yard outside came a buzz, then with a sharp crack and a shower of sparks from the top of the prison the lights went out. Fear gripped me, the knowledge that those things could be right outside the cell. But seconds later the prison was plunged into a pool of bloodred color again as the electricity came back on.

"What the hell is happening?" I asked, but this time I had spoken too softly for even Donovan to hear. I chewed my lip furiously, desperate to know where the gas masks were. Finally, I could bear it no longer. As quietly as possible, I lifted the covers from my bed and climbed out. The squeak that the bunks made seemed as loud as the siren, and as soon as he heard it Donovan shot up in bed, his eyes like daggers.

"Back!" he spat, fear severing his sentences. "Get us both taken." He glanced at the bars, his face a mask of panic. "Not too late, back!"

From somewhere below another unnatural shriek cut through the red night, this one followed by a mournful wail that was painfully human. The wail turned into a word, one spoken again and again and again like a mantra. "No, no, no, no, no, no, no, no."

The lights cut out again, the sparks that fell from above like a miserable fireworks show that did nothing to illuminate the prison. I took comfort in the darkness, getting onto my knees and crawling to the door. Donovan had given up trying to stop me. I heard a creak as he turned his back on the bars, and the rustle of his sheet as he pulled it over his head.

"Dead man," came one last muffled comment from inside.

With an electronic hum the lights rebooted. It took my eyes a second to adjust before I saw movement on one of the levels on the other side of the prison. I counted upward, noting that one of the hideous wheezers was on level five. I watched it make its way slowly past the cells, no sign of life from any of them as their occupants shivered beneath their blankets.

The figure stalked like a bird, taking huge, sweeping steps forward, its legs lost in the tails of its leather coat. The body seemed to twitch and shake as it progressed, the head jerking upward every five or six steps, the gloved hands clawing at its own face as if trying to remove the ancient gas mask that hung there. There was something wrong with the way it moved its limbs, but the heavy crimson light stopped me working out what it was.

I was so busy studying the monster that I didn't notice which cell it had stopped at until I saw movement from inside. There was a flurry of motion, then a plump figure flew forward and crashed against the bars. Monty collapsed in front of the gas mask, curling up in the corner of the cell and burrowing his head in his arms. Behind him I could make out Kevin clambering back into the top bunk, diving under his sheets.

The gas mask arched its back and screamed, causing Monty to curl even more tightly into himself, then it placed a hand into its trench coat. When it pulled it free again, it was smothered in what looked like tar, great gobs of it dripping to the metal platform. The freak wiped its filthy hand across the cell door twice, marking out an X on the bars, then it screamed again and froze, its dry wheeze the only sign it was still alive.

The prison went black for a third time and I squinted into the darkness in vain. From somewhere above me came another scream, another terrified protest. Then a fizz of static as the red lights struggled on again. My view of Monty's cell was blocked, and it took me an instant to work out why. When I did, my heart actually skipped a beat as the horror sank in.

Right in front of me, in all its sick glory, was a gas mask. I only looked at it for an instant before staggering backward, but the image was seared onto my brain for a lifetime. The monster was standing directly outside the cell, staring at me with eyes so deeply embedded in its shriveled face that they looked like black marbles. The contraption that covered its mouth and nose was colored with rust and verdigris, and this close I could see that the ancient metal was stitched permanently into the skin.

It inhaled noisily, then raised its arms, the movement parting the filthy, bloodstained trench coat and revealing a leather bandolier slung diagonally across its chest. The strap held six or seven huge syringes that looked like they hadn't been cleaned since the Second World War. I realized what it was about its limbs that was so unsettling. They were moving too fast, shaking by its sides as if they were being played in fast forward. Its head suddenly twitched with the same terrifying speed, shaking uncontrollably for a second before snapping back into place.

I hit the bunks and slid to the ground, feeling as if somebody had stripped the bones from my legs. As I met the stone the lights flicked out, the sparks silhouetting the monster outside the cell as it reached into its pocket. I heard somebody else crying out "no, no, no" at the top of his voice, but it was another few seconds before I accepted it was me.

The lights snapped back on, but they didn't hold. For a few seconds they strobed on and off—red, black, red, black—while the wheezer stood outside the cell. The flashing lights made my head feel like it was going to explode, and I was forced to screw my eyes shut, burying my face into the crook of my arm as if that would protect me.

Then, with a hum, the power reasserted itself. I looked up, expecting to see the nightmare still standing outside my cell. But it was gone. I scrabbled to my feet and flung myself at the bars to see the gas mask continuing down the platform, eventually reaching the stairwell and heading up.

I hadn't taken a breath for what seemed like hours, and sucked in lungfuls of air.

"Is there a mark?" came Donovan's voice. "A cross, on the door?"

I ran my hands up the bars, but they were clean.

"Nothing," I whispered. Donovan sighed loudly, muttering thanks to something or someone.

"Get your ass back in bed, Sawyer," he went on. "You were lucky, but don't push it. It ain't over yet."

I stared down at Monty's cell. The gas mask hadn't budged since it had marked the door.

"What are they doing?" I asked again. "They're not moving."

There was another scream from above, and this time all of the gas masks echoed it. Seconds later the siren blasted out again and I saw more shapes emerge from the vault door below. There were seven blacksuits in total, two of whom held a mutant dog on a leash, struggling to control the animal as it thrashed against its restraints.

Darkness again, and howling. The sound of footsteps against stone, then metal. A fresh round of screams from the gas masks and the same endless cry of "no" from the cell below me.

When the lights came back on I saw that the guards had split up, and were making their way to the marked cells. I crouched down as low as I could get and followed the blacksuit heading toward Monty. When he reached the door he called out for it to be opened. He was almost twice as tall as the shriveled figure beside him, but he eyed the wheezer warily as he waited for the door to slide open, never getting too close.

Monty was still curled up tight inside the cell, but I had never seen anybody look more exposed. The blacksuit reached in and grabbed the boy by his elbow, dragging him onto the platform as if he weighed no more than a sack of feathers. As soon as he was out under the red light Monty uncurled himself, flailing against the guard's iron grip. But the giant simply grabbed him by both wrists in a single mammoth hand and hoisted him into the air.

The gas mask screamed as if in delight. Then it snatched one of the syringes from its belt and thrust it at Monty like a knife. Right then I was grateful that the lights failed. But against the black canvas of darkness my imagination projected its own hor-rific conclusion to the story—the needle plunging into Monty's arm or neck, filling him full of rot and decay, of dirty chemicals, contaminated blood.

The prison was illuminated once more—just long enough for me to see the blacksuit dragging Monty's limp body toward the stairs, the gas mask right behind watching its prey like a hyena eyeing a corpse, the cell door sliding shut. On the yard below, the other blacksuits were slowly progressing toward the vault door— a sick procession of giants, freaks, and lost boys being dragged to a fate I couldn't even begin to imagine.

Then the prison went dark again, although from the pound-ing in my chest, the ringing in my ears, and the rush of air as I collapsed to the floor I knew that this time it had nothing to do with the lights.

AFTERMATH

I WOKE WHERE I'D FALLEN, bowed up like a baby on the hard stone beneath my bed. Opening my eyes, I saw Donovan on the toilet, but there were no jokes this time. He looked at me like I was something nasty he'd just expelled, then turned his attention to the toilet paper.

I hauled myself onto my bunk, my aching limbs protesting about a night spent on the freezing floor. My head was full of the horrors I'd seen during the blood watch, but due to an endless series of nightmares afterward I wasn't sure which of the images were real and which imagined. The wheezers with their dirty coats and filthy needles and gas masks sewn into their faces seemed like something only possible in a twisted dream, but the memory of them was so sharp that I knew they'd really been out there.

With a painful churning in my gut I suddenly remembered Monty, strung up and stabbed with that filthy syringe. Where was he now? What were they doing to him? I put the questions to Donovan, but he simply fixed me with that look of fury again and I quickly shut up.

A couple of sirens later and we all drifted down to the yard. I had never seen so many dark, tired eyes and drawn faces, so many nervous twitches and tear-stained cheeks. That morning, for once, everybody in Furnace looked their age. All the hard stares and swaggers had been replaced by frightened expressions and anxious shuffles as the children huddled in groups for comfort.

Donovan still wasn't talking to me, so I scanned the crowd for Zee. He was standing in a group that included his cellmate and a few others, but it took me a while to recognize him. The cocky smile had gone and his face had drawn in on itself, as if he'd lost half his body weight overnight. He saw me looking and walked over, meeting me halfway across the yard. We both opened our mouths to speak, but neither of us seemed to remember how to have a normal conversation.

The duty roster materialized on-screen, putting me and Donovan back in the kitchen but sending Zee to the laundry. I waited for Monty's name to appear but it had been stripped from the records as if the boy had never existed.

Hard labor was hell that morning. Donovan acted like he couldn't stand the sight of me, posting himself in the canteen serving up mush and leaving the processing to me and another couple of inmates I'd never really spoken to before. I tried asking them questions about the wheezers as we stuffed crate after crate of leftovers into the industrial blender, but they just sent back one-word answers that meant nothing.

To make things worse, Kevin Arnold had been assigned to the trough room too, and several times throughout the morning I was ambushed by flying chunks of rancid meat and mushy vegetables and barbed comments. I remembered the way he'd pushed Monty across the cell last night, sending him to his terrifying fate without a shred of remorse. I wanted to stuff his mouth full of rotten food until he choked, but instead I turned my back on him and suffered his abuse. What else could I do?

Umpteen hours later, after washing the slop from my hair in the showers and donning a fresh uniform, I found myself standing alone in the yard. I didn't realize how much I had come to depend on Donovan. Without him by my side I felt completely lost, utterly vulnerable. I saw him make his way up the stairs to our cell without a backward glance but I didn't try to chase him. Instead I picked an empty table toward the back of the yard and cursed myself for not just curling up in bed last night and ignoring the blood watch like everybody else.

Holding my head in my hands, I didn't hear Zee slide onto the bench opposite me until he coughed gently.

"You look like battered crap," he said as I lifted my head.

"You're no oil painting yourself, mate," I replied, wondering if I still had the ability to smile.

"Where's Big D?" he went on. "You two are like Siamese twins, weird not seeing you joined at the hip."

"I'm not in his good books," I replied after a humorless snort. "After last night. I wouldn't stay in bed, had to see what was going on. He thinks I drew one of them to our cell."

"Seriously?" Zee asked, eyebrows practically leaping from his forehead. "You saw one up close?"

I nodded, trying not to recall the experience in too much detail.

"He'll be okay," Zee went on, cracking his knuckles. "He can be a moody lug, but I'm sure he'll come around."

"I hope so. If he doesn't then I'm a dead man. He's pretty much the only thing standing between me and the Skulls."

"Don't forget me," Zee said with a grin. He flexed his arms, but the satsuma-sized bumps beneath his uniform didn't exactly fill me with confidence. "Could take them all on single-handed with these muscles."

For a moment it looked like we might break free of the gravity of the situation, but it quickly pulled us back in.

"What the hell were they doing last night?" Zee asked, leaning across the table so that his low voice would reach me. "What are those things with the gas masks?" I shrugged and shook my head. "I mean, they look like Nazi storm troopers with those masks and coats. I've seen them on TV. My folks used to watch war documentaries all the time. But why would they be here? And why do they need help breathing? I mean, it's not like this place is full of Zyklon B."

"They're attached to their faces," I told him. "The masks. I saw it last night. The metal is sewn into their skin."

Zee looked like he was about to hurl.

"No way," was all he managed, but I could tell he believed me.

"Whatever they're doing, it's bad," I said. "Donovan told me they took prisoners to a fate worse than death."

"Maybe they're using us as human guinea pigs," Zee suggested. I laughed at the idea but he was serious. "During the Second World War the Nazis and the Japanese army used to perform all these sick experiments on innocent people, civilians and prisoners of war and stuff. They'd cut them up while they were still alive, infect them with all these diseases, biological weapons and gas, blow them up—"

"Come on," I interrupted, but he held up his hand.

"No, seriously. They used prisoners as test subjects. They'd just think of things they could do to them and then they'd do them. They claimed it was all about science, but they were just butchers. I saw this on TV too, but Dad made me go to bed halfway through because it was too gross."

"But we're not in a war, Zee. I mean, this is one of the most advanced countries in the Western world; you can't even call somebody a pensioner now without it being politically incorrect. They're not just going to let somebody open a prison where a bunch of sick freaks do experiments on kids."

"What about a prison where mutant dogs chew up the inmates?" he asked. I didn't have an answer. "Everything changed that summer, Alex, all those gangs on the rampage and all those people who died. People got scared of kids, that's why they got away with building a prison like this, that's why those freaks can take us and butcher us and nobody gives a crap. Did you see who they took, anyway?"

"Monty," I replied. "They took Monty. I didn't see the others."

Zee swore beneath his breath and stared out across the yard. I thought I saw his eyes filling up for a minute but then he wiped his hand across his face and was back to normal.

"Do you think anyone on the outside has any idea?" he asked.

"I don't think anyone on the outside cares. We did the crime, we're doing the time. In their eyes we're just as bad as the kids who went around killing everyone. What was it that blacksuit said? As far as the outside world is concerned, we're already dead."

Somebody in the yard shouted and I looked over to see two inmates pushing each other, faces red and angry. But it died out after a couple of shoves, one of the boys walking away with his hands held up in submission.

"I'm not going to just wait here until I get taken, Zee," I said. "I can't just lie down and let them come for me, let them jab me with their filthy needles and haul me off to some butcher shop."

"Alex, what choice do you have? Throw yourself off the eighth floor? That's about the only way out I can think of, and it isn't pretty."

"I'm just not ready to give up, that's all I'm saying. There's always a way."

"There's a mile of rock in every direction, and those dogs will chew you up if you even piss the wrong way."

I slammed my fist down on the table in frustration.

"Didn't you tell me on the first day that you were getting out of here no matter what?" I asked, ignoring his guilty shrug.

"That was back when I had a little hope," he muttered.

"Well, don't lose it just yet," I said, leaning over the table and once again thinking of mountains, of fresh air. "I'm telling you, there's a way out."

ALL GOOD PRISON breaks need a plan. I'd seen them in films so many times—learning the guard rotation, bribing somebody for blueprints of the sewer system, getting your girlfriend to smuggle in a file so you can get through the bars of your window. One good plan, perfectly executed, that's all it would take to get us out of here.

But I had nothing. There was no guard rotation here, the monsters in their pinstriped suits seemed to patrol when and where they liked. The sewer system just led farther down toward the abyss, dumping its filth in the center of the earth. And even if I'd had a girlfriend, which I didn't and probably never would, we weren't allowed personal visits or letters. Hell, we didn't even have windows. None of the things I'd seen on-screen were going to work in Furnace, but that shouldn't really have been a surprise. I mean, television isn't real life.

On the plus side, my short career as a criminal had programmed my mind to find escape routes wherever I could. From the second I arrived at a target house I'd be scoping out emergency exits just in case I was found out. Which door would offer the quickest getaway, which second-floor window was a leap away from a tree branch or drainpipe, which bush in the garden would offer the darkest, safest hiding place if everything went wrong.

Inside, my mind worked in the same way. I'd take a mental snapshot of the house I was in, the layout, the location of furniture, how many locks were on the door. That way, even if the lights went out I'd know where to run to avoid tripping or crashing into a wall. There's no greater shame for a burglar than cracking your shins on a coffee table or doing cartwheels over a footstool that you'd forgotten was there.

The times I'd almost been caught, and there had been a handful, I'd only escaped because my brain had programmed in its routes and guided me to safety without me having to think about it.

It was like being on autopilot—the adrenaline would kick in and I'd fly along the safest possible route until I was outside. I could almost see the thread of silver light leading me to safety, a trail that I had to follow or my life would be over, a trail that led from the unbearable confines of an unwelcoming house to the utter relief of fresh air.

When I'd first arrived in Furnace the escape artist in my mind had set to work right away, taking a snapshot of every room in the prison, poking and probing everything I knew about the place in search of the path of least resistance, the best possible way of escape. It had drawn a blank every time—except one. Just once I'd imagined that silver thread, one occasion when I'd sensed fresh air and freedom beyond Furnace's impenetrable walls.

Room Two.

Zee wouldn't stop talking as soon as I mentioned a way out. He practically leaped over the table, grabbing me by my collar, his eyes wide with desperation. I clamped a hand over his squawking mouth before the entire prison heard him, then we walked to the most isolated part of the yard we could find and I told him what I was thinking.

"You hear anything more about the cave-in?" I asked, speaking as quietly as I could. There was nobody nearby, but in a place like this you never knew if the walls had ears.

"Just that it happened a couple of months ago," he whispered back. "I heard some kid talking about it in the laundry. Roof came down, killed thirty guys and sent a load more through the vault door, to the infirmary. They haven't come back, though."

I nodded. Donovan had told me the same. It had been the worst disaster in Furnace, apparently, but the blacksuits just acted like it never happened. The room was sealed and anyone caught talking about it got a day in the hole.

"Didn't you notice the smell when we were standing outside the room the other day?" I went on. He shook his head, confused. "Not so much a smell, just a sensation. Something different, like a breath of fresh air."

"It smelled less like sweaty teenage boys, I guess," was all he could manage. "Why, is that your way out?"

I didn't say anything, and he raised an eyebrow.

"Come on, Alex, think about it. For starters, we're who knows how far underground. Even the biggest cave-in in history won't have opened up a path to the surface. You'd need an earthquake measuring like a million on the Richter scale. It just isn't going to happen."

I opened my mouth to argue but it was no good, Zee was on a roll.

"Two: you think that if by some freak of nature and blessing of God a giant crack in the rock opened up to lead us to salvation, that the guards in here would let us hammer away with picks in the very next room? I mean, there isn't even a proper door on Room Two, just a few planks of wood. That's kind of like tempting fate if you run a prison, don't you think?"

I chewed my lip, my brow furrowed. Zee had caught me off guard. He was right, of course. What was I expecting? A miracle exit that nobody had spotted yet? But my mind kept circling back to the silver thread.

"I don't know what's in there, Zee," I replied, casting my eyes across the vast yard to the crack that led to the chipping rooms, guarded as always by an armed blacksuit. "I just know we need to find out."

NEW FISH

MY HEAD WAS BUZZING with possibility as we made our way back across the yard, but Zee was doing his best to undermine my escape fantasies.

"What next?" he asked, grinning. "The hand of God poking through the ceiling and offering us a lift to the surface?"

"Zee," I said, trying to ignore him.

"No, a magical escalator that the guards use to nip up and get their shopping. It probably leads to the local supermarket. We could just hop on and get some dinner for the walk home."

"That's not funny."

"A transporter!" he cried out, then: "Beam me up, Scottie."

"Give it a rest!"

"I know, why don't we just find one of Leonardo da Vinci's flying machines and soar up the ventilation pipes?"

"What?" I asked, turning around and raising my arms. "I have no idea what you're talking about."

"I'm just trying to show you how ridiculous the thought of escape is," he said, quietly this time. "I mean, you stand a better chance just running into the elevator as the doors are closing and hoping that nobody sees you."

I grimaced. That idea had occurred to me too. I was about to reply when, as if on cue, a gentle rumble came from above us, like distant thunder. The shouting and laughing and chatter in the yard instantly died away as the noise increased in volume, making the ground shake and dropping clouds of dust from the ceiling far above. The elevator was on its way down.

"Well, now's your chance," said Zee, walking toward the yellow circle in the center of the yard. I followed him, keeping my eye on the elevator doors as the lift lowered to our level. We'd seen it drop a couple of times now, twice with black-suits wheeling in massive trolleys of supplies and once with five ordinary Doberman dogs that were dragged squealing through the vault door. Other than that the elevator had remained sealed.

When it seemed it would never reach its destination there was a crunch and the rumbling stopped. Half a minute later the huge doors grated open revealing three kids almost lost in the enormous interior. They hesitated when they saw the hundreds of unfriendly eyes glaring at them from the guts of Furnace, and one of them started crying. I couldn't hear him from this distance, but the way his shoulders shook was unmistakable.

"More new fish!" came a shout from the crowd that was gathering in the yellow circle, followed by a series of whoops and whistles. I noticed the Skulls making their way toward the elevator door, one pulling a nasty black shank from the inside of his overalls.

"Looks like they're getting the same warm welcome we did," said Zee, thrusting his hands in his pockets and shuffling uncomfortably on the stone. "Poor bastards."

One of the new arrivals walked calmly from the elevator. He

was tall and well built, and the way he stood in front of Kevin and his posse made it clear he was no stranger to a fight or two. The Skulls stared him down for a few seconds then dismissed him, spreading out in front of the lift door to pick on the easier targets inside.

"Come on, you chickens," screamed Kevin at the top of his voice. "Get out here and get on your knees. I'm your boss now."

Two of the Skulls leaped into the lift and grabbed the inmates, pulling them out and throwing them to the stone. One rolled and tried to get back to his feet before getting a kick to the chest that sent him sprawling. The other, who had been crying, just lay there and howled. The Skulls laughed and imitated the sound. I felt my entire body burning with the desire to help, my muscles so tense that I thought they were going to snap. But what could I do? Charge in like an idiot again and risk someone else getting chewed to pieces?

Fortunately the horrible scene was cut short by the siren, which sounded for a good few seconds while everybody crowded into the yellow circle in the yard. Kevin saw me scowling at him and rubbed his eyes as if he was pretending to cry. Then he ran a hand across his throat and pointed to me before turning his attention back to the elevator. The two boys who had been dragged out were getting to their feet, the weeping lad being helped up by the other. Their faces were creased in agony and fear, and I shuddered, knowing that's what we must have looked like when we arrived.

With a hiss and a roar the vault door swung open to reveal the same horrendous group that had welcomed us a week ago. They prowled into the yard all growls and wheezes and muffled screams, and even though they were some distance away every single inmate in the prison shuffled backward.

Once again I found that I couldn't focus on the warden, my eyes slipping off him each time like two opposing magnets held next to one another. Frustrated, I turned my attention to the gas masks, who shuddered and shook like rag dolls as the warden introduced the three boys to Furnace. It was impossible to tell if the wheezers were feeling any emotion because their faces were covered with metal and scars, but I thought I could make out a gleam of excitement in their piggy eyes as they studied the fresh pickings before them.

"Maybe one of the new fish is a tunneling expert," Zee whispered to me as the warden gave his speech about rules. "That tall one looks like he might have already escaped from a couple of prisons."

I laughed inside, not wanting to draw any attention from the freaks as the warden read out a series of names and numbers. The tall kid was Gary Owens, the weeping one was Ashley Garrett, and I had to choke back a sob as the name of the third kid was read out—Toby Merchant. I didn't know him, but the name Toby was almost too much to bear. I was assaulted by the memory of my best friend lying on the carpet, his head blossoming, the same shade of red as a valentine rose. It could have so easily been him here, and me decomposing in a quiet graveyard. I guess we were both dead and underground.

One by one the boys drifted off with their cellmates, and as the warden and his ghastly crew vanished behind the massive door, the shouts of "new fish" and "fresh meat" rose up again from the crowd, serenading the terrified inmates to their new home. It was terrible seeing even more new faces shoveled into Furnace, more fuel for the horrors to devour in the dead of night, more innocent victims, no doubt, forced into their rawest nightmares.

The siren blew, letting the crowd disperse, and my attention returned to thoughts of escape. I jogged up the stairs toward my cell, Zee hot on my tail and still bombarding me with crazy ideas—including stuffing my sheet into my uniform and pretending to be one of the muscular blacksuits. I ignored him as I made my way down the platform, entering to see Donovan sitting on his bunk idly picking his nose. He looked at me distastefully, then flicked something in my direction.

"Haven't you got better things to be doing, Sawyer," he said with a sneer, "like trying to get us all killed? Why don't you start another fight? This time you might get lucky and bring the dogs *and* the wheezers up here."

I walked up to the bed and leaned against the wall, running a hand through my hair and sighing loudly.

"I couldn't just lie there not knowing what was going on," I said eventually. It was a lame excuse for something that could have got us both dragged away, but at least it was the truth. "Besides, you saw that thing. It wasn't interested in us. It knew exactly where it was going."

"You wouldn't be so damn cocky now if it had marked the door," Donovan spat back. "You'd be strung up somewhere beneath Furnace having your skin ripped off or your eyes skewered or something."

I felt my stomach turn and did my best to ignore his remarks. Donovan wiped a hand beneath his nose and sniffed loudly, looking me in the eye as if waiting for something.

"Okay, I'm sorry," I said quietly. "I really am. Come on, I've hardly been here any time, I didn't know how serious it all was." Donovan nodded gently but his eyes never left mine. "I just . . ." I paused, not quite sure what I was saying. "I just want to be doing something, something to help get us out of here. I don't want to be curled up and cowering in the dark when those things come for me. Okay?"

"What else is there to do?" was his emotionless reply.

"He thinks we can make a break for it," said Zee, smiling at Donovan as if he was talking about a silly child. "He thinks there's a way out."

"Oh yeah, there are plenty of ways," Donovan said, rummaging under his mattress and pulling out a small wooden shank. I was surprised to see it, but I guess everybody in Furnace needs some way of protecting themselves. He started scratching the rock wall, the homemade blade not even leaving a mark. "Just pick a spot and start digging. If nobody catches you, I reckon you could make it out in, say, a thousand years."

He tossed the shank back onto his bed then leaped nimbly onto the floor, barging past me and standing at the bars of the cell, looking down into the yard. I sat down on the bottom bunk and tried to ignore my frustration. In the relative silence I heard the sound of screaming from nearby but I tuned it out.

"Tell me what you know about the cave-in," I asked after a while. "In Room Two."

Donovan snorted.

"That was my reaction too," Zee said, sniggering. I wanted to leap up and slap him but I managed to control my temper and settled for a mean glare. He mouthed the word "sorry" and let me carry on.

"Something happened in there," I went on. "Those kids hit a fault line or something. I could smell it, Donovan, I could smell the fresh air."

"It was your imagination, you chump," he replied, resting his head against the bars. "Maybe someone let rip when you were standing next to them and you felt the draft."

"You were there too, the other day. Didn't you sense something? Anything?"

"Yeah, I sense it every time I walk into a room in here. I hope and pray that there might just be a hole in the rock and we can all make a run for it. Sometimes I hope so much that I can see the way out, I can smell the rain, I can hear the birds. But I can't, it's just an illusion. They say that hope can set you free, and I guess that's what it is. A tiny glimpse of freedom to keep us sane, if you follow me."

"It wasn't an illusion," I snapped. "I'm telling you, it was real. I didn't make it up."

I thought back, remembering the sensation of being outside, of mountains and wind and endless views. Maybe it had just been an illusion, my brain's way of coping with the thought of never going aboveground again. I guess it made sense. I mean, I knew that Furnace could do funny things to your mind. But something deep inside me wouldn't let it rest, was screaming at me not to give up. I knew that inner voice well, the instincts that I had followed all the time when I was robbing houses.

"Fine, maybe it was just my imagination," I said. "But what if it wasn't? What if there is a way out? Isn't it worth a look?"

"Feel free," muttered Donovan. "I'm not stopping you."

"But we need your help, D," I added. "We can't do this alone."

"You mean *you* can't do this alone," Zee said, looking at me with a concerned expression. "Less of this *we* business, please."

I looked at Donovan for a response but he had straightened up and was staring down into the yard with an expression of disbelief.

"No way," he said with a laugh. "No way is he taking on the Skulls."

I jumped off the bed and ran through the cell door to the platform. Six floors beneath me I made out a small circle of people, each wearing painted bandannas and unsettled expressions. In the middle of the circle, prowling around like a caged tiger, was the tall, calm new boy, Gary Owens. Donovan and Zee rushed to my side and watched as Gary raised his hands, inviting the Skulls to throw a punch. Some had pulled shanks from inside their overalls but nobody was making the first move.

"He is either the bravest kid or the biggest idiot on the planet," said Donovan, his tone almost respectful. I'm not sure why but I suddenly felt a surge of jealousy that my cellmate was so impressed with him.

"Idiot, I'd say," I muttered. "He's going to die down there."

I saw Kevin walking up to Gary. The new kid was almost a head taller than the leader of the Skulls but Kevin didn't seem to care. His face was red, his expression apoplectic—all bulging eyes and foaming mouth. He grabbed Gary by the collar and started screaming at him. The acoustics in the prison weren't great, but from up here we got the gist, just like everybody else in Furnace who had stopped what they were doing to see what was going on.

"Think you can march in here and take over?" Kevin

screamed, along with a few choice expletives. He was shaking
Gary, but the big boy wasn't folding. He was studying Kevin with
a look of cold detachment, a look that reminded me of a spider's
emotionless glare right before it bites into its prey. "Gonna kill
you, new fish. Gonna skewer you."

He pushed Gary back and a number of Skulls grabbed his
overalls, holding him in place. A length of gleaming silver had
appeared in Kevin's hand, and he waved it menacingly in front of
Gary's face.

"Even the tough kids learn the rules pretty quickly in here,"
Donovan said.

I wasn't so sure. With a twist of his body Gary sent one of
the Skulls holding him skittering across the stone floor, then
smashed his free fist into the face of his other captor. The boy's
legs buckled with the impact and he fell to the floor, his landing
spot already marked out by the blood gushing from his nose.

Kevin screeched like a wild animal and backed away, motioning for his henchmen to attack. But nobody moved. They weren't
Mafia enforcers, they were kids. Gary strode forward and
grabbed Kevin's arm, bending it in such a way that the shank fell
from his grip. The Skull was yelling in pain, his fury replaced by
fear.

"Kill him!" Kevin yelled to dead ears. "Cut his heart out."

"This is great," said Donovan. "Kevin's been asking for it ever
since he arrived. About time he got some himself. Hope the new
kid roughs him up a bit."

Gary kept twisting Kevin's arm, using both hands to bend
back the wrist to an impossible angle until, in horrible unison, a
crack and a scream echoed across the yard. The prison had been
plunged into silence, everybody watching as Kevin dropped to

his knees clutching his broken arm, tears streaming down his face. Gary placed a foot on Kevin's shoulder and sent him sprawling, and at once a huge cheer broke out from the inmates.

"This is great!" Donovan repeated with more enthusiasm. "How the mighty have fallen, eh?"

"You think this means we'll be free of the Skulls?" Zee asked.

"Reckon so," Donovan replied. "Maybe he'll take out the Fifty-niners too."

Gary bent down and snatched the bandanna from Kevin's head and the shank from the floor. He held them up in the air for us all to see, like trophies. Some of the other kids had gone right up to the boy, circling him as if he'd just scored the winning goal in a soccer match. One inmate had even put his arm around him and was jumping up and down.

"Wanna go join the celebrations?" Zee asked. But I stayed where I was. Something wasn't right. Gary wasn't smiling, he didn't look like somebody who had come to save us. He eyed the crowd around him with the same dead gaze that he had given the Skulls. Then, with a flash of silver and an arc of crimson, the boy who had been holding him staggered across the yard, looking at the wound on his arm with disbelief. The inmates turned their shocked expressions toward Gary as if there had been some mistake, but the new kid slashed out again, catching another victim in the chest.

For a moment the yard was chaos as the prisoners climbed over one another to get to safety. In the center of the maelstrom Gary tucked the stained shank into his overalls and pulled the Skull bandanna over his head. I felt my heart sinking. He wasn't a savior, he was a psychopath.

The siren blasted out across the yard, a fitting funeral dirge

for the boys who lay squirming in their crimson coffins. Donovan pushed himself off the railings.

"Like I said, Alex," he said as he watched the injured kids fold
into themselves, all sobs and snot. "It's the only thing we can do,
curl up and cower and wait for death."

ROOM TWO

THE THOUGHT OF FACING another evening locked down in our cells was almost unbearable, but a small part of me was relieved that there was a set of thick metal bars between us and Gary Owens.

As soon as the siren blew, the blacksuits had come running, one knocking down Gary with the butt of his shotgun and the rest hauling him and his victims through the vault door. After a couple of hours of restless pacing, I saw the massive portal swing open again and a couple of guards escort Gary, bruised and bloody, to his cell—which fortunately was on the second level, a long drop from mine.

Some time later Kevin was dragged back out into the yard, his arm in a rough cast that was the same shade of pale gray as his face. As soon as he emerged, Furnace's long-suffering inmates began whistling and whooping through their cell doors, calling out insults with a vicious ferocity fueled by years of abuse. Kevin made no effort to reclaim his air of menace—he let himself be dragged up the steps, never taking his wide eyes off the floor. Looking back, I almost felt sorry for him. Little did I know then that he had far worse coming to him than a few jeers.

When all fell quiet in the yard, I tried again to get Donovan interested in escape. It was like trying to get a hippopotamus interested in ballet.

"There's nowhere to go," he said for the umpteenth time.

"There must be, there's no such thing as a prison with no way out."

"Furnace is a prison with no way out, you plank."

"I can find a way, I know it."

"There's nowhere to go."

Around and around and around in circles. Shortly before lights-out he sat bolt upright in his bunk as if he meant to strangle me, his expression so incensed that it was scary.

"What?" I asked, backing off toward the bars just in case he'd finally lost it.

"Why are you so desperate to die?" was his reply. I tried to argue but he cut me off. "There's only ever been one escape attempt in Furnace, a couple of years ago. Was a kid a little like you, only cleverer, smarter. He spent months learning the way the prison worked, especially the elevator, you know. Nobody knows how he managed it, but somehow during a lockdown he got himself inside the air vents. He stayed in there for five days while the guards and the dogs hunted him down, then when they brought in more blacksuits from the surface he found his way onto the roof of the elevator and hitched a ride up."

"He made it?" I asked, my heart pounding at the very thought of somebody getting out. Donovan smiled wickedly and shook his head.

"Oh no. They found him. They caught him climbing into the vents of the Black Fort on the surface. He was so hungry and thirsty he'd gone delirious, was singing to himself. Guess what happened to him."

"The hole," I said, sighing.

"He wasn't that lucky. The warden, damn his soul, he brought that kid back down to the yard and tied him up good. Then he let three of his dogs loose." Donovan faltered, his mind somewhere terrible. "They treated him like a toy, tossing him back and forth like some teddy bear until he was limp and broken. Then they ate him."

"You're kidding," I said, certain that he was making the story up to scare me.

"Ask anyone who's been here longer than two years. They never talk about it but they all remember it. Scott was his name, Scott White. You wanna end up the same way as him, then you carry on talking about escape, kid. But don't say I didn't warn you."

"So the air vents," I went on, trying to forget everything I'd just heard. "They're still there, right?"

Donovan collapsed down on his bunk with a cry of frustration.

"Warden sealed them off the week after White was killed, replaced the tunnels with pipes so narrow you couldn't fit your hand inside. Why do you think the air is so thin down here? We're all suffocating 'cause of the last idiot to think of freedom."

He said something else but it was lost beneath the siren. With a snap the lights cut off, and I felt my way across the tiny cell to my bunk. Stripping to my underwear, I crawled under the rough sheet and tried to ignore the brutal images that paraded past my

open, sightless eyes. A kid like me, being chewed and dismem-
bered by beasts with bloody breath while the whole of Furnace looked on. It was almost enough to make me forget about
escape, to resign myself to a lifetime behind bars.

Almost. Surely doing nothing was the worst kind of death
imaginable—endless days rotting in the guts of the earth, dying
piece by piece by piece. As sleep blotted Scott White's violent
end from my mind, I resolved to find out what lay in Room Two,
even if it cost me my life.

As IT TURNED OUT, I didn't have too long to wait. The next
morning's work chart put Donovan and me back on chipping
duty, giving me the perfect opportunity to scope out the abandoned cave. After a hearty bowl of gunk we walked across the
yard toward the crack in the wall, Donovan giving me concerned
sideways glances practically every other step.

"I don't like that look you've got," he said as we reached the
entrance to the chipping rooms. There was a blacksuit on duty,
as always, his shotgun locked, loaded, and aimed directly at our
heads as we filed past. Donovan waited until we were out of
earshot before continuing. "Don't do anything stupid, okay?"

"As if I would," I replied, beaming at him with a kind of wild-
eyed insanity. He looked at me, openmouthed, then shook his
head and started selecting his equipment. I did the same, lifting
a pick from the racks and slapping a hard hat onto my head.
Switching on the lamp and pulling down the visor, I snatched a
look across the hall at the entrance to Room Two. It was sealed
up with thick planks, but they were just wood. I gripped the
pick, wondering how quickly I could hack my way inside.

"Levels one to three, Room One," bellowed the blacksuit,

pointing his shotgun at the black hole on the other side of the room. "Rest of you get into Room Three, now."

We shuffled forward with the same lack of enthusiasm we always did, and I let myself drift to the back of the crowd. The blacksuit was watching us go, his silver eyes never blinking, but I knew from experience that he wouldn't stand there all morning. Sooner or later he'd start patrolling the workrooms, and that was when I was going in.

Once we'd passed through the cracked portal into Room Three, I stationed myself as close to the door as possible. At this angle I could see back into the equipment room, where the long shadow of the guard sat heavy and motionless across the rock. After refusing once again to help me out, even by providing a distraction, Donovan swaggered over to the far end of the room and began hammering the rock. I added the sound of my pick to the familiar percussion, but there was no strength to my swings. I was saving my energy for when it counted most.

The snakelike shadow didn't budge for the better part of an hour, by which time my brow was dripping and my overalls were drenched despite my lack of effort. The adrenaline shot that rocked my body when I saw the guard move almost made my legs buckle, but I embraced the boost. I checked the room to make sure nobody was watching, then edged my way toward the door.

I could hear the blacksuit's footsteps growing fainter as he strode into the first chipping hall, but even when the sound had stopped it took me a good few minutes to build up the nerve to peek around the corner. With a shuddering sigh I saw the equipment room was empty, and I dashed across the stone floor to the wooden boards that sealed off Room Two.

There were eight long planks in all, each fixed to the wall like a ladder. They didn't do a great job of concealing what lay beyond. Through the gaps I could see a tunnel stretching out into blackness, and my heart soared as once again I sensed the wind blowing through the cracks, the fresh air making me euphoric after the long days spent in Furnace's stale passages.

I breathed deeply, feeling like the sensation could lift me off the ground. Then I remembered what I was doing. I checked the entrance to the first room, but there was no sign of the blacksuit returning. I jammed the head of the pick behind the plank closest to the ground then leaned on the handle, using it as a lever. The bolts securing the plank to the stone didn't budge.

Cursing, I tried the next board up, but it was equally stubborn. Taking another look in the direction the guard had walked, I steeled myself and swung my pick at the wall. The sharp edge struck the bottom set of bolts, sending a shower of sparks flying out into the room. Under normal circumstances, the noise would have been deafening, but it was easily lost against the backdrop of a hundred pickaxes hammering against stone.

I lifted the pick a second time and swung with every ounce of strength, gouging a hole in the rock where the bolt was secured. Wedging my tool back into the gap between the board and the floor, I pushed down again. This time, the bolt held on with a little less conviction, then gave up and pinged out across the room, leaving one end of the plank flapping against the wall. I pulled hard, creating a gap that looked big enough for me to crawl through.

Ramming my pick into the nearest tool rack and slinging my helmet across the floor, I got down on my hands and knees and pushed my face into the hole. A blast of cool air slapped me, giving me strength, and I squeezed my left shoulder through the gap, ignoring the sting of sharp rock slicing into my skin.

It was as I was pushing my other shoulder through that I heard the sound of footsteps, each louder than the last. I froze, peering through the gap to the entrance of Room One and knowing that the blacksuit was returning. I had seconds, at most. Push in, or pull out. I should have listened to my instincts, wrenched myself out of the hole, and run back to work.

But I didn't.

I forced my body forward, gritting my teeth with the pain. The steps were getting louder, crunching against loose pieces of stone on the floor. My sleeve caught on the plank, hooking me in place, and I desperately tried to wrench it free.

Crunch. Crunch. Crunch. No time.

With a rip my sleeve came free and I tumbled forward. I pulled my feet in with the speed of a rabbit disappearing into a burrow, the board snapping back against the wall just as the black shadow swept across the room.

The steps halted, and despite the endless hammering from the rooms next door it felt like I'd been plunged into a pool of silence. As gently as I could, I rolled onto my back then stood up, staring through the gaps in the makeshift door to see the blacksuit standing in the center of the equipment room. His head was cocked as if he was listening out for something, but he wasn't looking in my direction.

We remained like that for what seemed like an eternity, mirror images of each other's stillness. Finally, the guard straightened himself and paced toward the entrance to Room Three, eventually disappearing from sight. I breathed out as slowly and quietly as I could, then turned to see if this was truly my road to salvation.

It was then I realized my mistake. The tunnel that led into Room Two was darker than Furnace at night. I had absolutely no way of seeing where I was going.

I stood like an idiot for a couple of minutes, wondering what I'd expected—lights along the walls and a red carpet? I cursed silently again, wishing I still had my helmet with its lamp, then began edging my way forward. The lights from the equipment room sliced through the wooden planks to form faint stripes on the uneven floor, but the glow was powerless against the black heart of Furnace and by the time I'd taken a few steps I was smothered by cold, dead night.

I took comfort in the fact that there had been no cry of alarm from the blacksuit in the chamber next door, no blast of the siren. With tiny steps I pushed onward, running my hand along the wall for guidance. Every now and again I'd trip, but I managed to stay upright.

Eventually the wall arced away to my left, and from the slight change in echo I knew I'd entered the cavern. There was still no light, but the air here was definitely fresher, cooler. I felt certain that it wasn't my imagination. There was something down here, some chink in Furnace's armor. I just had to get back in with a light and I'd know for sure whether that chink was our way out.

That was when I heard it. It started so quietly that I barely even noticed it, then it began to grow in volume—a low hum, like a cell phone vibrating in somebody's coat pocket. I felt my skin break out in goose bumps. I wasn't alone. There was something in here with me.

The sound shifted in pitch, fading then reasserting itself. I couldn't work out what it was but it chilled me to the bone. I thought about the thirty kids who'd died in here when the cave collapsed—thirty angry spirits charging back and forth across the deserted cavern for all time looking for somebody to take their anger out on. Maybe the hum was their collective screams, so loud and furious that it breached their ghostly plane and entered ours.

I took a step back and the noise changed again, growing louder. It toyed with my hearing, playing tricks on my tortured imagination. I couldn't tell whether it was far away or close. If distant, the noise could have been a roar. But it also could have been a whisper in my ear from something right next to me. No, not a whisper—a growl.

I suddenly panicked. The noise grew louder, a guttural snarl that could only have come from one creature. It was a dog, one of the warden's monstrosities. He'd obviously put one in here to devour anyone stupid enough to try to escape.

Blind and terrified, I swung around and ran. But I'd lost track of where I was, and with a crunch I slammed into the rock wall. Something hot dripped into my mouth, choking me, and I spat out my own blood, gripping the rough stone for support.

The growling was getting closer, and I saw the darkness begin to take shape, morphing into a nightmare creature that bounded toward me. I felt so sick that I thought my stomach was going to flip inside out, and I held up my hand to ward off the monster. But as soon as I did, the illusion vanished back into the night.

I blinked hard, my throat slick with blood and bile. The wall had to lead back to the equipment room so, doing my best to ignore the persistent growl, I fumbled my way along it, expecting to feel daggerlike teeth sinking into my shoulder at any minute.

But nothing came for me. Each time I looked back and thought I saw the beast in the blackness, it vanished with a blink of the eye, a hallucination brought on by fear and fatigue.

I rounded the corner of the corridor and found myself staring at the boarded door, light squeezing through the cracks like golden fingers trying to embrace me. I took one last look into the cave, then crawled through the bottom board, staggering back into the equipment room.

Too late I realized I should have checked the room first. I heard feet pounding on rock and swiveled around in time to see a massive black shape swoop toward me. The blacksuit had just emerged from Room Three, and like a speeding train he rammed into me, wrapping his hamlike fist around my throat and lifting me off the floor.

"Better have a good explanation for this, Sawyer," he hissed. I saw the mole, knew it was the same giant who always seemed to terrorize me. His fingers were like iron, squeezing my windpipe and refusing to let me draw a breath, let alone reply. I felt my vision cloud as I stared into the twin silver portals of the freak's eyes. In them I caught a glimpse of my own reflection—the bottom half of my face smeared with the blood that still gushed from my nose, my eyes the very essence of terror. Seeing what I'd been reduced to was infinitely more terrifying than the man who held me.

"Been fighting?" the blacksuit went on, and despite the pain I felt a massive wave of relief. He hadn't seen me climb out from the tunnel. I did my best to nod, and with a glint of shark teeth he threw me to the floor. I landed on my back, winded.

"Back to work," Moleface said, pointing the gun at me. "If I see you out here again during hard labor, then I'm going to splatter you all over the walls."

"Yes, sir," I said. Somehow I managed to pull myself to my feet, lifting my pick from the rack again and my helmet from the floor. I barely had the strength to stagger back through to Room Three, but beneath my crimson mask I was smiling.

A REVELATION

THE REST OF THE MORNING felt like a dream. The adrenaline had robbed my body of any sensation, leaving me completely numb, and I seemed to float back into the chipping room. As soon as Donovan saw me, he dropped his pick and ran over, taking my arm and helping me to the far wall. After checking to see that the blacksuit hadn't followed me in, he lowered me down onto the rock, using his sleeve to wipe the blood from my face. I just lay there, helpless as a baby, looking at him but not really seeing him.

"Christ," he said eventually, speaking over the pounding of picks. "I won't say I told you so. What happened? Guards? Dogs?"

I opened my mouth to speak, but instead of words I suddenly found myself spewing my breakfast all over Donovan. He reeled, disgusted, but his expression quickly snapped back to one of concern.

"You all right?" he asked. "For God's sake, don't get sick. They'll take you."

"I'm okay," I slurred. Puking seemed to have removed the lead ball from my stomach, and feeling gradually ebbed back into my body. I struggled to a sitting position and wiped the acidic drool from my lips. "Sorry about that."

"Little warning would have been nice," he muttered. He glanced toward the door then back at me. "You better get up. That guard will rip your guts out if he catches you sitting down on the job."

Taking a deep breath, I heaved myself upward, using my pick as a crutch. I looked at the solid wall before me, and the thought of smashing through it for the next few hours almost made me chuck again. Donovan lifted his pick and brought it down hard, bathing us in sparks and debris. He struck a couple more times before looking at me impatiently.

"Well?" he said. "What did you find?"

I grinned and shrugged. "I thought you weren't bothered."

"I'm not, just curious is all."

I started to reply, but he suddenly looked back toward the door and gently shook his head. I lifted my pick, glancing out of the corner of my eye to see Moleface standing in the doorway. I couldn't make out his expression, but something told me his silver glare was aimed right at me. I took a halfhearted swing, and when I looked again the guard had gone.

"I'll tell you later, big guy," I said, swaying unsteadily as I prepared to swing again.

Donovan just sniffed and muttered, "If you live that long."

SHOWERS, FRESH UNIFORMS, march to the canteen. I could do it blindfolded now, without thinking, which was just as well since I was on autopilot for the rest of the day. I couldn't stop going over what I'd done. It didn't seem like it could have happened, none of it. The memories sat in my mind like the tendrils from some half-forgotten dream, fragments that couldn't possibly have been real.

But they were. I had done it, dashed beneath the boards and entered the forbidden room—a crime that could easily have been my last. And for what? All that effort just so I could panic and flee at the slightest noise.

We arrived in the trough room to see that Zee was already there—positioned as far as possible from the bench occupied by the Skulls and staring mournfully at his lunch. Gary Owens was sitting at the head of his table, bandanna still perched on his shaven head. The other gang members sat around him like caged animals, not moving or talking and looking like they regretted ever joining the Skulls.

I cast my eyes around for Kevin but he was nowhere to be seen. Knowing this place, he was probably lying in a crypt of shadows in a dark corner somewhere, already forgotten. Scanning the room further I made out the two other new kids, Toby and Ashley, sitting in a corner sharing food from a single plate, pressed against each other for comfort. Both their faces were bruised.

Zee saw us approaching and shuffled along the bench to make room. He smiled at Donovan, but did a double take when he saw me. I'd washed off all the blood in the showers, but I was guessing my face was pretty pale.

"Where'd you find Casper the Friendly Ghost?" Zee asked Donovan as we sat down.

"Haunting Room Two," he replied softly.

"No way," said Zee, his eyes like pickled eggs. "You didn't?"

"Got busted too, the fool."

Zee's eyes bulged even farther from his face. I thought they were going to pop.

"I wasn't busted," I explained. "But it was close."

"You looked like someone had shot you in the face," Donovan said, his brow creased. I couldn't help but laugh.

"Well, I kinda had myself to blame for that," I muttered sheepishly. "I ran into a wall when I heard the growling."

"Growling?" Donovan asked, but Zee held up his hands and started waving.

"Whoa, whoa," he said. "Start from the beginning."

So I did. In hushed tones I told them how I'd got through the wooden boards into the room, how I'd felt the blast of cold air, and how it had been pitch-black—a revelation that got a laugh from both boys. I told them about the hum that I thought had been a growl. Lastly, I filled them in on my near escape from Moleface.

"You know he'd have probably shot you on the spot if he'd seen you climbing out from under those boards," Donovan said when I stopped talking. "I'm telling you, it's just too damn dangerous."

"So what was the noise? That hum?" Zee asked, ignoring the comments.

"I have no idea," I replied. "I couldn't place it. I know now that it couldn't have been a dog. I mean, I'm still alive, aren't I?"

"Something electrical maybe?" Zee asked. "The prison generator?"

Donovan shook his head.

"Nope, there's no way the generator would be through there. That room was carved from scratch by the inmates."

"Air vents?" Zee asked. "Maybe it was the sound of wind in the pipes. That might be where the draft came from too."

"What did I just say?" said Donovan. "There isn't anything in there. No wires, no pipes, no vents. Nada."

"No, you might be right," I said to Zee, trying to recall the sound in my head. "What if it was wind? I mean wind from the surface. Maybe the cave-in cracked open a rift in the rock. If fresh air is getting in, then we can get out."

"You're a little more substantial than thin air," Zee replied. "Besides, like I've said before a million times, if there was a route to the surface, then don't you think they'd have sealed it off with something more secure than a few planks?"

I ground my teeth together, exasperated.

"Well, I sure as hell didn't imagine it," I hissed after a moment's silence. "I heard something in that room, something big enough to make a roar or a growl or whatever. I'll figure it out."

Donovan snorted and rose to go get some food. After scanning the trough room, however, he collapsed back down onto the bench.

"Incoming," he whispered.

I glanced up to see that Gary and his henchmen were making their way across the room toward the exit to the yard. The inmates were scampering out of his way with a deference that they'd never shown toward Kevin. The former Skull leader had been violent, yes, but there was something different about Gary. Kevin had tortured and killed to prove something, because he knew that life was valuable, something precious to take away. But Gary lashed out and killed as if life was nothing, meaningless, like he was crushing a bug.

"Don't look at him," Zee whispered, and I lowered my eyes to the table. When I raised them again, however, I found myself staring right into Gary's face. He was standing on the other side of the table, behind Zee, eyeballing me like I'd just killed his dog.

"I hear you've got a problem with the Skulls," he said in a voice that turned my bones to water. "Picking fights you got no business picking."

My tongue had turned to sandpaper, my limbs to lead.

"Well come on, then," Gary challenged, raising his hands. His knuckles were swollen and bloody. "You think you're so tough, then why don't you step up and take a crack at me?"

He pushed Zee out of the way and leaned on the table. This close I could see a line of blond hair on his top lip, like a tiny wig over his cracked and yellow teeth. I thought for a moment that I was going to puke again. At least I'd humiliate him before I was shanked. I swallowed hard and stared at the table.

"Look at me when I'm talking to you," he spat, grabbing my chin and wrenching it up. His fingers were rough against my skin. "I'm telling you to come on, let's see what you've got."

"Not enough," I breathed.

"What?"

"I'm sorry," I said, louder this time, then added "sir" for good measure.

"Too late." He pushed my head back so hard that I felt something pop in my neck. Then he slammed his hand on the table, sending Zee's food and drink flying. "You're marked. You're mine. You'll get your fight, little man."

And with that he turned and pushed through the Skulls, making his way toward the exit. I lowered my head and winced as pain cut through the tendons. Rubbing my neck, I saw Donovan and Zee staring sheepishly at the table.

"You okay?" asked Zee, not looking up.

"Oh yeah, that was fine," I replied, doing my best to hold back the tears that were building up behind my eyes. "No problem."

I put my elbows on the table and cupped my head in my hands so that nobody would see my glassy eyes. But I couldn't stop the floodgates from bursting. I blinked, and a tear dropped from my face to the plastic surface, winding its way gently toward the other side of the table. It wasn't alone, merging with the trail of water that had spilled from Zee's plastic cup. I watched the little stream meander through the piles of brown slush, flowing inexorably toward the edge.

And then it hit me, a revelation so bright and wonderful that it was as if the lights in the room had doubled in strength. I sat bolt upright, so quickly that Zee and Donovan both flinched.

"The noise. I know what it is."

They looked at me as if I'd gone mad.

"It's water," I said, pointing at the mess on the table. "It's an underground river."

THE RETURN

WE ARGUED ABOUT MY revelation through practically the whole of trough time, Donovan scoffing at the idea with his usual disdain. As soon as we'd sat down with our trays of mush, he began listing the reasons why it was impossible.

"They didn't just pick a spot in the gorge and plonk the prison down inside it," he ranted between, and often during, mouthfuls. "I mean think about it, they must have done a hundred checks first, a million. Rock samples, scans of the tunnels, analysis of the caves already here, probably even psychological tests on the bugs that live underground. They'd have seen a river if there was one."

I poked my plastic food with my plastic fork and mulled over what he was saying.

"And if the cave-in had breached the river, then surely we'd all be floating by now," he went on.

"Not if it's beneath us," added Zee, using his fork to steal some of my mush. The idea of escape seemed to have finally filtered through his skepticism, and he was at last taking my side. "I mean, the cave-in could have opened up a rift that went down, not up."

"So what use is that?" Donovan asked. "Burrow even deeper into your own prison, head farther underground. Great idea."

"Well, that water's got to go somewhere," I said.

"So you think you'll just pop up in the girls' showers at the local gym, then," Donovan hounded. " 'Hello, ladies, don't mind us, we're just escaping from jail. By the way, you've missed a spot, allow me.' "

We all laughed at the idea.

"Okay, it probably won't end up there," I said. "But what if it goes up top?"

"What if it stays underground for a hundred miles?" Zee said, shuddering. "We could end up drowning."

"Better that than this, right?" I asked, but both boys were shaking their heads.

"Got life here, Alex," said Donovan. "Ain't much of one, but I'm still breathing. Just isn't worth the risk."

"He's right, you know," muttered Zee. "I'm not much of a swimmer, and I don't much like being stuck in small places neither. I think we should just stick it out here. You never know, they might close this place down tomorrow."

"They might come and take you tonight," I retorted, but it was no use. Zee started talking to Donovan about soccer, and I tuned out the conversation, retreating into the comfort of my own mind. The more I thought about it, the more the noise made sense—the distant, muted rush and roar of a million tons of water speeding past beneath our feet. If I could just get to it, maybe it would carry me home.

AFTER LUNCH WE headed back out into the yard. Donovan claimed he wanted to go to the gym, so Zee and I jogged up the stairs to my cell, sitting down on the bunk and preparing for another afternoon of mind-numbing boredom. We'd only been chatting idly for a few minutes before Donovan came storming into the cell, his eyes full of murder.

"They wouldn't let me in," he fumed, pacing up and down as best he could in the tiny space. "That new kid has taken over. Now the gym's out of bounds for anyone who isn't fighting. He's got the Fifty-niners on his side too; they're too scared to argue."

"So why not go in and knock his block off?" Zee asked. "I mean, you're easily as big as him, go and teach him a lesson."

"Not worth it," said Donovan, sighing loudly then climbing onto his bunk. "It's just not worth it. I don't mess with them, they don't mess with me."

Zee and I looked at each other as we listened to Donovan punching the wall in frustration, then he fell silent.

"Plenty of gyms on the surface," I hinted, but there was no response.

We sat there as the minutes ground by, life running in slow motion. In here, even time seemed moribund. My mind was already beginning to rot. I'd forgotten half the books I'd ever read, lost the TV shows I once loved. I struggled to even remember what certain colors looked like, as Furnace's relentless palette of reds and blacks and grays had long since rendered blues and greens and oranges a distant memory, as vague and delicate as a spider's thread.

To pass the time Zee and I summarized our favorite films, doing our best to act them out to one another. I ran through the Indiana Jones saga, impersonating my hero and even using a pillow as his hat and the sheet as a whip. My amateur dramatics had

Zee in stitches, and even woke Donovan from his funk as I acted out the plot of the seventh film, which he'd never seen.

Zee picked a trilogy about some kid inventors, although his memory was useless and he was forever stopping and going back to fill in a vital piece of the story that he'd missed out, or revealing the end before he'd reached the middle. By the fifth time he'd said, "Oh, wait, that never actually happened," Donovan and I were rolling around on our beds, tears streaming down our faces. They were good tears, though.

The siren blew for dinner midway through my account of the third Darren Shan movie, but we deliberately waited as long as we could before traipsing downstairs. Our delay worked, and by the time we reached the trough room it was almost empty, the inmates behind the canteen already starting to clear away. We grabbed the last few plates of swill and wolfed them down as quickly as possible.

The only other boy in the room was Kevin, who sat alone on a bench near the door, devouring his food with a nervous twitch that reminded me of a rat eating trash. He saw me looking and snarled, but soon broke eye contact, pathetic in the absence of his gang.

From there, we headed back to our cells. Zee claimed he was beat, and disappeared down the platform on level four. Donovan and I continued upward but we walked in silence, both too exhausted to bother with conversation.

As soon as we entered our cell, I lay down on my bunk and felt my eyelids droop. I didn't struggle, letting sleep gather me up in her gentle arms and carry me far away from Furnace. I should have stayed awake. I had no idea that she was about to betray me, that she would carry me to the most horrific thing I'd witnessed since I descended to the bottom of the world.

IT ALL STARTED with a dream, the same one I'd had so many times since I arrived here. I was trapped inside a glass prison, one that looked out over my old home. Each night I had the dream, the house looked different, less solid. It was like a little piece here and there had been erased from existence, forgotten.

My parents were inside, as always. They were strangers to look at, my unconscious mind no longer able to picture them as they once were, but I knew it was them. It was always them.

And it was always the same sequence of events. I watched through the glass as the blacksuits and the dogs approached my front door, the beasts crashing through the windows, gripping my mom and dad in their dripping muzzles, sucking the crimson life from their veins.

The wheezer slammed on the other side of my prison, a twisted reflection that I still didn't understand. I beat the glass and screamed until my throat was raw, but nothing could stop them dragging my loved ones away, throwing their writhing, stained bodies into a prison meat wagon.

This time, however, something was different. I kept beating on my transparent prison cell, my bleeding fists creating cracks in the glass. The cracks spread across the entire wall, each one letting in a trail of clear liquid, as if the prison was submerged underwater. The harder I struck, the bigger the cracks got, until the glass cube began to fill up.

On the other side, the wheezer was writhing as though in agony, its scarred hands ripping the gas mask from its face. I couldn't bear to look, but in my dream I was unable to turn away. With a grotesque sucking sound the mask came free, revealing a wet, raw mouth with no lips and no teeth, just a gaping hole in its head that seemed to have no end. I screamed again, and as I did the prison wall exploded inward, the weight of the water like a giant fist knocking me backward.

A siren broke out, different from any I had heard so far—endless bleats that sounded more like a car alarm. The wheezer began to scream, its filthy maw growing impossibly large, stretching so that it was wider than its head, wider than its body, wider than the glass cell. The water began to change direction, disappearing into the creature's mouth, flooding down its throat. I fought against the flow but to no avail, and I was carried wailing into the fleshy wound, its color the same as the rock walls of the prison.

I woke moaning, clawing at my face and almost tumbling out of bed. For a moment I thought I was still in my dream, as I could hear the unfamiliar siren, but as the last vestiges of sleep retreated I found myself wide awake.

Everything was red. It was the blood watch, they were coming back.

"Donovan," I whispered, knowing that he would probably just tell me to shut up but desperate to hear his voice, to know that I wasn't alone. "Donovan?"

"Quiet, kid," came his hushed reply. "Told you once, ain't gonna put up with this again."

He wouldn't have to. After last time there was no way I was getting out of bed.

"They're coming," I hissed. I was surprised to see Donovan's head appear from the top bunk, his features the color of blood.

"Not for us," he said. "That siren, it means they're bringing someone back."

"Back?" I said, startled. I sat up in bed, looking through the bars down into the yard. I saw Donovan's hand fly out, slapping me around the ear.

"Doesn't mean they won't take you if they catch you ogling them," he said before disappearing.

I remained upright, trying to stretch my neck to see the vault door. Bringing someone back? It didn't make any sense. I'd always assumed that once you'd been taken, that was it, that there was no return.

"I thought nobody came back alive?" I risked.

"I didn't say they were bringing him back alive. Now shut the hell up."

This time I did as I was told. Down below, I heard the hiss and boom of the vault door, followed by an all too familiar screech. It was the wheezers, twitching and convulsing into the yard. I heard another noise from behind them, a long, low moan that spilled out into the prison and made my heart bleed.

I stared into the shadows of the door as some more figures materialized from the darkness. Two blacksuits strode forth, each holding a metal pole connected to something behind them. As they entered the yard I saw that they were leading a creature that writhed and twisted against its restraints, an animal that moaned and howled as it fought to break free.

The flickering red lights made it impossible to see what the monster was, but I assumed it was another of the warden's dogs. It was about the same size, and thrashed around on all fours, but there was something about it that set my nerves on edge, something that wasn't quite right.

The group headed slowly toward the staircase on the far side of the prison, the blacksuits struggling against the sheer ferocity of the animal. At one point it pulled so fiercely on its poles that it managed to gain ground, charging into a cell door with such power that the bars buckled. The guards pulled on their poles and dragged it back, one smashing his gloved fist into the creature's distorted head—an attack that only seemed to make it angrier.

I counted the floors as they rose to the fifth level, and by the time they were halfway along the platform, I knew where they were going. So did Kevin. He peered from the bars of the cell he once shared with Monty, his fear so intense that everyone in the prison could see the whites of his eyes.

"No, no, no, no!" he screamed, over and over again as the procession drew near. "Get it away, get it away! It's not fair. Get it away!"

His pleas did nothing except make the blacksuits grin, their shark smiles glinting in the red light. One shouted for the cell door to be opened, and with a clatter it began to slide back. Before it had budged more than half a meter, Kevin made a break for it, squeezing between the gap and almost getting past the guard. But the blacksuit was too quick, snatching out his bear-trap hand and snapping it around the boy's neck, hurling him back into the cell. Kevin hit the bunk and scrabbled to his feet, but by then it was too late, the door was open.

Laughing, the two guards twisted their sticks and pushed the thrashing creature into the cell. They twisted again and the poles detached from the beast's collar, and after another call the door began to slide shut. The blacksuits stood to one side to allow the wheezers to see into the cell, but I wish they'd stayed where they were. Now I had a front-row view of the horror.

The hunched animal that I had thought was a dog threw itself against the bars, bending them outward. Then, to my horror, it stood up on its hind legs, rising to well over six feet in height as it hurled itself at the door. It was moving so quickly I couldn't get a good look at it, but what I saw told me exactly what it was. Or at least what it had once been.

The creature's face was human—ravaged and mangled and broken, yes, but still with eyes and a nose and a gaping mouth. The skin was marked with fresh wounds, as if a child had been trying to decorate it with a knife. It was naked, but there was something wrong with its skin, like it had been cut open and had something stitched underneath. Muscles bulged everywhere, flexing each time it moved and occasionally even splitting the skin with their size.

Tired of thrashing against the door, the monster turned its attention to the back of the cell. It didn't take it long to spot Kevin, cowering behind the toilet. With a roar that made me think of dragons, the freak leaped across the tiny cell, gripping the toilet and tearing it from the rock like it was made of tissue paper. Water burst from the severed pipe, obscuring my view even further. But I saw the creature grab Kevin, lifting him off the ground and throwing him into the far wall.

By the third time he'd done it, Kevin's screaming had become a soft groan. Five times and the boy was no longer moving. I kept watching as the monster went to work on the corpse, but my brain refused to acknowledge what I was seeing, editing it out as if it knew the images would drive me insane. I couldn't tell you what I saw in there, even though I watched the whole damn thing.

Some time later the blacksuits called for the door to be opened, jamming their metal sticks into the creature's collar with a spark of electricity. The murderous freak fought against them but the giants were too strong, dragging it out of the dripping mess in the cell. They pulled it back along the platform, eventually disappearing from sight down the stairwell.

But not before I'd seen something that filled me with terror.

On the creature's arm, distorted and pale but still unmistakable, was a birthmark.

It was Monty.

A DISTRACTION

THAT NIGHT I BEGAN to wonder if I actually was in hell. I'd never been a believer, skipped Sunday school and scoffed at the kids who prayed in assembly. I always figured that if there was a God, then he'd have stopped me doing bad things, but there were never any signs, any warnings. Until now, of course.

I lay there in the pitch black, Monty's inhuman cries still echoing through my skull, blending with the sobs and screams that played endlessly from outside my cell. I wondered if maybe I had died on the night we broke into that house, tripped as I climbed in through the window, snapped my neck or something without even knowing it. Maybe the blacksuits had been angels of death, come to trap my soul and drag it down to the pits of hell.

I was so tired and scared that my mind was delirious, and the more I lay there thinking about it the more I was convinced that Furnace was Hades, Gehenna, the pit where sinners are sent to rot away for all eternity. It made perfect sense—the warden and his devil eyes, the blacksuits with their superhuman strength, the wheezers that looked like the tortured ghosts of Nazi storm troopers, and the way that poor Monty had been scoured of everything recognizable, forced to become a demon that thrashed and ripped and killed. What if that was the fate of all of us, turned into the very basest of creatures, the very essence of evil?

So if this was hell, where did the river go? I thought back to school, to the stuff we'd learned about Greek mythology. This was back when I'd wanted to be a magician, to live a good life, a free life. I'd devoured all that stuff, fascinated by stories of myth and legend and magic. I remember the picture of Hades we looked at, the Greek underworld. To get there you had to cross a river, I forget the name. Once you'd crossed it, you were in hell, but if you could get back over from the other side, maybe you were free.

Half dreaming, half awake, I saw myself diving into the river, its water clean and pure and cold, carrying me through the raw red tunnels of Furnace, buoying me upward toward the light on a surf of bubbles and foam. I saw myself laughing as I breached the surface, emerging on a crystal clear night with all the stars of heaven welcoming me back and the cool wind speeding me across the world, taking me home.

I was still chuckling gently when Donovan woke me the following morning, but not for long. As soon as I opened my eyes the four walls of my cell slammed down on my memories of freedom, cutting off the air and making me struggle for breath. I sat up in bed, shocked to find myself back behind bars after such a vivid dream, clutching my throat and gasping for oxygen.

"Easy there," said Donovan, sitting on my bed and placing a hand on my shoulder. "Deep breaths, don't panic."

I inhaled the hot air as deeply as I could, my whole body shuddering with the effort. My lungs filled, the fear ebbing away.

Looking out of the doors, I saw people in their cells reluctantly getting ready for another day in Furnace.

"Did I sleep through the siren?" I asked, yawning. Donovan nodded, pulling on his overalls and standing by the door.

"You were away somewhere nice," he replied. "Giggling like a baby all night. God knows why, though, after . . ."

The pause was just long enough to bring back the horrors. They flooded the silence, ripping through my brain like razor wire and settling in the tender flesh of my stomach.

"It was Monty," I said, picturing the beast as it tore through the cell, through Kevin. "That thing, that monster."

Donovan didn't move, just stared in silence.

"I know," he said eventually. "It's not the first time someone has come back."

"What happened to him?"

Donovan turned slowly, then slid down the bars until he was sitting on the rocky floor. He ran his fingers through his hair, then let his head fall gently into his hands.

"I don't know," he said quietly. "No one here does. It's only happened a few times, five or six maybe. I don't know, maybe more. Most of the time people get taken, they never return, they just disappear. Dead, most likely. Sometimes, though . . ."

"They come back," I finished unnecessarily.

"The first few times I saw them I thought they were creatures, animals. Like monkeys or something. They were brought in just like Monty was last night. I never saw what happened before, they were always out of sight. I just thought they whaled on the inmates a little, taught them a lesson.

"Then one time I saw this kid get taken. Real nasty one. He was young, but he had all these tattoos of guns and knives and death and things, all over him. Gang ink, you know? Well, a few days after he was taken, the blood watch brought in this monster, like last night. They dragged him to a cell on this level, only a few away from ours. Walked right past the bars, and I saw these things weren't no monkeys."

He wiped his eyes and I saw he was crying.

"Its skin was all ripped and stitched, all bulging in weird places with all those muscles underneath. But I could still see those tattoos. It was him, that kid, no doubt about it."

"But what happens to them?" I repeated. "Monty was taken two nights ago, what the hell could they have done to him to change him like that?"

"Don't know," was his reply. "Don't want to neither. Only one way of finding out for sure, if you follow me, and by that time it's you who's ripping through your old cellmate."

"But why bring them back? Just to scare us?"

"To scare us, to kill us, to give us something to talk about in the morning. How the hell should I know? This is Furnace, Alex, they can do what they like." He paused for a minute, then lashed out, smashing his fist against the bars hard enough to draw blood. "Christ, that thing killed Kevin. I mean, it tore him to pieces."

I saw my chance and took it.

"You still sure you want to stay here?" I asked. Donovan looked up at me, his dark eyes boring right into mine.

"Can you promise me that river exists?" he whispered.

"No, but I'm pretty sure."

"Can you promise me it will get us out of here?"

"No, of course not."

"Can you promise me they won't catch us?"

"No, Donovan. I can't promise anything, except that dying while trying to break free is better than being killed by one of those things."

"Or becoming one of them," he added. He sucked the blood from his knuckle, deep in thought, then turned his face toward the ceiling. "Okay, I'm in."

BY THE TIME we'd made it downstairs we had a plan. Now that Donovan had finally accepted the possibility of escape, he was on fire, his mind blasting out idea after idea in hushed tones as we made our way to the trough room. I could barely get a word in edgeways, but it was a relief to finally hear someone else as optimistic as me.

Zee met us at our table and we hunched together over our plates of mush, doing our best not to look too much like co-conspirators. After a quick check to make sure nobody was in earshot, I filled Zee in on the details. He was as surprised as I was to see Donovan's change of heart.

"It's about time, big guy," he said through a grin.

"We're going back in to scope out Room Two," I whispered.

"With a light this time, presumably?" said Zee.

"Yeah, I'll keep my helmet on," I replied. "I may be an idiot, but I do learn from my mistakes."

"What about the guard?" Zee asked. "I mean, he nearly caught you before."

"That's my job," added Donovan, licking his lips and leaning in even farther. "I'll distract him. Won't give you long, but should be enough time to work out what's in there."

"Distract him how?" said Zee. "Do the old feeling sick trick?"

"No, I've got something a little more dramatic planned," he

said, flashing us a look halfway between a grin and a grimace. "Just stay by the door in the chipping room, you'll soon see. Five minutes, that's about all you've got. Make it count."

"We will," I said. Zee nodded, then his brow suddenly creased.

"Hang on, *we*?" he asked, looking frantically between Donovan and me. "Surely it's better if just you go. I mean, not that I wouldn't do it, but isn't it twice the risk if two of us break into the room?"

"But it will take twice as long to search it if it's just me," I responded. "Besides, I want someone to keep me company in the hole if we get caught."

"Alex is right, Zee, it's a big room and there's probably still rocks everywhere. If you're gonna find where that noise is coming from, you need as many pairs of eyes as possible. Hell, if you don't wanna do it, you can always distract the blacksuits instead."

Zee blanched and shook his head.

"Right," I said, pushing my untouched breakfast across the table and cracking my fingers. "Let's do it."

FORTUNATELY, DONOVAN AND I had been assigned to chipping duty that morning. Zee was scheduled for the laundry, but Donovan told him to ignore the duty roster.

"People don't always stick to their jobs," he explained. "The guards make sure everyone on the list for chipping is there, but they don't check to see if there's an extra body in the halls—they figure no one would be stupid enough to do this if they didn't have to, y'know?"

We followed the usual routine, selecting our equipment and marching like drones into Room Three. Zee and I stayed as close to the entrance as possible, but Donovan made his way toward a group of Skulls who had already started hacking at the wall. I wondered what the hell he was doing, and prayed it wouldn't be anything too dangerous. He turned and winked at me, then nodded toward the ceiling prop that was wedged between him and the Skulls.

"Oh no," I said. "He wouldn't."

He did. With a swing of his pick he smashed the wooden prop into pieces. The Skulls all leaped back, yelling at Donovan to stop as a curtain of dust and rubble fell down from the unsupported ceiling. He swung his pick again, sweeping it upward and letting go of the handle. It struck the ceiling where the prop had been, dislodging a massive chunk of rock that crashed to the floor, narrowly missing the nearest Skull.

By now everybody was watching with terror in their eyes, including me. Donovan reached down and picked up a melon-sized piece of rock, then lobbed it toward the Skull who'd almost been flattened. It struck him square in the nose, and he crumpled earthward.

"Cave-in!" yelled Donovan at the top of his voice. "Man down!"

The call worked. The blacksuit ran into the chamber so quickly he was almost a blur. He dashed across to where the Skull was lying, leaning over him and watching the blood drip from his nose. The boy was out cold, and none of his friends seemed able to pluck up the courage to speak. Donovan looked at me from the other side of the hall and mouthed something: "Make it count."

"Time to go," I said, running for the door. I didn't wait to see if Zee was following me, just flung my pick onto the equipment room floor and dashed to the wooden boards sealing off Room Two. The bottom board was still unfastened, the missing bolt obviously unnoticed. Pulling it out as far as I could, I hissed for Zee to get inside. With a quiet curse he did, squeezing his body through the gap. Once clear, he used his foot to keep the board away from the wall while I clambered in.

"Piece of cake," he said, his voice shaking.

The hard part was over and I breathed a sigh of relief, staring into the mouth of the abyss that had so terrified me yesterday. We stumbled forward a few paces, keeping our lights off until the equipment room was out of sight. Halfway along the tunnel we heard movement behind us and ducked down. Through the gaps between the boards we saw the blacksuit dragging the unconscious Skull toward the yard, and waited for him to vanish before pressing on.

"Man, I hear it," said Zee as we reached the end of the tunnel. It was pitch-black ahead, but the faint roar filled the darkness. Once again I panicked, thinking that the sound was a growl from the warden's dogs, or the wheeze of a gas mask. But when I flicked on my helmet lamp the only thing it illuminated was rock.

"Jesus, look at this place," Zee whispered, switching on his light. The twin beams did practically nothing to combat the dense blackness of the room, the pale tendrils of light reaching no more than a few meters before surrendering to the shadows.

"Five minutes," I said. "That's all we've got."

"Well, far as I can tell, it's coming from that direction," Zee said, turning his helmet and pointing a trail of light toward the back left-hand side of the cavern. The roar seemed to come from everywhere, but I took Zee's word for it. My hearing never was my strong point.

We made our way across the cavern, forced to scale the massive boulders that littered the floor. Every now and again I'd see a shard of white, or a suspicious stain on the floor, but fortunately the bodies of the kids who'd died here had been removed. Once again I wondered if their souls still remained, but quickly put the thought out of my head.

I wasn't sure how many minutes it took us to cross the hall. Too many, I knew that much. More than once we had to double back after reaching a blockage, or duck under a treacherous archway formed by unstable blocks of stone. But with each step we took, the roar got louder and more distinct, the sound becoming less like a growl, more like the thunder of a waterfall. The closer we got, the fresher the air became. I could have sworn that there was even a fine mist suspended in the cavern, one that clung to our skin and gave us the strength to proceed.

And then, like finding an oasis in the desert, we rounded a truck-sized mound of stone and saw it. Our way out. It was a crack in the floor of the cavern, one that stretched over twenty paces from the far wall to our feet. There was nothing but darkness through the rift, but we didn't need to see. Where we were standing we could practically feel the river that raged beneath us, the torrent that would set us free.

"We were right!" I shouted at Zee, no longer caring about the noise. "I don't believe it, there's a way out!"

But he didn't share my enthusiasm.

"Are you seeing something I don't?" he muttered. "I mean, did you happen to bring a crate of dynamite with you?"

I looked back at the cracked rock and frowned. Then, feeling like someone had just punched me in the gut, I saw what he meant. The rift in the floor may have split the cavern wide open lengthways, but the solid stone had only parted a few centimeters. Our way out was no wider than a fist.

MY DARKEST HOUR

ZEE PRACTICALLY HAD TO drag me back through the rocky labyrinth of Room Two. The sudden switch from thinking we were home free to knowing there was no way through the slit in the ground was unbearable. In the space of a second I had lost the will to carry on, and with it had fled the part of my brain that could remember how to do simple things like walk and talk. I must have bumped into a dozen rocks, scraping my shins and arms and even my face. But I didn't care. It was over.

Several wrong turns later and we found our way back into the tunnel. Zee switched his lamp off, then mine, leading the way toward the wooden planks. Beyond them the equipment room was empty, but we had no idea where the blacksuit was. He could have been right outside, waiting for us to emerge so he could pump us full of shot. The thought didn't bother me. At least it would be quicker than festering away in Furnace for the next seven decades.

I dived down onto the floor and pushed my way through the loose board, ignoring Zee's frantic protests.

"Wait, for God's sake!" he hissed, but by the time he'd repeated himself I was already out. The coast was clear, the guard nowhere to be seen. Zee pushed himself through, scrambling to his feet and grabbing our picks from where we'd left them. "Let's get back."

"What's the point?" I asked, not moving. Zee grabbed my sleeve and hoisted me forward, pulling me into Room Three. With the heat and the noise nobody even saw us enter.

"Come on," he said, his words almost lost in the hammering. "Did you really expect it to be that easy?"

We spotted Donovan hard at work and shuffled over. He took one look at our expressions and his shoulders slumped.

"No river, then?" he said matter-of-factly.

"It's there, but the gap is too narrow and the walls are too thick," Zee explained when I didn't open my mouth.

Donovan nodded then returned to work, mumbling something like "too bad" over his shoulder. Zee shrugged at me, then started hacking away at the wall. I lifted my pick halfheartedly and took a swing, but I just couldn't find the energy to make it count. I mean, why bother? If a lifetime in this sweaty room was all I had to look forward to, was all any of us had to look forward to, why didn't I just ram the pick into my brain?

I'm sorry to say that my thoughts were like that for the rest of the morning—a slide show of ways to put myself out of my misery. Not that I think I ever would have gone through with it, but I'd been so set on an escape that was now impossible, and the only form of freedom left to me was death. It was a terrible kind of freedom—one from misery and pain, yes, but also one from lightness and laughter and life. It was an absence of everything.

We walked from the chipping rooms with all the enthusiasm of death-row prisoners going to the electric chair, showering and dressing without a word. Silence followed us as we grabbed our food in the canteen and sat down at an empty bench. We all made a good job of thoroughly poking our mush, but nobody seemed to be eating it.

"So are you saying we need to lose a little weight before we fit in the crack?" asked Donovan after a few minutes, pushing his plate away and folding his arms. " 'Cause I think I can do that."

"Even a baby wouldn't be able to get through," Zee replied, holding his hands a few centimeters apart to demonstrate the size of the gap. "My cat wouldn't be able to squeeze its bony ass into that hole."

As usual, lunch was interrupted by the sound of crashing plates and yelling. I peered over Zee's shoulder to see the Skulls going to work on some kids in the middle of the room. From here it looked like the other new fish, Ashley and Toby. They were getting food poured down their overalls and rubbed in their faces, but I didn't even think about trying to help. After dreaming of escape the reality of Furnace seemed even heavier, even more claustrophobic than before. The oppressive air pushed down on me like a weight, I felt like I couldn't move a muscle.

"And we couldn't chip it?" Donovan went on.

"Even if we could all get in there it would be too noisy," Zee answered. "Besides, it would take us weeks to break through."

"Any of you guys know how to make a bomb?" Donovan went on, smiling, but he got no response. "How about the gas tanks in the kitchen? They'd blow a hole in anything if they were lit up."

"You've seen those things," Zee countered. "They're bolted and strapped and secured tighter than the gold in Fort Knox. There's no way you'd be able to get them loose, let alone smuggle them across the yard."

Donovan wasn't willing to give up.

"Come on, you get me all excited about this, then you're telling me it's impossible? That's just cruel."

"Well, boo hoo," I suddenly snapped. "Poor you. You've been wasting away here for half a decade, Donovan. Why didn't you find your own way out? What do you want from me?"

He stared at me like he was going to lash out, then his face fell and he got to his feet.

"Wait, Donovan," I said to his back as he walked away, but it was no use. The world was falling to pieces, and I was crumbling right along with it.

It was over the next few days that I started to understand how people survived knowing they'd never again be free. It was as simple as just switching off, forgetting that you were alive, that you'd ever existed outside of Furnace's red walls. You just made your way from place to place, did what they told you, ate and slept, but you stopped thinking of yourself as human. We were robots, automatons who had every appearance of humanity but who were dead on the inside.

By some twist of fate, it was Zee and Donovan who did their best to keep the idea of freedom alive. Every time I saw them they talked about ideas they'd had—trying to melt the rock with laundry detergent, trying to chip their way down to the river in Room Three, greasing themselves up with canteen fat so they could squeeze through the gap. I just scoffed at their plans the same way they had scoffed at mine, the idea of getting out now laughable to me.

But there must have been a part of my mind that still dreamed of escaping, because the image of the river never truly left me. I'd find myself thinking about it while working, while my conscious mind was engaged with chipping or bleaching the laundry or cleaning the filth off the toilets. I'd suddenly notice that I was trying out different scenarios in my head, testing escape plans without even knowing I was doing it.

I tried to stop the images because they were so painful—like wishing for something you knew you could never have. But they just wouldn't go away. My body and my mind were confined here, but my soul, or my imagination, or whatever, wouldn't rest until I was breathing surface air.

A week passed since Zee and I broke into Room Two, a week where I barely said a word to anybody, barely even made eye contact. Donovan and Zee started spending more time alone without me, giving me cautious glances whenever I approached. I didn't blame them, I was a shadow of my former self and my dark eyes were haunted by something that scared my friends. As if my resignation were a plague that would spread to anyone close by.

Two weeks passed, another visit by the blood watch, five more kids dragged into the vault, their veins pumped full of darkness and death. I didn't watch, just lay awake in bed—half hoping they wouldn't take me, half hoping they would. Anything to break the monotony. None of them returned this time, and there was no further sign of the creature that had once been Monty.

It would have gone on like that forever, an eternity of hopelessness and misery, but for one instant of madness. One beautiful, crazy moment in the canteen's kitchen.

DONOVAN AND I were on trough room duty, both of us working the processor and blending the trash to put in our meals. We hadn't said a single thing to one another for almost two days, and I wasn't planning to do anything to change that. Donovan, though, had other ideas.

"Remember that day?" he asked, his voice so unfamiliar that it startled me. I didn't respond, didn't even look up, but he went on anyway. "Monty's big brunch? Man, I wish he was still here. That was some tasty trough."

I couldn't bear even thinking about it, so while he chattered I crouched down to turn on the stove. I suddenly felt a hand on my shoulder pulling me back up.

"What the hell happened to you, Alex?" Donovan asked, gripping my overalls as if worried I'd make a run for it. "I thought you said you'd never let this place beat you. You were a breath of fresh air in here, man. For a little while back there I actually thought you were gonna do it, gonna get out."

I wrenched myself away so hard that Donovan's rubber glove came loose, sitting limply on my shoulder. Grabbing it, I threw it at him by way of response, getting down on my haunches again to switch on the gas. With a hiss it started feeding through to the burners, and I hurried to get to the lighters, cracking my head on the counter as I stood up.

"You just gave up," Donovan spat. He was furious, I could tell from the specks of spittle crowding in the corners of his mouth. "Like some gutless wonder, some chicken." He reached down onto the counter and picked up a handful of rancid white meat. "Yeah, this is what you are, Sawyer, chicken. Processed, dead."

I ignored him, lifting the chained lighter to the burner and sparking it up. I heard a squelching sound and turned to see Donovan stuffing his glove full of the wet flesh, his face twisted with some strange delirium. I was about to break my silence to ask him what he was doing when he pulled back his hand and launched the disgusting missile in my direction. At that distance he couldn't miss, and the packed glove slapped me right on the cheek, trails of chicken fat dripping against my lips.

I reeled backward, wiping my face in disgust.

"Jesus," was about all I could splutter. The glove had fallen on the burner, and I picked it up to lob it back in Donovan's direction, feeling the meat inside soft and cold against my fingers. But something stopped me, a flash at the back of my mind that was bright enough to blow away the shadows of the last fortnight.

I looked up at Donovan, feeling my skin prickle and tighten, feeling my blood fused once again with adrenaline. He recognized the expression straightaway and grinned.

"What?" he asked. "What brought you back?"

"This," I replied, holding up the dripping glove.

"You planning on battering your way out with a meat-filled rubber glove?" he said, raising an eyebrow.

"Not quite."

I picked up the lighter again and held it to the burner, watching the air around it explode as it ignited. Then I pictured the crack in the rock that led to the river, saw it packed full of rubber gloves just like this one.

Only filled not with meat, but with gas.

JUMPERS

"OH. MY. GOD," said Donovan when I whispered the idea in his ear. "That's genius. Why the hell didn't I think of that?"

"You did," I answered, rummaging under the counter and picking up a box of rubber gloves. There were a hundred pairs in each carton, more than enough for what we had in mind. "If you hadn't splatted me with that meat missile, I never would have had the idea."

Donovan scratched his head and looked at me apologetically.

"Yeah, I'm sorry about that. I kinda just lost my head. Speaking of which, you've still got a little . . ." He pointed at my face, guiding me to a white worm of chicken tendon that had dried to my upper lip. I peeled it off and flicked it at him.

"So how do we do this?" he asked, brushing the flesh from his overalls. "I mean, it's gonna be hard to smuggle the gloves out; we go straight from here to the showers."

"But we're not under guard here," I replied, pulling a glove from the box and blowing into it. It expanded like an udder, then deflated with a farting sound. "I've never once seen the blacksuits watch to make sure we shower after being on trough duty.

It's not the same as chipping, no sharp rocks or mining equipment to smuggle out."

"I guess they're not too worried about someone getting stabbed with a carrot," he replied. "Okay, so we smuggle the gas out and hide it in the cell. Then take it with us for chipping."

I nodded.

"The only problem will be getting it into Room Two," I said. "Every time we go in there we're risking our lives. And they only have to catch us once to know what we're doing."

"And there's only so many times I can threaten to bring down the roof before the guards start getting suspicious."

I swept my eyes around the room, checking to make sure nobody was watching, then puffed hard to blow out the burner flame. Wrapping the opening of the glove around the gas vent I watched as it began to expand, the main body bloating first before each of the five fingers stretched out like an unfolding hand. When it looked like it was ready to pop, I plucked it off and tied a knot round the base, then held it up triumphantly.

"Alex," said Donovan as he clamped his own glove around the gas vent. "I think I love you."

I laughed, tucking the makeshift balloon into my overalls. For once I was grateful for the baggy prison uniforms—the glove made it look like I'd put on a bit of weight but it wasn't too obvious. Donovan pulled his glove free and tried to tie a knot, but it was too full. With another rude noise it spat gas into his face, half emptying before he managed to secure the opening. Coughing, he held up the bedraggled glove.

"Not bad," I said. "But please don't kill yourself."

"How many do we need, you think?" he asked, tucking his

first attempt down his overalls and wrapping a second glove around the vent.

"Probably dozens," I answered. "But we can't take more than three or four each at a time without looking like the Michelin Man. We can't risk giving the game away."

"Four at a time. You, me, and Zee. We can do this in a couple of weeks if the hard labor shifts are right."

"A month at most," I replied, trying to calculate it in my head. Donovan sighed loudly as he pulled the bloated glove free.

"Month's a long time in Furnace when you've got a secret like this," he said, doing a better job with his next knot. "You really think we can do it?"

I pulled another glove over the burner and tried to think back through the last couple of weeks, my endless depression, the sense of utter futility. But the feelings had vanished, as if my mind had been waiting to bring down a shutter and seal them off for good.

"Yeah," I replied, feeling like it was the first time I'd smiled in a lifetime. "I really think we can."

WE WERE SO pumped up with hope that we almost forgot all about the trough. By the time the lunch siren blasted we'd only made a handful of pots of food and were forced to serve the hungry inmates with uncooked mush. From the sounds of it there were a few violent complaints, but they were directed at the unlucky kids who were serving, not us.

We almost learned the hard way how dangerous our plan was. Once we'd stuffed our overalls with flammable gas we lit the burner again, and came very close to being blown to smithereens by a stray spark. Next time we knew to fill up the gloves at the end of hard labor, not the beginning.

Walking out of the canteen and through the trough room was the most terrifying part of the operation. I felt like the globes of gas pressed between my skin and my clothes were visible to even the most shortsighted person in Furnace, and as we crossed the yard toward the staircase I started to panic, knowing that a guard or snitch was going to discover us at any moment. But Donovan steered me on with a firm hand on my back, and we made it to the cell without incident.

I hid the gloves underneath the mattress at the base of my bed while Donovan kept watch. I wasn't too happy about the idea of going up in flames in the middle of the night, but we had no choice. It was either there or in the toilet cistern, and the thought of being blown up while taking a dump was infinitely worse.

Once the miniature bombs were secure we set off to find Zee, bumping into him halfway along the third-level platform. He was red-faced and sweaty with a nasty-looking burn on his neck.

"Gary," he hissed as an explanation. "Had laundry duty with him today. He wanted me to do his share while he napped on the clean bedding. I won't be saying no to him again, he's a psycho."

"Well, we've got something that will cheer you up," I said.

"It must be something big if it's pulled you out from that mother of all sulks," was his reply. I clipped him softly on the ear then started walking, waiting until we were in the clear before we filled him in on the plan. He just about danced a jig on the spot, the excitement too much for him.

"Holy Mother of Jesus," he said, clutching his hair in his hands. "You pair of crazy, wonderful nutters. The gloves, of course!"

I clamped a hand over Zee's mouth while Donovan held a finger to his lips.

"Don't want the whole prison to know," he said.

"Yeah, that's essential," I went on, leaning in and whispering to Zee. "If this is going to work, then we can't tell a soul. It's got to be us three, nobody else. I trust you guys, no questions asked, but I wouldn't trust anyone else in here as far as I could throw them. One word to anyone and it's over, we'll end up in the hole, or crapped out the backside of some dog."

"Word of honor, boss," said Donovan, holding out his hand palm down. Zee nodded and placed his hand on Donovan's.

"Feels like the three musketeers," I said, adding mine to the pile. Zee laughed.

"All for one and let's get the hell out of here," he said.

I know it was just my imagination, but I could have sworn there was some sort of electrical pulse charging through our linked fingers. Maybe it had been so long since I'd gripped someone else's hand, so long since I'd felt that contact with anyone. But I sensed it, a force that united us right there and then, a bond of trust, of friendship, of hope.

I guess that's why it came as such a huge surprise that out of the three of us, I was the one who broke the vow first.

IT WAS AS we were heading down to the yard that I heard someone shouting, pointing to the platforms above our heads. I looked up into the shadows of the upper floors, scanning the cells and the walkways. At first I couldn't work out what had caused so much consternation, but then I spotted them—two bodies clinging to the railings on the eighth level.

"Jumpers," said Donovan. "I wouldn't watch this if I were you."

There were three blacksuits in the yard, but none of them moved. They simply gazed up at the two boys as if watching a movie, their booming chuckles audible even from where I was standing. The inmates around us were similarly unconcerned, shouting and jeering as they ran from the place the boys would hit if they let go of their perches.

"Why isn't anyone doing anything to stop them?" I asked.

"Like what?" said Donovan. "Put up a safety net? It's their choice, just let them go."

"No," I whispered, then without thinking about what I was doing, I bolted back up the stairs. I leaped up the first flight three at a time, bounding round the corners so fast I nearly toppled over the side. I made it up the second and third flights in seconds, by the sixth level I was gasping for breath, and I almost didn't make it up the eighth set of stairs, tripping on the last one and sprawling out across the landing.

I pulled myself up, desperately gasping for breath. The lights were off up here, the cells unoccupied and shut tight. But by the weak glow that rose up from the yard I saw the two pale figures twenty or so meters down the platform. They were standing on the other side of the railing, only their trembling fingers stopping them from spilling into the void.

Both boys were eyeing me nervously, and I could finally see who they were. It was the new kids, Toby and Ashley.

I stepped slowly toward them, hands up to show I didn't mean any harm. Ashley shuffled on the ledge, looking ready to leap at any time. Toby was a little more secure, his eyes locked on mine, pleading for me to help. Behind me I heard two more sets of footsteps and knew that Donovan and Zee had my back.

"Toby, right?" I said. "And Ashley?"

The first boy nodded, the larger of the two marking out his landing site eight stories below. I stopped walking when I was an arm's length away, and realized I had no idea what to say.

"Don't jump," was the first thing that came out of my mouth. What a great help that was—I should have been a Samaritan. "I know it's bad down there, but you don't have to do this. There's people who'll look after you, you can get by."

I reached out toward Toby but quickly pulled back when Ashley started screaming at me.

"We can't get by. Every day it's the same, every day we're pushed and punched and spat on. Some guys even wet my bed the other day."

I laughed, which only seemed to incense him further.

"No," I explained hurriedly. "It happened to me too, not long after I got here. It probably happens to everyone."

"I didn't even kill him!" the boy screeched. "I shouldn't even be here."

He leaned backward, his arms straining with his own weight. Donovan and Zee rushed to my side, ready to grab for the boys if they jumped.

"Come on, Toby," said Ashley. "Let's do it."

"Wait, Toby," I said, turning my attention to the smaller boy. He was young, maybe eleven. He looked nothing like the Toby I'd known, but when I stared into his sad eyes I saw the same boy, the friend I'd let down, whose death I'd caused. He looked

like he was going to jump, and I didn't blame him. I'd been thinking the very same thing until this morning.

I thought about our plan, our way out. I thought about our
promise to keep it secret. I thought about my friend Toby, lying
dead on a stranger's floor. I thought about this kid, the way he'd
soon be lying in a pool of his own blood as well. I couldn't let it
happen again, not when I had the chance to save him.

"Look, there's a way out," I said as quietly as possible. I felt a
hand grip my arm and turned to see Donovan staring at me, the
tendons in his neck strained with anxiety.

"Don't," he said. "We made a deal. One word, remember.
That's all it could take."

"There's a bunch of us," I went on, ignoring him. "We know
how to escape."

Both boys jerked their heads in my direction.

"Really?" said Toby. It was the first time I'd heard his voice, a
musical lilt with an accent I couldn't place. "A way out of Furnace?"

"It's a lie," spat Ashley. "He'll lure us down and then they'll kill
us, turn us into one of those things. There's only one way out."

I extended my hand again and nodded at Toby. He returned
the nod, and his dark eyes suddenly glowed. He started to climb
back over, but Ashley loosened his grip from the railing and
snatched his clothing.

"I can't go on my own," he snarled, then with a noise halfway
between a snort and a sob he fell. Toby lurched out over the yard
and I threw myself toward him, grabbing his outstretched hand
an instant before he dropped. The weight of both boys pulled me
into the railings but I held on tight, refusing to let go.

The pain in my arm was unbearable. Looking down I saw

Toby holding on to my hand with everything he had. Clinging to his waist was Ashley, wailing and tugging on his captive to try to pull them both loose. Far below, several hundred inmates were watching from the yard, cheering for us all to drop.

I screamed to Donovan and Zee to help, but they didn't move.

"Just let them go," Donovan whispered. "They know about the plan, they could ruin everything."

I screamed with the pain. Zee took a step toward me but Donovan stopped him.

"I'm telling you, Alex, let them go. We don't know anything about these guys."

"You can trust him," I said through gritted teeth. "I'll lay my life on it. You can trust Toby. Now help me!"

"You'll lay all our lives on this," Donovan said, then both boys ran forward, Zee grabbing me and Donovan gripping Toby's arm. We all pulled together and managed to shift them up a fraction. But Ashley was still throwing himself around. If we couldn't dislodge him, then we were all going over.

"You got him?" I asked. Zee threw his arms over the railing and grabbed Toby's wrist. I let go of the boy and ducked behind Donovan so I had a better view of Ashley.

"Let go," I said, but he showed no sign of hearing me. "I said let go."

Ashley just looked at me with unrestrained contempt, then doubled his efforts to pull Toby loose.

"I can't die on my own!" he screeched.

"Quick," hissed Zee. "I can't hold on much longer."

"Last chance," I said, leaning over the railing, my fist bunched. Ashley spat at me, the gob arcing up then landing back on his own chin. He thrashed around, eyes wild, and I knew I had no choice. I lashed out, my fist connecting with his cheek. His head snapped back, his arm slipping. I punched him again, and this time he let go, seeming to fall in slow motion as if his endless scream was a parachute.

I staggered back from the balcony before he hit the yard, collapsing against the wall as Donovan and Zee pulled Toby onto the walkway. We all sat in silence for a while, trying to understand what had just happened, then Donovan threw me a cold look.

"I hope you're happy," he said.

But how could I be? In the space of five minutes I'd broken the vow and put us all in danger. Worst of all, I'd just become a killer for real.

THE RED HAND

WE WERE SERENADED BACK downstairs by the sound of a hundred voices cheering and screaming, calling for us to jump as well. It was sick, the way the inmates and the guards saw Ashley's final moments as entertainment, a performance to brighten up their day. He'd been a living, breathing kid; he hadn't deserved his fate, even though he'd chosen it.

"Breathe a word of this to anyone, kid, and I'll kill you," Donovan said for the fourth time as we reached our level. "I'm not joking."

He and Zee pulled ahead, disappearing into my cell. I stopped walking and turned to Toby. He wasn't crying, but it looked like his insides had been pulled out, leaving a white, shivering shell that seemed on the verge of collapse.

"Just ignore him," I said. "It's my plan and you're part of it now. But you really can't say anything, not if you want to get out of here."

"I do," he said. "I won't, I swear."

We walked into the cell. Donovan was lying on his top bunk fuming quietly, and Zee was sitting at the foot of my bed.

"I really wouldn't sit there if I were you," I told him. His eyes widened and he shot up, looking at the bulge that concealed the explosive gloves. He smiled nervously, then glanced at Toby.

"More hands means we can do this quicker," he said eventually. "Right?"

"No," said Donovan without lifting his head. "We don't tell him what we're doing. He can come with us on the day, but the less he knows the less he can give away."

"I'm not going to say anything," Toby said. "I just want out of here. I promise, my mouth is sealed. And I can help."

Donovan just snorted.

"Zee's right," I said. "The more of us there are, the quicker we can get out."

"Well, why don't we just tell everyone?" Donovan spat. I ignored him, checking to make sure there was nobody outside the cell before filling Toby in on the details of the plan. By the time I'd finished, he was grinning from ear to ear.

"You're all crazy," he said.

"Welcome to the club."

MY DREAMS THAT night were as bad as ever. I was back in my glass prison, only this time it wasn't my house I was looking at but a stranger's. The blacksuits pulled someone screaming from it, a figure I recognized as Ashley, throwing him in the cell with me. Instead of thumping the glass, I found myself banging on the boy's face, ignoring his sobs and his pleas as his skin cracked and split. Eventually he smashed into a thousand pieces, and beneath them on the glass floor I saw my reflection, all piggy eyes and rusted mask.

I woke with a cry to find myself encased in a darkness that was almost solid. Shivering, I crawled from my bed to the cell door and lay on the stone staring at the screen in the yard far below, the rotating Furnace logo a beacon in the night. I don't remember falling asleep again but I must have done so, because I woke when the siren blew, my entire body aching from the hard floor.

When the doors grated open, Donovan sprinted down to the yard to check the work chart, then legged it back up the stairs.

"Me and you on laundry," he said, obviously disappointed. "Zee's chipping, Toby's in the kitchen but I don't think he should be doing anything."

"I can handle it," came a voice from the cell door. It was Toby, and behind him stood Zee. "Just tell me what to do."

I told Toby how to fill the gloves while Donovan helped Zee squeeze the balloons under his overalls. We managed to get five in without him looking ridiculous.

"I'm glad Furnace is a no-smoking establishment." He grinned, giving us a twirl to show off his new curves.

On the way down to breakfast we made a plan just to throw the gloves through the wooden slats into the tunnel leading to Room Two. When we got the chance, we'd go through and carry the stockpile to the crack in the floor. Doing it this way was much less risky than breaking into the tunnel every day, and so long as the gloves were out of sight it was unlikely they'd ever be found. Donovan wasn't keen on the idea, but only because it was Toby's suggestion. Anyway, he was outvoted.

"Great," he muttered as he sat down with his breakfast. "Now we're a democracy."

We split up after leaving the trough room, wishing each other good luck. Donovan and I didn't say more than a handful of words to each other as we bleached and washed the sheets, too anxious about the plan. There were so many things that could go wrong—Toby could be caught filling the gloves, Zee could be spotted pushing them through the boards into the tunnel, one of us could explode while walking through the yard, and of course somebody could just mess up and spill the beans. Each of those scenarios went through our minds a million times that morning.

After showering we practically sprinted back to our cell to see Toby sitting on the bottom bunk, pale but happy. Making sure we were alone, he lifted up the mattress and proudly displayed eight fresh gloves, all bloated with gas.

"Holy crap," I said. "How'd you get so many?"

"There are certain advantages to being so skinny," he replied, pulling on his overalls to display just how baggy they were. "You could fit an elephant in these and there'd still be room for little old me."

Donovan made some comment about not pushing it, but he was obviously impressed. Some minutes later Zee came running into the cell looking just as pleased with himself.

"Massive. Piece. Of. Cake," he said. "Just pushed them through the boards when the guard did his rounds. I checked, it's so dark in there you can't see a thing. Nobody will find the gloves unless they're looking for them."

I felt some of the anxiety leaving me—like a bit of the black cloud that had obscured my thoughts for so long just breaking off and floating away. The whole thing seemed like a dream, but it was real—the plan was actually coming together.

For the rest of the day we wandered impatiently through the prison, dreaming wordlessly of what we'd do if we ever reached the surface. We must have looked like giddy kids, and several times we had to warn each other not to grin so hard for fear of someone getting suspicious.

The days rolled by with the same monotony, but for the first time since I arrived at Furnace I actually looked forward to hard labor in the morning. I'd always be awake before the siren and the first one down into the yard. The third day of our plan Donovan and I smuggled a combined total of nine gas-filled gloves from the kitchen while Toby dumped more in the tunnel and a furious Zee scrubbed the toilets. Day four we were all on trough duty and my mattress was almost falling off the bed with the sheer number of makeshift balloons beneath it. Day five Toby finally won Donovan over by stuffing ten gloves into his overalls and somehow managing to waddle to the tunnel without being seen.

Each day the stockpile grew and each day we became more confident. The blacksuits occasionally flashed us a wicked grin, but they never once stopped or searched us. The gloves were just too inconspicuous, invisible unless you knew where to look.

After ten more days we made the decision to start moving the gloves from the tunnel to the rift. Donovan and I were the only ones on chipping duty, but we'd got so used to the movement of the guard during hard labor that neither of us was worried. Well, that was a lie, we were permanently worried, but no more than usual.

We stuck to our routine, positioning ourselves by the door to Room Three and waiting for the blacksuit to start his rounds. As soon as his shadow had disappeared we ran around the corner, pulling the loose board away from the wall and scrabbling inside. Ahead of us, looking like bulbous sacs of insect eggs in the muted light from the equipment room, were the gloves. There were more than I remembered.

"Um, you didn't bring a duffel bag with you by any chance?" I asked Donovan in a whisper.

"I left my suitcase in the cell."

I swore under my breath, wondering how many trips it would take to get the gloves to the back of the cavern, then suddenly noticed that Donovan was stripping out of his overalls.

"Is there something you're not telling me?" I asked, a little concerned by the boy standing before me in his prison-issue underpants.

"Well, you know when I said I loved you . . ." he said, laughing quietly. "No, you dope, we can use them to carry the gloves."

He tied the ends of both legs, then began stuffing the gas-filled globes into the opening. After a while he looked up at me and nodded at my clothes.

"Come on, don't be shy."

I stripped, sealing the legs of my overalls and picking up a couple of gloves by their fingers. I could smell gas, but they all looked intact, and thankfully stayed that way as I squeezed them into my makeshift bag. By the time we'd located any strays that had rolled to the edges of the tunnel, I'd counted thirty-three gloves and Donovan had twenty-eight.

"Lead on, Macduffer," he whispered, hoisting his stuffed overalls over his shoulder.

We made our way into the tunnel, taking extra care not to trip. When the equipment room was out of sight we switched on our helmet lamps and I headed off in what I thought was the right direction. My memory may not have been great, but it was impossible to ignore the freezing air against my skin, and my goose bumps did a great job of locating the crack. We stood above it for a moment, savoring the roar of the river and the smell of the air.

"You really weren't imagining it," Donovan said quietly, staring at the fist-wide ravine as if he could see right through it to another life.

I placed my overalls on the rock, then got down on my knees. Pulling out a glove I eased it gently into the crack until it was completely below the surface, wedged perfectly between the two sides. Donovan followed my lead, squeezing his stash into the gap.

"Stick to a small area," I said. "We don't have to blow the whole thing, just a hole big enough for us all to drop through."

It took us no more than a few minutes to finish laying the gloves into a section of the crack roughly ten feet in length, layering them so that they were five or six deep.

"That enough, you think?" Donovan asked. I shook my head.

"One more lot like this should do it, then we're ready to blow."

"Which reminds me," he went on, turning and blinding me with his lamp. "How exactly are we going to light these mothers? I mean, I sure as hell don't want to be doing it with that piddly kitchen lighter. I'm attached to my beautiful arms and I want it to stay that way."

I untied my trousers and slipped back into my overalls without replying. To be brutally honest, that part of the plan hadn't even occurred to me.

"We'll think of something, D," I said as we started walking back. "It's what we do."

The blacksuit was back at his post when we returned to the

tunnel, and we watched him from a distance until he walked into the first chipping room. Squeezing under the loose board we sprinted back into Room Three and started hammering at the walls with glee, trying to ignore the sparks that hit our gas-scented overalls.

I was so excited that I didn't see the figures approaching from my side until it was too late. I felt a hand grip my neck, twisting my head around, then another slap me hard across the cheek. I dropped my pick and stumbled backward, only staying upright because Donovan caught me.

When my vision had cleared I saw Gary Owens standing right in front of me, flanked by two snarling Skulls. I reached up to touch my stinging cheek and my fingers came away red, although somehow I knew that it wasn't my blood.

"Red hand," said Gary, his face impassive as always. "Time for you to get your fight, little man."

"What?" I asked, genuinely confused. Gary stepped toward me and held up his right hand, which was smeared with blood. I knew it must have left an imprint on my face.

"You been marked by the red hand, little man. Gym, this evening, when my boys come get you." He walked off, the inmates parting like the Red Sea to let him through. "Fight to the death, little man," he shouted over his shoulder as he returned to his station. "Time to die."

THE ARENA

I WAS IN A STATE of shock for the rest of hard labor, hacking at the wall without knowing what I was doing while my exhausted mind tried to picture what was going to happen later that day. I knew all about the gym, about the bodies they dragged from there, the Skulls and Fifty-niners who came out grinning with bloody knuckles and bloodstained shoes.

I was no fighter, they'd throw me to the wolves and I'd be eaten alive. Why now? Two more weeks and maybe we'd have been out of here, riding a river to a fate other than Furnace. Instead I was going to be slaughtered by an ugly psychopath with a taste for murder.

While we worked Donovan tried to teach me everything he knew about self-defense, telling me to go for the eyes and the throat or the groin. But even the thought of it made me feel queasy. Admittedly I'd sent Ashley tumbling to his death less than two weeks ago, but that had been different. I had taken a life to save a life, and it wasn't like it had been a proper scrap or anything. Against the Skulls I'd fold like paper.

We met up with Zee and Toby in the yard. They'd both been on kitchen duty, smuggling another batch of gloves up to the cell, and were desperate to know how we'd got on that morning. They only had to ask a couple of times before they saw something was wrong.

"We lost them, didn't we?" guessed Zee. "The gloves. I know it."

"The gloves are fine," said Donovan. "Got them in place no problem."

"Well, you obviously weren't caught," Zee went on. "What the hell's wrong?"

"Them," said Donovan, nodding toward a group of Skulls heading to the gym. "They've challenged Alex to a skirmish, tonight."

Zee's face fell.

"They'll kill you," he said. "Alex, you can't do it."

"He doesn't have a choice," Donovan went on. "I've seen this happen a million times. If you don't show up when you've been marked, they come after you and stick a shank in your back."

"Well, we'll hide you then."

"Where?" I snapped. "The garden shed?"

We held our tongues as a blacksuit strolled past, his eyes glinting with an evil smile as if he knew I was toast.

"Whatever happens," I said when he had moved on, "the plan goes ahead. Even if I die in there, you know what to do, right?"

All three boys looked reluctant, but they nodded.

"You never know," I added. "I might win."

This time, nobody responded.

IT HAPPENED SO quickly. I thought that time would slow down, the seconds so heavy with fear that it would take each one hours to pass. But one minute I was sitting in the yard talking to the boys, the next I was yanked off my seat and practically dragged across the stone toward the gym. I fought against the two Skulls who held me, but they didn't even flinch from my pathetic blows. What good was I going to be in the arena?

I heard a familiar voice by my side and saw Donovan walking with me, telling me just to go with it. We reached the door, manned by a Skull and a Fifty-niner, and I was shunted inside, tripping over my feet and landing hard on the floor. I thought for a minute that they were going to stop Donovan from entering, but I soon felt his hand under my arm, lifting me back onto my feet.

Ahead of me lay the gym, roughly half the size of the trough room and filled with various pieces of rusting equipment— weights, benches, even an ancient-looking exercise bike. The kit was arranged in a rough circle around a ring of bare floor that looked a much darker shade of red than the rest of the room.

What shocked me most about the scene was the sheer number of people packed into the small space. Most had Skull bandannas or painted cheeks, and were sitting on the equipment waiting for the show to begin. Others had no gang markings and crowded around the back of the hall, nudging each other for the best view. There must have been fifty people in there, all waiting to see my blood spill.

I spotted Gary when he jumped off a bench into the circle, his arms raised as he addressed the crowd.

"Little man come to show us how tough he is," he shouted, then he turned to me. "Get in here."

"Eyes and throat," whispered Donovan. "Just don't go down. If you stay on your feet you might get through this."

Easily said, but my legs already felt on the verge of giving out.

I walked slowly to the edge of the circle, trying to ignore the whistles from everyone around me. Gary walked up until my eyes were level with his chest. He bent his head toward me, his quivering blond lip-hair spattered with spittle.

"Poor little man," he said. His face was expressionless, as it always was, but when I looked him in the eye I saw something moving in there, something primeval that swirled and swooped in the darkness of his pupils. He turned away, back to the audience. "Who called this challenge?"

Three Skulls leaped into the ring. I recognized them immediately as the ones I'd fought before in the canteen, the ones whose friend had been chewed to pieces by the warden's dogs. For a second I managed to snatch a ray of hope. If it was just these three, then maybe I did stand a chance. I'd given as good as I'd got the last time I faced them.

"All yours," Gary said, starting to walk away. Then, without warning, he spun around and punched me square in the jaw. I felt like my head had exploded. Fireworks burned my vision as I fell back, their color giving way to shadow as I fought to stay conscious. The blow had been like a sledgehammer, I could barely even remember where I was.

Somehow I managed to stay on my feet. I shook my head, clearing my vision in time to see Gary walking back to the edge of the circle. The three Skulls moved quickly to fill the space, the first running at me with his fist raised, ready to strike.

I stepped back, arms held up to block the blow, and more by luck than anything else I managed to weave out of the way. The momentum of the missed punch carried the Skull past me, flying into the crowd, who turned him around and pushed him back. The second thug advanced, feigning a strike to my face but changing his angle of attack at the last minute and raising his fist into my gut. It hurt, but he'd missed his target and I wasn't winded.

Fueled by adrenaline and fear, I lashed out, my fist scraping the side of the Skull's head. Before he could recover I struck again, this time connecting more firmly. I wasn't sure whether it was my knuckle or his nose that broke, but he reeled backward clutching his face. I went to finish him off with a kick to his stomach but before I could I felt something slam into my lower back. I tried to turn but the pain came again as one of the Skulls rammed his fist repeatedly into my kidneys.

I shouted, looking into the crowd to see Donovan stepping forward. But the inmates blocked his way, a wooden shank held at his neck to ensure he didn't break the rules by entering the ring.

I swung an elbow around, missing my attacker but forcing him back. I'd only been fighting for a few seconds but already my energy was fading, my limbs seizing up. I screamed, then threw myself at the boy, arms wheeling like a toddler in a tantrum. He raised his hands to defend himself and I took the opportunity, kicking him hard between the legs. A collective groan rose up from the crowd as the kid collapsed.

Spinning around again I saw the last Skull run toward me. I jabbed my fist at him but he was too quick. The punch missed and he grabbed my arm, twisting it until I was bent double. I saw a shadow approaching from behind, the strike almost shattering my spine. My legs buckled and I collapsed onto my knees. Another blow caught me on the back of the head and I sprawled forward.

If I didn't get up I was a dead man, but every time I pushed myself off the ground a foot sent me crashing down again. After a couple of attempts I gave up, curling myself into a ball as the kicks rained down. My head, my back, my stomach, my chest, nothing was out of bounds. They landed everywhere, each sending a bolt of pain through my body until it seemed like every part of me was broken.

I felt like I was sinking into the ground, blackness creeping over my vision. I heard the jeers and the cries as though through a coffin lid, muffled and distant and growing increasingly faint. I risked one last look at the arena, seeing past the blurred legs to Donovan. He had moved around the ring, and was pleading desperately with Gary. The psycho wasn't listening, he wouldn't take his eyes off me as I was pounded closer and closer to death.

Then, as if he'd been stung, Gary snapped his head around and stared at Donovan. I knew what my friend had said, I knew what he was doing, and I tried to call out for him to stop. But it was no use, I could barely even breathe, let alone shout.

I watched Gary grab hold of Donovan's throat, watched Donovan nod frantically. Then the Skull jumped into the ring and wrenched my attackers away from me, pushing them back out into the crowd. There was a chorus of boos from an audience denied their bloodlust, but Gary didn't seem to care. He bent down and grabbed my dripping overalls, pulling me up until his face was an inch away.

"Your lucky day, little man," he hissed in my ear, confirming my worst fears. "Looks like I'm hitching a lift out of this place with you."

BACK TO WORK

"What was I supposed to do?"

It must have been the tenth time Donovan said it as we made our slow way out of the gym. I was so battered and bruised that I couldn't even pick myself off the ground, Donovan had to haul me up and drag me from the arena. I tried to put one foot in front of the other, but even the smallest of movements made me cry out in pain. It felt as if all my joints had been filled with grit, my bones laced with razor wire. I spat out a mouthful of bitter blood and tried to tell him it was okay. What came out was a low groan.

"I couldn't let them kill you, man," he said, helping me across the yard. Zee and Toby were waiting by the stairs, and ran over when they saw us, but none of the other inmates looked the least bit concerned.

"Oh no," said Zee when they reached us. "Is that him?"

"Of course it's him, you moron," said Donovan. "Who else is it going to be?"

"It's just . . . his face."

"What's wrong with my face?" I tried to ask, but all that emerged was another groan.

"Let's get him back to the cell," Toby said. "You think you can get him up the stairs?"

"You think you can help?"

Together they pushed, pulled, and carried me up six flights of steps. A couple of times they folded under my weight and I almost toppled over the railings. Right at that moment the agony was so great that I didn't really care. Let me fall, let it be over. But a few minutes later I ended up on my bed, trying unsuccessfully to find a comfortable position to lie in while Donovan recounted my embarrassing attempts to defend myself. He left out the deal he'd struck with Gary, eyeing me nervously as he told them that the Skulls had just let me go after a beating.

"You were lucky," said Zee, perched on the bed next to me. He reached out as if to touch my face, then pulled his hand back. "You don't look it, but you were lucky."

I ran my tongue over my teeth. One of the bottom ones was missing. By the way my face was throbbing I thought that was the least of my worries.

"I wasn't lucky," I said, the words coming out like I was chewing a mouthful of toffee as I spoke. "Donovan saved me."

"Donovan?" said Zee, looking at the bigger boy who stood by the cell door, staring out into the yard.

"He saved my life," I went on.

"Nice one, big guy," said Zee. "You go in and show 'em who's boss?"

There was a moment of uncomfortable silence, then Donovan spun around and faced us all.

"What was I supposed to do?" he shouted. "Leave him to die?"

"Whoa," said Zee. "I don't blame you, I'd have done the same thing if my arms were as big as yours."

"He didn't fight," I said. "He made a deal."

"A deal?" Both Zee and Toby looked worried. "What kind of deal?"

"We've got another passenger," I slurred. "Gary."

"No way," said Zee. "No way, Donovan. You didn't tell him?"

"It was that or Alex died," Donovan spat back. "You want that?"

"Well, what . . . I mean, we all get a plus-one now or something?"

"Zee," I said. "It's fine, it just means one more person. Donovan did the right thing."

"But Gary's a psycho, he'll tell all the Skulls and then there's no way we'll get out. We're all going to the hole. Either that or he'll stab us in the eyes just to get out first. This is a bad idea. This whole thing's a bad idea."

Donovan slammed his hands on the bars and stormed out of the cell, disappearing down the walkway.

"Leave it, Zee," I mumbled through swollen lips. "He did the right thing."

Zee just snorted, but his expression was one of fear. If my face had been able to move at all, it would have probably mirrored it. The thought of having Gary on board was terrifying. He really would snap our necks if he thought he could get out alone. Hell, he'd probably snap them even if we made it to safety, just for fun. But I couldn't complain. The alternative was having my guts spilled out across the gym floor.

"It will be okay," I said. But I wasn't sure how much I believed it.

THE REST OF that day I spent drifting in and out of sleep, with endless dreams of being beaten senseless. Each time I woke I thought the pain had been part of the nightmares, until I tried to move.

Donovan only returned when the night siren blew. I didn't ask him where he'd been, but he apologized for storming off and reassured me that he hadn't told Gary anything about the escape except for the fact that it would be happening soon.

"He can't give anything away and he can't do it without us," he said as the lights shut off.

I went to hard labor in the morning even though I thought I was going to die. I didn't have a choice—anyone too injured to work was dragged off through the vault door to the infirmary, a place that few returned from. Fortunately we were on trough duty and Donovan sat me in the corner, happy to do my share of the work as well as his. Despite the fact that my skin was purple and unbearably tender to touch, I still managed to squeeze a couple of gas-filled gloves against it. Donovan managed to smuggle out eight, and we were back on track.

It was on that morning that Donovan had a brain wave about the fuse for the explosion. He spent an hour trying to weasel off the end of one of the giant stove lighters, draining the fluid inside into a glove and filling it with string from one of the crates. He slipped the flint free from one lighter as well.

"Something to spark up with," he said.

"Nicely done," I muttered weakly as he stuffed the fuse into his overalls.

We didn't have many run-ins with Gary for those few days. Every now and then we'd see him in the yard and he'd track us with his insect eyes, and four days after the fight he came over as we were sitting in the trough room.

"Better not be going anywhere without me," he said, leaning over the table.

"As soon as we know when it's happening we'll tell you," I replied. "You've got my word."

He just stared at me for a few seconds until I thought my blood was curdling, then he walked off. He threw another comment at us over his shoulder as he went, one loud enough for most people to hear.

"I'll kill you if you try and leave without me."

"He's going to ruin it for all of us," said Zee when Gary had left the room. "Half the hall must have heard that."

If they had, they showed no sign of understanding it. For most, the idea of escape from Furnace was so unthinkable, so impossible, that they'd probably have dismissed it even if there was a hole in the wall and a staircase marked "To Freedom."

"Relax, Zee," I said. "There's only a few more days."

THERE WERE EIGHT, to be correct. Eight days of fear that everything would go horribly wrong. Eight days of panic that we'd be caught, tortured, then executed in the most violent ways possible. But also eight days of hope that we'd actually manage to break free of our prison, that we'd be able to see sunshine once again.

For the next week it was the hope that carried us. Even though I was exhausted, and never fully recovered from my beating, it was the smell of fresh air that kept me going. So many times I thought I couldn't go on, couldn't handle the stress of smuggling out any more gloves or secreting them behind the panels in Room Two. But just when things seemed at their bleakest I'd recall something from up top—birdsong, the feel of the grass on my bare feet, the sight of the sea bounded only by the horizon—and the hope would be like fuel, urging me on.

It was the same for the rest of them. Where there should have been tired faces there were always smiles, jokes instead of tears, bravery when we should have all been cowering in our cells. We pushed ourselves to the limit. By day two we'd smuggled another fifteen gloves into the tunnel. By day five it was thirty-three. By day seven the pile was fifty-one deep and more than big enough to blast us out of here.

Day eight found Donovan and me back in Room Two, stripped and dragging our gas-filled overalls across the rough floor to the rift. We were relieved to see the rest of our stash still in place. A couple had deflated slightly, but it looked like they were all fit to go boom.

"You start slotting them in," Donovan shouted above the roar of the river. I could swear the sound was louder now, like it knew we were coming for it. "I'll get the fuse sorted."

He rummaged through the gloves until he found the one full of lighter fluid. Giving it a shake for good measure, he opened it up and pulled out the string, which reeked of fuel. Tying the strands together, he laid one end by the balloons then walked backward and unwound the rest, the fuse snaking for several meters until it disappeared behind a massive chunk of rock.

"That should be enough," he said, his head popping out from the stone. "The explosion will probably set off another cave-in and kill us all anyway."

"Better that than any more time in the cell," I replied, struggling to squeeze another glove into the packed rift. "Especially with your farts."

Donovan laughed as he made his way back over. He looked at the bulging crack in the ground, then at the twenty or so gloves we still had left in his overalls.

"Spares?"

"Looks like it," I said, grimacing as I tried to stand up. "You want to just scatter them around?"

Donovan scratched his chin, then shook his head.

"No, I got a plan." He picked up his overalls. "Let's get back to the tunnel."

"The tunnel?" I asked, but he just grinned at me and set off across the cavern. I followed, my limbs screaming at me with every step, and arrived at the passageway to see Donovan wedging the remaining gloves into the crevices in the ceiling. He wasn't having much luck in the dark, as they kept dropping to the floor with a wet slap.

"I'm sure there's a good reason for this," I whispered. The equipment room was dead ahead; deserted, but you never knew when the blacksuit was going to return. Donovan managed to cram a couple of gloves into a particularly big crack above his head, then turned to me.

"What if we have to leave in a hurry?" he asked. "The guards'll be on our tail like rats after cheese. If we demolish this tunnel after we've got through, then we'll have all the time in the world to blow the floor and get into the river."

"Makes sense," I replied, nodding. I picked up a couple of gloves and looked for suitable holes in the ceiling, stretching up with considerable pain to fit them all in. By the time we'd finished, the top of the tunnel looked like the underside of a mutant cow—all bulging udders and no legs.

"Moo," I said, as Donovan unwound the last of the fuse, jamming it between a glove and the wall, then running it down and out into the cavern. There wasn't much string left, but hopefully enough to give us a bit of distance before the tunnel collapsed. He tucked the lighter flint under the end of the fuse so he'd easily find it again.

"So," he said, climbing back into his overalls and rubbing his hands on the material to get rid of the pungent smell of lighter fluid. "We're done."

"Finished," I added. "All we've got to do now is get everybody here without anyone seeing us, blow a hole in a solid rock floor, and jump into a raging underground river."

"Easy," he added, laughing quietly. I couldn't really see his expression in the dark, but he suddenly fell silent, and I could sense an intense gaze in my direction.

"You don't just wanna go now?" he asked. I stared into the shadows where his face was.

"And leave the others?"

"We might never get another chance," he went on. "What if something happens?"

"Donovan," I said gently. "I know you don't mean that. You risked everything to save me the other day. I know you're not the kind of guy to abandon his friends. I know it."

"What did I tell you when you first got here, Alex? You don't have friends in Furnace."

"Yeah, right," I said. "Play the hard man all you like, but I know you're not going anywhere without Zee and Toby."

There was a moment of silence, then Donovan laughed.

"Jeez, look what you've done to me. You've turned me into a sentimental old fool!"

"Come on," I said, leading the way back to the wooden boards. We'd left the tunnel so many times it was almost automatic now, and we returned to the chipping room without incident. It was only when we'd started hacking at the walls with our picks that Donovan winked at me.

"So . . . tomorrow then?" he asked.

I rested my pick over my shoulder and nodded.

"Tomorrow."

THE LAST NIGHT

AFTER HARD LABOR WE showered and ate, then retreated back to our cell. Toby and Zee were already there, chatting excitedly about something or other when we strolled through the door. Their heads jerked up, their faces creased with anxiety.

"So?" asked Zee, drawing the word out.

"Guards caught us," Donovan answered. "They destroyed the gloves, sealed off the room, and took Alex and me through the door. They turned us into monsters, and now we're back to eat you."

He threw himself at the two smaller boys and they jumped back to avoid him.

"What's got into him?" Zee asked as Donovan fell onto the bottom bunk, giggling. "Did he inhale some gas or something?"

"I'm not sure," I answered, pushing Donovan out of the way and sitting on the foot of the bed. But I did know: he was drunk on hope, on excitement. We all were. "Everything went to plan, though. It's all ready to go. Tomorrow's the day."

"Tomorrow?" Toby said, turning pale. Zee grabbed his shoulders and shook him.

"Don't cave now, Toby old boy," he said gleefully. "Too late to back out."

"I just didn't expect it to be so soon," he replied as the color slowly returned to his face. "Are you sure we're ready?"

"Nope," I said. "You're welcome to wait here for a couple of years, but I'm going now, ready or not."

"And me," said Zee, adding a soft little whoop as he punched the air.

"So what are you gonna do when you're out?" asked Donovan. "First thing I'm gonna do is grab the biggest burger I can find, all relish and onions and bacon and—oh mamma, my mouth is dripping."

"I just want the air," I said. "Give me a beach and a sea breeze and the sound of seagulls and I'll be the happiest man on earth."

Zee budged me over and sat down.

"I'm going to head home, sleep in a proper bed for once," he said dreamily.

"And wait for the police to arrive?" I asked. "Come on, Zee, as soon as we're out of here, they're going to be looking for us. If we go home, they're just going to cart us straight back here, and straight into the hole."

Zee's face fell, as did Toby's.

"So what do we do then?" asked the new kid, sliding down the wall and drawing his knees up to his face. "I've got nowhere else to go."

"We're all kids, Toby," I replied. "None of us do. We just have to stick together. We'll be okay."

"Long as I get my burger," added Donovan, smacking his lips.

"What about this place?" asked Zee. "I mean, do we tell anyone about it? About what goes on here?"

"Yeah," I offered. "We have to. We can file an anonymous report to the police or something."

"Like they'll ever believe it," said Donovan.

"We have to try," I added. "What about everyone else here? We've got to do something to help."

"Feel free," the big guy said. "You go off and be heroes while I sit and eat my burger."

"Enough about the burger!" I yelled, laughing. "There's more out there than fast food. Come on, D, we'll be free, we can have anything we like."

"Free?" came a voice from the door. I snapped my head around so hard I thought I'd broken my neck. Standing there was Jimmy, the beanpole kid that Zee, Monty, and I had ridden down to Furnace with in the elevator. He was even skinnier now, his overalls hanging off him like a tattered shroud on a skeleton.

I'd hardly seen him at all since that first day, he'd been hanging out with a group of kids that kept themselves to themselves. He'd walked past my cell a few times, but never stopped to say hi. I guess he'd never heard us talking about escaping before. I mentally kicked myself. Anyone could have been outside, even the guards.

"Where are you going?" he went on. "You getting out of here?"

"Nowhere."

"No," Donovan and I said in tandem.

"Just dreaming," added Zee. "Talking about what we'd do if we ever got out. You know, you must have done it."

Jimmy stared at us like he could see right through our lies.

"Everyone knows you guys have been acting weird," he said. "Rumor is you know a way out and you're not saying. Figured

you'd tell me though. We got here together, we can leave together."

"Ain't no way out, kid," said Donovan, getting up from the bed
and walking up to him. "Got your head screwed on all wrong.
Now scram."

Jimmy kept staring at me. One more, I thought. Surely one
more person wouldn't hurt. But it was one more person to spill
the beans, one more to ruin everything. It wasn't worth the risk.

"Sorry, Jimmy," I said eventually. "Donovan's right, we're not
going anywhere. There is no way out of Furnace, remember."

"Now scram," Donovan repeated. This time he planted his
hands on Jimmy's chest and sent him stumbling backward. The
boy hit the railings but his eyes never left mine.

"Last chance," he said. "Take me with you."

I just turned away. We all did. And when we looked back at
the platform it was deserted.

WE SPENT THE next couple of hours panicking. What did Jimmy
mean when he said everyone knew we were acting weird? And
what rumor? If the inmates were starting to suspect something,
it meant the guards might be too, and if that was the case, then it
was all over.

But there had been no alarms, no blacksuits at the door, no
dogs chasing us from our cells. If the warden even suspected we
were planning to make a break for it, then the chances were we'd
already be dead.

We voted on what to do about Gary. Zee and Toby figured we
should just not tell him, make a run for it and hope he didn't figure out what we were doing. Donovan and I thought it was prob-

ably best to let him know. We'd made a deal, after all, and the Skull had let me keep my life. Besides, he was big and strong and he might just come in handy if things got tough. The vote was a tie but Donovan only had to put a little pressure on Toby to make him change his mind. Physical pressure, that was, in the form of a Chinese burn.

Nobody else was willing to deliver the news, however, so I ended up traipsing down the stairs. The Skulls were nowhere in sight, and I made my way to the gym. From the howling inside I didn't really want to go in, but when I told the two sentries on duty I had some important news for Gary, they let me pass.

Inside was a bloodbath, a Skull and a Fifty-niner going to work on each other with unrestrained fury. Gary was watching, but when he saw me he jumped off his bench and walked over.

"Something to tell me, little man?" he sneered. He wiped his hand across his face, his swollen knuckles leaving a trail of blood on his lips.

"Tomorrow," I said. "During hard labor. We're all going in the chipping room. Get in there too. You'll see when we make our move, just follow us."

He looked at me, and for the first time I actually saw a hint of emotion. To my surprise, it resembled anxiety, there for a second then gone.

"What if I'm put somewhere else?" he asked. "You're not going without me."

"Doesn't matter," I replied. "They don't check. Just get in there, Room Three. Stay close. And don't tell a soul, okay?"

He didn't move, just stood there with his dark eyes fixed on mine. Then he turned and walked off, climbing back on his bench and watching the fight as if nothing had happened. The Skull in the ring was on the floor, the Fifty-niner stomping on his chest, and I made my way from the gym as quickly as I could to escape the sound of snapping ribs.

Back upstairs we went through the last few details of the plan, with Toby posted outside to make sure there were no more eavesdroppers. There wasn't really much left to say, however, and after a period of silence Zee and Toby decided to head back to their cells for some rest. Neither Donovan nor I could face the thought of dinner, so we just lay on our bunks and waited for lights-out.

"You know what it means if we fail, don't you?" he asked.

"Yeah, we die."

"In the most horrible way possible," he added. "Truly in the most horrible way possible."

"I'm not sure if it really matters though," I said quietly. Donovan protested but I just carried on. "I mean, even if everything goes wrong and we end up in the hole, or worse, we still managed to beat Furnace."

"How's that?"

"Well, we figured a way out. We actually found a way of escaping. It doesn't matter if we make it or not, we still beat the system. Right now, Donovan, right now we're free."

"I don't really get you," he said. "But I hear what you're saying. We'll be legends, man, whatever happens."

He didn't really understand, but then neither did I. It was just a feeling, a weight lifted from my chest. Furnace's walls seemed a little bit weaker, the air a little bit lighter, the space a little bit bigger. It was still the same place but it didn't have the same power. We'd found a way to break it before it had found a way to break us.

At least that's what I thought when the cells locked and the prison went dark. Everything changed when I woke up some time later, deafened by the siren and bathed in a pool of blood-red light.

TAKEN

I SAT BOLT UPRIGHT in bed, my head spinning. It was the blood watch, here for another harvest. I couldn't believe it, they couldn't be, not tonight.

The crimson light made the entire prison shimmer like I was seeing it through a heat haze, as if the fires of hell were burning right beneath us. I stretched my neck and looked down into the yard as the vault door swung open, unleashing a series of screams and wheezes that could only come from the gas masks.

"Alex," came Donovan's voice from above me, laced with fear. "Just don't move, okay? For once, just stay in bed and keep your head down."

I lowered myself back and pulled the sheets over my head. Donovan was right, just stay quiet, stay hidden and they'd pass right by. There was a series of wet cries as the wheezers split up, each heading for a different flight of steps. I pictured them jerking and convulsing as they made their way along the platforms, their piggy eyes picking out victims to be devoured.

There was a scream, distant. It was on the far side of the prison. The first wheezer had chosen. A second cry followed, like a dying bird, from below us. Two down, three to go. Another shriek, followed by a chorus of pleas from the chosen inmate. A fourth, this time way above, the sound echoing down the prison walls in case any of us missed it the first time around. Only one wheezer left. One more victim.

"Not us," I prayed, so softly I couldn't even hear myself. My breath hit the sheet over my mouth, the air stale and warm. "Please, God, just one more night. Not us."

A scream, so close it could have been from inside my bed. I curled up even more tightly into my sheets. Stay quiet, stay hidden, they'll go away, they'll just go away.

I heard another scream, but it wasn't from the gas mask. It was a cry of rage, of anger, of despair. It was Donovan. I pulled the sheets off my head and sat up to see the monster standing right outside the cell, all rust and stitches and glass eyes, all leather and syringes and dried blood. It had one hand in its pocket, and pulled it free with a sucking sound.

"No!" screamed Donovan. "NoNoNoNoNo!"

Its soiled hand struck the bars of the cell, marking out a crude X on the metal. Then it slung back its twitching head and screeched, the sound quickly mimicked by its twisted siblings.

I jumped out of bed and looked at Donovan. He was peeking from his sheets, his eyes like white moons against his dark skin, his mouth foaming. I'd never seen him like this before, filled with utter terror, and it broke my heart.

"What do we do?" I asked. The wheezer had frozen, but it wouldn't be long before the blacksuits made their way here with their dogs. "Which one of us is it taking?"

Donovan didn't move, didn't speak. I ripped the sheets from him and he still didn't respond. Desperate, I grabbed his arms and hauled him out of bed. He was halfway over the edge before he realized what was going on, snapping out of his trance in order to flip himself over and land on the floor.

"Donovan," I said. He looked at the wheezer, then at me. "What do we do?"

"I don't know," he replied in a voice as soft as breath.

"Which one of us has it picked?"

"I don't know," he repeated. "You only know when the black-suits come."

I cursed, slapping my hands against my forehead. I should have been more scared, but for some reason my head was clear. I guess it was because it didn't seem real, I expected to wake up any second. I threw myself at the bars, finding myself face-to-face with the wheezer, but it was motionless, not even a twitch to show that it was still alive. The prison was plunged into darkness and I backed away from the bars in panic.

"Think!" I shouted as soon as the red lights snapped back on again. "It can't end like this."

"But it has," Donovan said. "It's come to nothing."

I paced the cell, glancing down into the yard to see more figures emerging from the vault door. I counted seven blacksuits, two dogs. Then, to my surprise, the warden strode into the middle of the yard, staring up at the cells. He'd never come out during the blood watch. Something was wrong.

"They know," I said, my shoulders slumping. "They've come for us. They've probably got Zee and Toby too."

"No," replied Donovan. "That's Zee's cell down there. No wheezer."

I looked down and, sure enough, Zee's cell was unmarked. I couldn't make out any sign of life in the bruised shadows but I was sure Zee would be watching me. Maybe the warden didn't know. Maybe this was just some sick joke, a perverse coincidence. The lights flickered, then went out again, the only sign I was still alive the terrifying noises outside the cell—growls and footsteps and wheezes.

"Look," I said, taking Donovan's shoulders. "They only take one cellmate at a time, right?"

"Right."

"Then one of us is left. We still go ahead with this, okay? One of us makes the break. Once I'm free, I'll go straight to the cops. Doesn't matter if they throw me back in here, just so long as they investigate. If I'm quick, I might be able to save you. If you hurry, you might get back in time to save me."

Donovan nodded as the lights rebooted, then he flung his arms around me, squeezing me so hard I gasped for breath.

"Thanks," he said, his eyes filling.

"For what?"

"Thanks for giving me hope."

"It's not over yet," I said. I could hear footsteps crashing down the platform, the howl of the mutant dogs.

"I know," he replied. Then they were there. A command from the blacksuit sent the cell door crashing open and in a blink of an eye the guard was inside, a massive hand wrapped around Donovan's throat, pulling the boy out as if he weighed nothing, holding him up above the ground. I threw myself forward but the giant used his other hand to swipe me away. I felt like I'd been hit by a car, sliding across the floor and smashing into the bunks.

By the time I'd got to my feet again, the cell door was rattling shut.

"Donovan!" I shouted. The gas mask was sliding a needle from his belt, a syringe full of blackness and death, a cloud that swirled like a galaxy, full of flickers of yellow light. "No!"

But it was too late. The wheezer stabbed the needle into Donovan's neck and the boy went limp and silent.

"You can't do this!" I shouted. "Donovan, I'll come for you. I'll come for you!"

My words tried to give chase as the procession made its way down the platform, but they were powerless to stop this nightmare. I could do nothing but watch as Donovan and the other victims were dragged down the stairs and across the yard, my best friend disappearing through the vault door, swallowed by the shadows that would escort him to his death.

The warden was the last to leave, and as he stepped through the door he turned and stared up at the cells again. From this distance his eyes were just pools of blackness lost in the red leather of his face, but I could swear he was looking right at me. I felt my vision twist and flicker, a hundred terrible images flashing before my eyes—blood and bone and teeth and chains and screams—then the warden turned away and the carnage ended.

As the door closed behind him I struggled to cling to my sanity, to my reason, to my consciousness. But it was no use. I collapsed to the floor, calling Donovan's name and wishing with all my heart that they had taken me instead.

BREAK

MORNING CAME RELUCTANTLY, afraid of breaching the darkness that embraced both the prison and my thoughts. I hadn't returned to sleep after Donovan was taken, I just sat on the bed at the mercy of a million different emotions—crying then screaming then pounding at the bars then laughing hysterically at the night like a creature of madness.

My last words to Donovan never left my head. *I'll come for you.* My exhausted mind pictured me charging back into Furnace at the head of an army, shooting the blacksuits where they stood, stringing the warden up by his neck, pulling Donovan from his cell and embracing him with the same strength with which he'd held me. *I'll come for you.* And I would.

As soon as the lights came on I was up and standing by the bars, staring out at the yard with cold eyes. It was like a piece of me had been taken along with Donovan, the side of me that felt compassion, that felt fear. All that was left was hatred. I was going to get out of Furnace, then I was going to burn it so that nothing remained but a smoking crater filled with the corpses of its demons.

The cell doors opened with a deafening rattle and I made my

way down into the yard along with hundreds of inmates. It was as if the other prisoners sensed something different about me too, an edge that hadn't been there before, like I would explode if anybody even touched me. They moved out of my way as I marched toward the canteen, throwing wary glances at me when they thought I wasn't looking and turning their heads when they saw that I was.

I was sitting at an empty table when Zee ran up to me. He slid onto the bench opposite, checking over his shoulder. His face was pinched, his eyes still red with tears.

"They took him," he said. He seemed like he wanted to say more, but gave up and hung his head. I didn't reply, just stared out across the trough room to see Gary taking a seat along with the Skulls. He nodded at me and I nodded back, and in that moment of symmetry my expression was identical to his— empty, inhuman.

"I'll come back," I said, looking away. "I promised him I would. I can't leave him."

"So it's still on?" Zee asked, raising his head.

"It's still on."

Toby met us just as we were leaving the trough room. He was red-faced and stressed.

"My cellmate," he said through strangled breaths, "wouldn't let me out until he knew where we were going. I didn't tell him, Alex, but the whole prison knows we're up to something."

"It doesn't matter," I replied, leading the boys across the yard. We joined the crowd for the chipping rooms, avoiding the inmates who were eyeballing us with a strange mixture of hatred and hope. Jimmy was there too, his sickly gaze never leaving me.

I ignored them all, focusing on the task ahead. We had one shot at this, just one. If we messed up, then we were all dead.

Slowly the crowd shuffled through the passage into the equipment room. The blacksuit watched us all with his silver eyes, finger permanently on the trigger of his shotgun. I thought for a moment that he might be able to hear my pounding heart as I passed him, but he showed no sign of even noticing me.

Inside the equipment room I slammed on a helmet and lifted a pick from the racks. Zee and Toby did the same. I thought for a moment that Gary hadn't made it, but he came in at the tail end of the crowd, his eyes narrowed with the same sliver of anxiety I'd seen yesterday. He spotted us and the expression vanished.

"Levels one to three, Room One," bellowed the blacksuit, waving his shotgun toward the portal. "Rest of you into Room Three, you know the drill."

We headed into the chipping room, our hearts in our mouths. Every few steps, I'd look up and meet the eyes of Zee or Toby or Gary. It was like there was a line linking us, one that only we could see. Or maybe it wasn't that invisible—the looks from the other inmates were growing increasingly hostile, like they could sense how close we were to making a break for it, to leaving them to rot.

We positioned ourselves near the front of the cavern, pulling our visors down to conceal the sweat that already ran freely down our faces. We started attacking the wall the same way we always did, Zee keeping an eye on the shadow that sat fat across the equipment room floor. As soon as that shadow disappeared we would make our move.

It seemed to take forever. We chipped and we hacked and we

sweated, and all the time our blood pressure rose, our tempers frayed. Much longer and I felt like my heart was going to implode.

"Come on," hissed Gary in between swings. "We gotta move now."

"We wait," I said, my voice heavy with an authority I never knew I possessed. "We leave when I say."

He gripped his pick so hard that his deformed knuckles went white, but he didn't argue, just kept swinging and cursing.

"Alex," hissed Zee a few minutes later. "The guard, he's going."

I looked to see the black shadow sweep across the floor of the equipment room as the guard disappeared into the first chipping hall. I turned and nodded to the three expectant, terrified faces in front of me, and after checking that nobody in the room was watching us, we walked calmly toward the door.

So far so good, it was all going to plan. Until I heard a voice call out from behind us. I swung around to see Jimmy legging it across the cavern floor, his face twisted into a mask of panic. He didn't even wait until he was in earshot before shouting out.

"Don't you dare," he yelled. "I know what you're doing."

"We're not doing anything, Jimmy," I replied as calmly as I could. "Just working."

He ran right up to me, then grabbed my collar with his bony fingers. The other prisoners in the room were turning to watch, looking at us like we'd stabbed them in the back.

"I knew it," he spat. "You're doing it now. Take me with you or I swear I'll scream my head off."

He never got the chance. From nowhere Gary moved in, jabbing the handle of his pick toward Jimmy's face. The wooden pole made contact with one of the most sickening sounds I'd ever heard, and the boy crumpled, groaning.

"Let's go," Gary said. "No time."

I looked at Jimmy, struggling to get up and hold his broken nose at the same time, then I turned and fled toward the equipment room. We rounded the corner to see that it was deserted, and it was all I could do not to cry out with joy. I skidded to the floor and yanked on the loose board, pulling it away from the wall. Zee went to climb in but Gary shoved him out of the way, diving through the gap headfirst. Zee followed, and it was just as Toby started climbing in that all hell broke loose.

I heard panting behind me and turned to see Jimmy standing there, the front of his overalls drenched in blood, his whole body shaking. He pointed at me, his eyes full of the strength that his body lacked.

"Escape," he said. His voice was weak, but the word hit me like a slap in the face. I saw him take a deep breath, then he repeated it with more force.

"Jimmy," I called out. "It's not too late, just come with us."

But he wasn't thinking clearly. The blow to his head had scrambled his thoughts. All he cared about now was making sure we didn't leave. He called out again and again, each time the volume of his cry escalating until it became a shrill shriek that echoed around the equipment room.

"Get in," I said to Toby. "Now."

He hesitated a moment longer, then scrabbled past the loose board, vanishing into the darkness. Jimmy was still screaming the same word over and over again. I had seconds until the black-suits appeared.

Not even that. As I bent down to climb through the hole, I spotted the guard emerging from the first chipping room. The giant paused, his silver eyes squinting in the light as if he didn't quite believe what was happening. It was all the time I needed. By the time he'd raised his shotgun I was halfway into the tunnel, the shot kicking up the dust where my feet had been an instant before.

Toby was waiting for me on the other side of the boards, his eyes so wide I thought they were going to fall out. I looked back into the equipment room to see the guard charging toward us, his vast body a blur. Behind him, coming through the door from the yard with equal speed, was another blacksuit.

There was a sparking sound ahead, from the other end of the tunnel.

"Oh no," I said, my heart sinking. Gary had found the fuse, and was trying to light it. "Run!"

We sprinted up the tunnel just as the blacksuits smashed through the boards behind us. They just charged right through the massive wooden planks, sending splinters flying into the air as they raised their shotguns again. I hurled myself to the ground as the guns fired, pulling Toby down with me, the shot slicing the air above our heads.

Ahead there was a hiss as the fuse lit. I watched the flame hurtle along the string, up the wall toward the gas balloons that were right above our heads. I hauled myself up, grabbing Toby's hand and throwing myself along the tunnel. Only a few more steps and we'd be free.

But the blacksuits were too quick. Just as I saw the end of the tunnel ahead, I felt an iron grip around my throat, hoisting me from the floor. By the squawk from my side I knew that Toby had been caught too. It didn't really matter now anyway. I watched the thin blue flame travel along the ceiling, almost brushing the first glove. We were going to burn.

The blacksuit turned me around to face him, narrowing his silver eyes at me. It was Moleface—the same guard who had tormented me ever since that first day in the house so long ago. His face split open into the shark's smile I knew so well.

"Got you," he said. Over his shoulder the flame flickered, almost went out, then burned fiercely as it reached the first glove. I willed it on. At least if we died here we'd take some of them with us.

"No," I replied, grinning insanely back at my captor. "*I've* got *you*."

The first glove swelled and burst into a ball of light and heat. Then the world exploded—darkness into a radiance that burned my eyes, silence into a thunder so intense it felt like my body had been crushed to dust. The rest of the balloons followed suit, the resulting fireball sweeping down the tunnel like the fist of God, a shock wave that catapulted us all into the cave.

I blacked out for a moment, the sound of ringing in my ears the only thing letting me know I was still alive. That and the pain, so agonizing that it forced me to regain consciousness. I snapped open my eyes to see the tunnel in ruins, slabs of stone and a curtain of dust and flames where there had once been a passageway. Somewhere in the distance I could hear a siren and the sound of people shouting, but Donovan's plan had worked, there was now a wall of rock between us and them.

I tried to get up but I couldn't move. Fears of paralysis flooded my mind, the thought that I would have to lie here until the guards clawed their way through the demolished tunnel. But looking down I saw a huge weight slumped across my legs. It was Moleface, although he was no longer a man in black but a man *of* black. He had caught the brunt of the blast, the fire burning off his suit and leaving his body a charred mess. I realized that he'd probably saved me, shielding me from the flames, and I smiled at the irony of it.

I tugged at my legs and finally managed to free them, using a nearby rock to pull myself up. My helmet lamp was smashed to smithereens, but the fires painted the cavern in a weak light. I made out a mangled shape in front of me, a broken boy that had once been Toby. It took me a moment to notice there was another person hunched over the scene.

"Zee?" I asked, peering into the gloom. The other boy stood and ran over to me.

"Alex! Jesus, man, I thought you were dead."

"Is Toby?"

"No, he's got a pulse, but he's smashed up pretty bad. Ain't no way he's getting into that river."

"Gary?"

"Ran ahead, the idiot," Zee said. "I tried to stop him lighting the fuse, Alex, I really did. He just shoved me out of the way. Only a matter of time now before he finds the river."

I limped over to Toby. His eyes were shut but he was breathing weakly, a trail of blood running from the corner of his mouth. I knelt down beside him and touched his cheek, and very slowly he opened his eyes.

"Did we make it?" he asked as his vision focused. "Are we free?"

I took his hand and squeezed it, but it just made him wince.

"We made it," I said. "But you can't go any farther, Toby. You'll die if you do."

"I don't care," he answered. "I don't care, I just want to get out of here. Don't leave me. Please don't leave me."

I looked at Zee but the boy just shrugged.

"He's had it if he goes in that river," he said.

Behind us I heard the sound of shifting rubble, a series of wet growls. It was the dogs. I could picture them tearing into the stone with their killer claws. It wouldn't take them long to break through.

"He's had it if he doesn't," I said. "Let's get him up."

I put my hand under Toby's armpit and pulled gently, Zee doing the same on the other side. Together we managed to haul him up and keep him steady. He screamed as he tried to walk on his broken leg, but he managed to stay conscious.

"Let's go," I said.

We had only just started walking when I heard a groan from behind us. I peered over my shoulder to see a shape rising out of the darkness, a giant hauling itself up from the debris and dust. It was Moleface; somehow, he wasn't dead. If he managed to get to his feet, then we were history.

"Can you hold him?" I asked Zee. The boy nodded and I slipped out from under Toby's arm. I ran over to the injured man, looking around until I spotted a block of stone light enough to lift but heavy enough to do some damage. I hefted it above my head, and was about to bring it down when the shape moved, fast. It swung an arm out, catching me behind the knee and making my legs buckle. I collapsed to the floor, the block of stone almost braining me.

Moleface grunted as he stood, wiping the blood from his eyes
and patting out the fires that still burned on his exposed flesh.
His injured face quivered and shook, and it took me a moment to
grasp that he was attempting to smile.

I tried to get up but the giant placed his foot on my chest,
pinning me like a butterfly. Then he bent down and picked up
the same piece of rock I'd been struggling to lift, holding it
effortlessly in one mammoth hand.

"Alex!" came Zee's voice behind me. I could barely breathe, let
alone yell, but somehow I managed to answer.

"Just go."

Was it really going to end like this? So close to escape yet
about to be crushed by the very guard who'd made it all happen,
the one who'd shot Toby and framed me. I struggled against his
weight but it was just too much.

I was distracted by a shape materializing behind the giant,
another face, a single gleaming silver eye. I couldn't believe it,
the blacksuits were indestructible. I looked up and saw the rock
held above my head, waiting for the moment it would fall and
snatch away my life. At least it would be quick. I fixed the blacksuit with the fiercest gaze I could muster. I wouldn't go screaming and crying and begging for my life.

The stone block dropped, smashing into pieces millimeters
from my head. I thought for a minute that his aim had simply
been poor, but something else was going on in the shadows
above me.

The second blacksuit had his burned hands around the throat
of his twin, a grip so fierce that it forced Moleface down onto his
knees. With the weight off my chest I rolled to my feet, backing
away but not taking my eyes off the scene.

Moleface threw an elbow behind him, connecting with his attacker's hip so hard that it sent a crack echoing around the cavern. But the man wouldn't let go, tightening his grip around his victim's neck. Gradually Moleface's flailing arms dropped to his sides, his body tumbling to the rock.

The other guard stood unsteadily for a moment, then crashed earthward as well. I noticed that his injuries were even more extreme than Moleface's. Without his suit I saw that the man was just a mass of scars, some still containing stitches. Under the skin muscles bulged and twitched helplessly, as if trying to escape the broken body. I didn't understand what had just happened, but there was no time to try to work it out. I was about to make my way back to Zee when the giant spoke to me.

"Alex?" he said. The voice was as deep and booming as always, but there was no malice in it this time, no evil. He sounded scared. The figure turned his head to me, and I saw that only one of his eyes remained silver. The other was normal, a pale green that looked at me in desperation. It was too dark to see clearly, but I thought I recognized that eye, and the look it threw me— fierce and defiant.

"Alex," the guard gurgled through a mouthful of blood. The voice raised and lowered its pitch, like it was breaking. "Don't forget your name."

"What?" I asked.

"If they catch you, just don't forget your name."

"Come on!" yelled a voice behind me. I heard the scrabbling from the tunnel. The dogs were getting nearer.

"Who are you?" I asked. But I didn't need to. I knew that voice, I knew that eye. A massive explosion rocked the other side of the cavern as Gary blew the hole, filling the entire room with light. I saw past the guard's twisted face, his stitched skin and spasming muscles, saw the grapefruit-sized birthmark on his arm, now so familiar.

"Monty . . ." I said, moving toward him. But it was too late. With a sigh the man—the boy—lowered his head, his one silver eye fading along with the dying light of the explosion.

"Come on!" came Zee's voice again. I ran back to them, my head spinning so fast I thought I was going to be sick. The scrabbling and growling behind us was growing louder by the second, and we hobbled across the uneven ground as fast as we could.

Fueled by fear we took less than a minute to find the crack in the rock. It was no longer a sliver. The explosion had ripped a massive hole in the floor, and way below it raged a river. We walked to the edge of the drop and peered down. It was impossible to tell how far below the water was—its flow just a gray streak in the shadows. But the air was sweet and cool, the foam settling on our skin and easing the pain of our wounds.

There was no sign of Gary.

"You sure you want to do this?" I asked Toby. "You can't even stand, let alone swim."

"I don't care," he replied. "I just want to get out of here."

I nodded.

"You ready?" asked Zee.

I closed my eyes and took a deep breath. In that second a thousand thoughts flashed through my mind—the day I was caught, the day I arrived here, the guards, the dogs, the warden, Kevin being slaughtered, Ashley falling to his death. Monty, taken and twisted and turned into a monster, into a blacksuit.

Then I thought about Donovan, snatched in the middle of the night, awaiting the same horrible fate.

I'll come for you.

"I'm ready," I said. Taking one last look at Zee and Toby, I leaned over the edge and let the cold air embrace me. There was nothing but death behind me, and probably nothing but death ahead, but at least this way I would be free.

And smiling at the thought, I jumped.